DEATH'S WHEREAF...

Do you want to live forever? A few of the characters you'll find in the pages ahead do. Did. Or do you fear staying this side the mortal coil? Some of those you will read about sure did. Do. Turn the page and discover Gothic Sword & Sorcery tales about immortals who return from Death, victorious over its sting—or horrifyingly despite!

Inside this heroic anthology are stories featuring protagonists in the vein of Karl Edward Wagner's Kane, Barry Sadler's Casca, Steven Erikson's Rhulad Sengar and Kallor, and Dennis O'Neil's Rā's al Ghūl. Dark tales of Death defeated, held at bay by willfulness, and desperately sought, its peace denied. Immortality may sound appealing, and if given the choice, it may be just the dream you've sought . . .

Beware! Its charms can mislead, condemn, enslave . . . or Rejoice! And open vistas of delights, powers, and curiosities.

Rogue Blades Presents
DEATH'S STING— WHERE ART THOU?

A HEROIC ANTHOLOGY OF IMMORTAL PROTAGONISTS

as selected by
JASON M WALTZ
& edited by
TY JOHNSTON

BOERNE TX
2020

Published by
Rogue Blades Entertainment
www.rogue-blades.com

This is a work of fiction. All the names, characters, places and events portrayed herein are either the product of the authors' imaginations or are used fictitiously. The publisher does not have any control over and does not assume responsibility for the content of author or third-party websites.

Rogue Blades Presents
Death's Sting—Where Art Thou? A Heroic Anthology of Immortal Protagonists
Copyright © 2020 Rogue Blades Entertainment
ISBN-13: 9798612896180 (print)
ASIN: B084VGSVPX (Kindle)

Cover Art: Célestin Nanteuil. Historiated initial N with Death holding a scythe [Wood engraving]. In Ludovico Ariosto's epic poem *Orlando furioso* (or *Roland furieux* or *furious Roland*) (p. 446). Paris: Morizot, 1864. Public domain @ https://www.oldbookillustrations.com/illustrations/death-n/
Cover Design: Jason M Waltz
Reading Team: Eadwine Brown, Bruce Durham, Robert Santa
Story selection by: Jason M Waltz
Edited by: Ty Johnston

First Edition: February 2020
0 9 8 7 6 5 4 3 2 1

All rights reserved. No part of this publication may be reproduced, scanned, or distributed in any form without the prior written permission of the publisher and the individual authors, excepting brief quotes used in connection with reviews. Please do not participate in or encourage piracy of copyrighted materials in violation of any author's rights. Copyright for individual works reverts to the individual authors and artists.

Contents

Immortality, a Poisoned Chalice? _____ 1
   by Adrian Cole
Red Horse, White Horse _____ 3
   by J.B. Toner
Ghosts of the Staked Plains _____ 13
   by Keith West
The Hungry Castle _____ 25
   by Liam Hogan
The Bull and the Djinn _____ 37
   by Logan Whitney
Just Add Holy Water _____ 58
   by Dawn Vogel
To Walk on Worlds _____ 71
   by Matthew John
The Immortal Contract _____ 86
   by D.K. Latta
Idol of the Valley _____ 103
   by Daniel Loring Keating
A Thousand Deaths _____ 131
   by Kate Runnels
The Death of Sleeping Beauty _____ 149
   by Brandie June
The Soldier _____ 163
   by KT Morley

Bhailgeth's Ransom *193*
   by Alfred D. Byrd
Sand-Devil *204*
   by Eadwine Brown
Shadow's Crossing *224*
   by Tony-Paul de Vissage
Rogue Blades Presents Titles *239*

Immortality, a Poisoned Chalice?

The drive for survival is probably the most powerful expression of the life force on our planet: in human terms it has often manifested itself as a yearning for immortality, or at least protracted longevity. Psychologists have described the human organism as a machine that seeks to be immortal, infallible, indestructible and irresistible, through a balance of its creative and destructive urges: certainly Man's gods have all these attributes. From the earliest tales ever told, down through the ages, our heroes and champions have often embodied them, or striven for them.

Two of strongest archetypal characters shaped in this mold are Mary Shelley's creature of Frankenstein—whose monster defies death and also bestows god-like powers on its creator—and Bram Stoker's Dracula, the superhuman vampire. However, both creatures are cursed, for immortality is a double-edged sword, its price inevitably isolating and earning the vilification of its abuser. We see it in Wilde's Dorian Gray and it is a shadow that constantly stalks Maturin's grim Melmoth. Even Rider Haggard's She falls victim to her obsession with everlasting life and youth.

Perhaps Edgar Rice Burroughs' Tarzan fares better, although he is a paragon, a fine example for us all, god-like in his distribution of wild justice. His powers are not corrupted by greed and self-aggrandizement, idealized by Burroughs to shape a better world.

My own immortal warrior, the Voidal, is necessarily enigmatic. He recognizes the dreadful powers working through him, just as Moorcock's Elric is a slave to his treacherous sword, Stormbringer. The Voidal constantly fights against the Dark Gods, at times desperate to win back his identity and thus his destiny from them. There is no joy in the terrible omniscience he has over men and gods alike, and he understands only too well that he is merely a conduit for it.

In *Death's Sting* the authors have explored this theme in many ingenious ways. Our love/hate relationship with Death is courted or cursed, mocked or praised, in fourteen thought provoking tales. The protagonists herein may be battle-hardened warriors, sell-swords, men of god, even gods themselves, but they all face a unique destiny, one which they may think they can control, but which invariably teaches them the ultimate, unavoidable truth. Death is master here. It may be averted for a time, used as an ally, won over as an apparent equal, but Man—even a superman—has his place in Death's master plans.

It is a tribute to the writers that they have between them concocted a collection that never flags, offering a feast of ideas as they examine the consequences of immortality, whether through longevity, the transmigration of souls, or in dark pacts with even darker powers. The style of writing varies from breathless violence to the more subtle, from the brutality of furious battle to the nuances of individual conflict, clashes of wills across the ages in settings that reflect an understanding of old legends and newly created ones, no less convincing for that.

Here you will find, I am sure to your great pleasure, a gathering of wonders. Enjoy this repast, but savor it slowly. It is a rich, heady mix.

Adrian Cole

October 2019

Red Horse, White Horse

by J.B. Toner

They crucified me in the desert. A long time I hung there. There was frost on my naked limbs each morning when the sun brought scourging fire. Thirst and bugs and hungry birds, and the never-ending anguish in my hands and feet. Those ropes were thick, and the nails heavy: my foes had learned red lessons of my strength. A long time I hung there before I worked myself free.

I'm Kalagor of Sorrowfen. I've been in this bent world for many dark and lonely seasons, and the Final Scythe is chipped with hacking at my spine. When I drink alone in alleyways, often with the cooling bodies of footpads for company, I cast my gaze back through a long, long corridor of memory, echoing with agony and carpeted with bone.

After I flopped down from the cross and crawled like a gutted jackal through the desert, I wanted only rest, a respite from the fighting and the pain. At the sand's edge, I found berries and clean water; there I waited while my flesh re-knit itself and my powers returned. It wasn't far to Kenoma, where I could take ghastly vengeance on my torturers. But instead, I turned east. I made a rough garment out of brush and bark, and I headed for the living lands. For the fair city of Sendroval.

At Argamore Bridge, I met a traveler who paid me a few coins to lift his wagon out of a mud-trap. I bought new clothes, a tunic and breeches of plain brown cloth. Outside of Jastor, I won a bet with a mariner who doubted I could raise a fallen tree. I now had tavern money.

It was a day of mist when I came pacing through the grasslands to the western gate. The Sendrovese pikemen came on guard as I approached, for I'm bigger than most and my face no longer smiles.

"What brings you hither, and whom does it bring?" a dark-haired fellow asked.

"I'm Cooran of Travisham," I said in the voice I use with people I don't plan to kill. "No business brings me, but to see my cousin Vash." There's no such fellow.

"How are you armed?"

"With nothing, as you see. I'd like no trouble in your town."

He nodded, and the others put up their blade-points. "Very well, pass. And keep those bludgeons you call fists in your pockets."

The streets were clean in Sendroval. Public buildings wore cheerful paint, and the lampposts wore flowered garlands. Strangers smiled at one another. It was the city of temples, where every god and goddess had a sacred place. Here, folk came from all the kingdoms to pray and to play. It was a happy city, and most days I muttered with distaste at the thought of it. But this year had been a grim one.

I found a small dim tavern on a back street, and took a mug of lager to a corner table in the shadows. *First of all, let's get drunk.*

The beer and whiskey were improbably good here. Patrons came and went, including passels of the bards for whom Sendroval is famed, singing of merriment and strife by turns. The mist outside deepened into drizzle, and the barkeep lit a fire in the hearth. I sat in my corner, warding off would-be companions with my glower, and a rare contentment filled me like the smoky warmth of the common room.

And then, of course, the door burst in.

Two intruders, man and woman, tall and pale and clad in black. Before the debris had even settled, the barkeep emerged with a broad-winged crossbow. "Last call," he growled, and shot the pale man through the head.

A spray of gore and bone chunks splashed the wall behind the intruder. I'd seen it hundreds of times, and I barely glanced up from my drink. But then the pale man smiled. Reached up, languidly, and yanked the bolt from his brain pan. The wound was already closing.

"We're not here for the wine," he said, and the woman began to laugh. Her fangs glittered cat-like in the half-light.

Ugh. More of *these* things. I'd massacred a nest of them in Babblebrook decades earlier, and hadn't seen any since. But Death's a fickle bitch. Or lazy.

As the other patrons stared and backed away, I finished my drink and got to my feet. "You two fucking weaklings. Why don't you go crawl down the sewer and find some rats to drink? I came to this town so I wouldn't have to fight anyone for a week or two."

The woman hissed: "And we came to desecrate the temple of Death, who has no power over us. You have no idea what you're dealing with."

"Well, actually, I do. And that's my aunt you're talking about. She and I have our differences, but I can't let every random passerby insult my family."

The pale man snarled and lunged at me, his fingernails extending into claws. Casually, I caught his wrists and held him at arm's length as the snarl became a stare. Then I stomped a foot into his chest and ripped his arms off. Everyone screamed. I started to chuckle.

The woman lunged as well, and I swung the spurting arms and knocked her flying: she smashed through a curtained window and went tumbling into the street. I started to laugh. Just days since my last battle and I already missed it. Why do we fight who we are?

"You'll regret this," gnashed the pale man, cowering.

"I already don't."

"That—that doesn't even—"

I grabbed him by the head. I wrenched and twisted, flapping his armless body like a trout, until the skull popped off, still trailing half his spinal cord. Decapitation's one sure way to kill these undead freaks. The body kicked, quivered, and withered into dust.

I drew in a long, satisfied breath through my nose. Glanced around the room and spied an untended tankard of ale on a nearby table. Grabbed it, gulped it, gave a happy sigh.

"Right, I'm off to save this pretty pink city of yours. Send my tab to the Priestess of Death."

The drizzle had become a heavy rain. The afternoon was ebbing into evening. And the dead girl had fled to save her life.

But I'm too old for pity. Everybody dies. She shouldn't have told me where they were going; she might have lived another night or two.

Part of my power and curse is perfect recall. With every breath, I strategize. High ground, blind alleys, sniper's vantage points: I knew these streets, these structures, from of old. The temple of Hyrule, Sun-God. The temple of Drimslip, Bard-God. The temple of Gordash.

And there, up ahead: the temple of Yyrkana, Goddess of Death.

I paced on patiently, as thunder-ushered twilight veiled the rooftops. If I were hunting people, I'd be formulating tactics—recollecting ingress points and tallying last-known troop numbers. But these things, these half-things, didn't rate the honor of being treated as warriors.

The huge ebony double doors burst open at my shove, and I strode through the vestibule with a scowl. Beyond, in the sanctuary, were a dozen of the unrotting cadaver-folk: grinning, hissing, caterwauling. Three priestesses lolled in their clutches, bleeding out.

"Who dares?"

A dark, broad-shouldered figure stood on the altar, white hair haloed in the candlelight.

I glared up at him. "I'm Kalagor of Sorrowfen. Son of Gordash War-God."

The figure on the altar leered.

"Bastard half-breed son, you mean to say. I can smell the human in your veins from here."

I shrugged. "Say what you like, I'm not here to banter. I'll give you five seconds to make whatever worm-chewed peace you can."

A blaze of lightning outside the stained-glass windows. "Kill him!"

They came scuttling forward, swiping their talons, each hoping someone else would finish me. Blood-sucking vermin: keen for murder, cowards in a half-fair fight. I grabbed the first one, raised it high, and snapped it over my knee, ripping out its cervical vertebrae with an old, long-practiced motion. It shrieked and shriveled into drifting flakes of ash.

The others scattered like rodents.

Slowly, with smoke rising and blood falling from my hands, I stalked down the center aisle. "You were a fool to come here, vampire. Yyrkana obviously has no interest in you. You should have crouched in the corpse-pits of Goblinsmoor till the end of days."

"Hide from what I don't fear? That would indeed be foolish. But you mistake me, son of War. It's no mere vampire that you face tonight."

"Goodness, how embarrassing. I beg your pardon."

"Oh, you'll beg. I'm Wolf of Travisham, son of Yyrkana."

"Well, gods will be gods. But you've got some cheek to call me half-breed when—"

"And Kazregoth Demon-Lord."

I stopped. Another facet of my dubious inheritance is a severely underdeveloped sense of fear; but my sense of wariness had been abruptly kindled into conflagration. The power of a demon brooks no mockery.

"Running low on quips, fighting man? A bit late for apologies, I fear."

"If you're what you say, then why in all Thirteen Hells would you waste your time on a childish prank like this?"

"Prank? This is a declaration. I wish the Kingdoms to know and fear my name. Every temple in Sendroval will be hallowed to Wolf before the night is out. But if I take a bit of juvenile delight in choosing Mother's sanctum as my starting point, what of it?"

"Fair enough," I said, and flung an oaken pew at his head. Conversation wouldn't settle this dispute.

He had time for a fanged cackle as he blurred out of the way and came streaking down the aisle in my direction. The pew smashed against the stone altar behind where he'd been standing, knocking it askew, and burning black candles clattered to the floor. The purple carpet began to smolder.

I was prepared for his speed; most high-level undead have it. I also knew his strength and durability would be, at minimum, the equal of my own. My one advantage (I hoped) was in tactical thinking. I'd walked in here underestimating my enemies, but it wasn't too late to rectify that error. You see, I never thought I'd actually hit him with that massive projectile.

Backing into the space where the pew had been, I created a waist-high corral for myself with the remaining pews on either side. Wolf zipped right into that space and started slashing at me with his claws, opening long gashes on my arms and torso—but he'd already given me what I needed, by sacrificing his speed advantage. In this cramped space, he couldn't maneuver well enough to escape my grapple. And as I'd expected, he was stronger than I was; but as I'd also expected, he had no martial training whatsoever, hence no idea how to use his strength to its potential.

We reeled back and forth, crashing into pews and pillars, his limbs popping back into place as fast as I could break them. His nails and teeth tore long wet strips of flesh from my bones and sent them flying through the dim space to slap against walls and columns, sticking in place or sliding redly to the floor. And above us on the altar, the flaming rug threw sparks at the curtains as the sons of War and Death played out their ugly destiny.

"This is meaningless, Kalagor. I haven't shown even a tithe of my true power!"

Chokes were useless, obviously. And I couldn't hope to pull off his head with him fighting back at full strength. I needed something to neutralize his celerity while leaving my own hands free.

"I'm going to hang you from my steeple on a spike for a thousand generations, half-breed!"

His senses. Speed wouldn't help if he didn't know where he was going. I leaned into his face and bit off his nose, and as he screamed with pain and rage, I squished my thumb-pads through his tear ducts and scooped out the eyeballs, snapping the retinal cords with a jerk. That distracted him long enough for me to stomp-kick the kneecaps off his legs, and that in turn gave me half a second to box his ears, grip the lobes, and rip them off his yowling, squirting head.

"*Kalagor!*"

I lifted another pew, and this time I bashed its full weight down on top of him, pinning him to the floor for one precious moment. Seized his skull in both my hands and planted my feet on his shoulders like a turnip farmer squaring off. And for the tiniest fraction of an instant, I thought my vicious yank had done its work, as he exploded into flame.

Then we blasted upward through the cathedral dome and out into the seraphic pandemonium of the skies. To the west, the indigo inferno of the dusk; to the east, a sweeping darkness. Far below, the dwindling rooftops—the vast empty plains—the roads and rivers fading into the silver lines of a distant map. Then out through the clouds, and all was crystal black and gleaming stars.

Wolf was a cyclone of fire, titanic, filling the heavens,

and I spun helplessly in his grip, scorched to the marrow, a paper ship in a tidal wave. At the summit of the miles-high tower of billowing, bellowing flames, I was tossed even higher into the air—and then he vanished. And there I hung, for just a heartbeat, in the heavens. And then I fell.

Half-blinded by the wind and the blaze, I squinted through the night as I went plummeting. The lands below were beautiful and wild. No mountaintop could offer such a view, no hawk had flown half so high. A strange celestial joy enfolded me. The night air was like a membrane, pushing against me, as if I were squeezing forth from a new mysterious womb. With half my body scarred and melted from the melee, I came hurtling out of the moon's vault and shattered myself against Yyrkana's burning temple with a smile.

"Kalagor."
"Mm."
"Kalagor of Sorrowfen. Can you hear me?"
"Mmmmm."
"My name is Nella, High Priestess of Death. We met once, you know, when I was a child. You look the same."

I felt comfortable. My fingers clenched reflexively, and silk sheets crumpled underneath. Soft light rested on my lids. With a drowsy blink and frown, I gazed about the chamber.

"We're in the temple of Gordash. High Priest Crylok has offered me accommodations for the nonce. And you, of course, are honored here for your parentage."

"I lay no claim to divinity," I mumbled. "I'm just passing through."

Her face was old, lined with grimness and gaiety alike, kindly but stern. "So I gather. It is well for us that you happened to pass through when you did."

The cyclone of flame arose in my memory, and I stirred sharply. "Wolf of Travisham."

"Yes. I have spent the night in meditation, conferring with my Mistress. It seems your opponent was provoked into unleashing his ultimate form, thus breaching the detente between the gods and demons. Both sides now call for his ruination. He has fled into exile, and his undead followers have been routed. It was an ill-considered plan to assail Sendroval."

"He underestimated his enemies. When you can't be killed, it's an easy mistake to make."

She nodded. "He'll be back. Doubtless with greater numbers and foresight."

"Doubtless. You should probably make some preparations." I sat up with a groan and rubbed my face. "But if you'll excuse me, it's time I was on my way."

"You have a place here, War-son. There's no need for you to wander like a wolf."

I spotted a jar of wine on a nearby table and helped myself. "Oh, I don't plan to wander. I have business to the west."

"As you will."

Pulling on a clean shirt that hung over a chair, I paused and looked at her face. "Nella, the earl's daughter," I said finally. "You loved my stories of bloodshed."

The old woman smiled. "I'm glad you remember me, Kalagor."

"I don't suppose we'll meet again. Have a good death, Priestess."

"And to you, happy warfare."

It was a lovely day out, and my spirits were high. Time to head back to Kenoma, where they nailed me down in the desert. And Hell would be riding with me.

~ J.B. Toner ~

J.B. Toner studied Literature at Thomas More College and holds a black belt in Ohana Kilohana Kenpo-Jujitsu. He has held many occupations, from altar boy to homeless person, but has always aspired to be a writer. His first novel, *Whisper Music*, was released by Sunbury Press in April of 2019. Toner currently lives in Massachusetts with his lovely wife Ellen and their octopus' handful of a daughter, Ms. Sonya Magdalena Rose.

Ghosts of the Staked Plains

by Keith West

Llano Escatado, 1803

The wind was picking up again, bringing with it dust that stung the eyes and made breathing uncomfortable. It whipped around the flames of the small campfires, sending sparks out into the night.

Miguel shifted the blanket he had pulled over his shoulders to protect himself from the wind's chill and looked toward the cattle beyond the tiny fire's glow. They were restless, and several lowed, a deep-toned nervous sound that was carried away by the wind almost before it could reach the ears. Miguel was afraid they would stampede again.

Something had spooked the cattle the last two nights. Both times the vaqueros had managed to get the herd under control. They'd been lucky. Miguel was afraid they wouldn't be so fortunate if it happened again.

At times it seemed as if the wind were calling someone. *"Con-quis-ta-dor."*

The conquistadors were all long gone, dead these hundreds of years. Miguel had to be imagining things.

He turned back to the fire and met the gaze of the new vaquero, Esteban. The man carried a sword with him everywhere he went, even though Joaquin, the trail boss, had told him not to. Esteban just ignored him, and no one, not Joaquin, not Felipe, the bravest man Miguel had ever known, nor any of the others had had the nerve to try and take it away. Esteban leaned back against his saddle. His saddlebags were on the ground next to him, and he took a whet stone from a compartment inside the bag.

Esteban looked up and met Miguel's eyes just as Joaquin threw a shovelful of dirt into the fire pit. Esteban continued to look Miguel in the eye as Joaquin put out the fire.

"The last thing we need is start a grass fire," the trail boss mumbled before going to put out another campfire.

"*Como esta, muchacho?*" Esteban asked Miguel. His whet stone glided along the blade. As Esteban turned the sword, its edge caught the last glow of the coals, giving it the appearance of a line of blood.

Miguel swallowed. "*Bien.*" Something about Esteban made Miguel nervous. Miguel's father had been a hard man, one who would beat him and his mother when he'd had too much tequila. And every year he drank more and more tequila. At least until last year, when Miguel had turned fourteen. His father had been about to take a knife to his mother, and Miguel had shot him then fled on his father's horse.

Now Miguel was with the cattle drives, hiding from the alcalde's men and the certainty of a noose. The alcalde and his father had been drinking companions. He would send his men to find Miguel and bring him back. It was only a matter of time before they tracked Miguel down. He knew he couldn't hide forever among the vaqueros. The alcalde's men would take him when they found him, and one day they would find him. The alcalde held a grudge like no one Miguel had ever known.

Miguel didn't fear the alcalde or his men, he didn't fear Joaquin, and he didn't fear Felipe, just like at the end he hadn't feared his father. Esteban, on the other hand, Esteban got under his skin like no one ever had, even though the man had always been kind to Miguel and treated him like a man. Most of the other vaqueros treated Miguel as a boy.

As Miguel stared across the fire into Esteban's eyes, he realized that was what made him uncomfortable around Esteban. The man's eyes. As Miguel met their gaze, he thought they were old, older than his grandmother's eyes had been before she died. No man's eyes should look that old.

Miguel suppressed a shiver.

"You look nervous, *mi amigo*. What's bothering you?"

"I'm just worried about the cattle stampeding again," Miguel said softly.

"You are not alone in that."

Esteban continued to run the whet stone along the edge of his blade as he spoke. "The cattle, they are very nervous tonight. Moreno than the last two nights, I think."

"What's got them so spooked?"

Esteban shrugged. "*Quien dice?* Who can say? But I think we will find out before the night is over."

Miguel wasn't sure what to say in response to that. Esteban was different. Miguel wondered if he was a *brujo*. Esteban seemed to know more than he was telling. He acted as though he were expecting something, something no one else knew about. Perhaps he did know more about what was spooking the cattle than he was saying. That didn't make him a *brujo*.

They sat in silence for a time, the only sounds being the wind, the cattle lowing, and the scrape of Esteban's whet stone. Several brands lay beside the fire pit. Miguel picked one up and rolled it back and forth in his hands nervously.

Esteban set his sword aside. He rose to his knees and looked around. The wind, which hadn't been anything close to gentle, was blowing hard now. Flying dust added to the darkness.

Somewhere in the dust and darkness a cow lowed. One echoed it, then another. This was a different sound than earlier. Then the cattle had seemed nervous. This new sound they were making had a tone of fear to it, even terror.

The cattle began to move. Miguel could feel the vibration of the hooves through the seat of his pants. They were about to stampede again.

He could hear the vaqueros cursing. Joaquin was shouting orders. He said something to Esteban, but the man ignored him.

Miguel got up and started to run to his horse. Esteban grabbed his arm. The jerk as Esteban's hand stopped him nearly took Miguel off his feet.

"No, stay close to me. There is death in the night, and it is coming this way. I can't protect you if you are out there."

Miguel swallowed.

"How do you know?" Miguel's mouth was so dry and coated with dust he could barely speak.

"Because I have sensed them approaching these last few nights. They are here, and they have come for me."

Esteban slipped his whet stone into his pocket.

"Then shouldn't I be somewhere else, somewhere far away from you?"

"No, *muchacho*. They are making the cattle stampede. As long as you are with me, the cattle won't harm you. They control the stampede and will keep the animals away from us."

"Oh."

Miguel was uncertain how to respond to that. He looked up at Esteban, but the man's gaze was fixed on something out in the darkness that only he could see.

The wind howled again. This time Miguel was certain he heard a voice.

"*Con-quist-a-dor!*"

The sound was a long, drawn out word.

"I am here!" bellowed Esteban over the wind. Miguel jumped at the sudden sound.

Two figures moved out of the darkness. They were Indians. The first one was several paces in front of the other. He wore trousers tucked into knee-high boots and a long-sleeved shirt. His long hair was held back by a wide headband. A blanket clasped to his belt hung over his left shoulder.

Miguel stared at the Indian, sensing something was wrong. Then it dawned on him. Although the wind was blowing stronger than it had all evening, the blanket and his hair hung straight, as though there was no wind.

The second Indian wore only a kilt and moccasins. A drum hung from a strap from around his neck, and as he approached, he began to beat out a rhythm. His hair was also held in place by a headband, but a single feather was stuck in it. The first Indian wore no feathers.

The first Indian stopped on the other side of the fire pit from Miguel and Esteban. He stared at Esteban with a look that was both stern and satisfied. He never looked at Miguel.

"So," he said at last, "we meet again, conquistador."

Esteban didn't say anything.

"Your companions are beyond our reach, conquistador, but you are not. We will extract our vengeance on you now."

"Do not be so certain. As you know, I don't die easily. And what do you mean, my companions are beyond your reach? Are they not with you in the afterlife?"

"The afterlife is not like that. We are not able to reach the others of your kind, the ones who killed our warriors, enslaved our little ones, ravished our women and left them to lie in the dust with bloodied loins."

"I had nothing to do with that. You know I ordered my men not to touch your women. As for killing your braves, we were at war."

"A war to reclaim our lands and homes. A war to restore our freedom."

Esteban didn't say anything to that.

Miguel struggled to understand what he was hearing. It sounded as though Esteban and the Indian knew each other and were discussing something that happened centuries ago during the days of the conquistadors. But they were speaking as though the events in question had happened recently.

"We have come to take our revenge on you, conquistador."

While Esteban and the first Indian had been speaking, the second had continued to beat out a rhythm on his drum.

Now the tempo sped up and the sound of the drum intensified.

The first Indian let out a whoop and began to dance.

Esteban took a step back from the fire pit. Although the coals had ceased to glow, the area where they were standing was illuminated by a strange glow that seemed to come from everywhere. Miguel had no trouble seeing Esteban and the Indians.

As the Indian continued to dance, Miguel grew more frightened. Something was happening that wasn't natural. Esteban looked nervous. Esteban had always had an aura of confidence about him.

The dancing Indian began chanting in a language foreign to Miguel. The one drumming joined in. The air began to change. The wind died down, at least in the circle in which they were standing.

Then the dancing Indian put his hand into a pouch attached to his belt. Miguel hadn't noticed it earlier. He would have sworn it hadn't been there.

When the Indian withdrew his hand, it contained a serpent. Miguel hated snakes. Even more than he hated scorpions. This one was particularly frightening. It was white with red bands that seemed to shift as the snake coiled and uncoiled around the Indian's forearm. Its tongue flickered in and out, a red forked whip tasting the night air. The eyes glowed red, but they weren't the most frightening thing to Miguel. What scared him the most were the two horns on the snake's head. They were red like the stripes along its body.

The tempo of the drumming increased, and as it did, the dancing Indian became more frantic, jumping and leaping and chanting in his unknown tongue. Miguel was too frightened to move. Esteban was motionless as well, but not from fear. At least it didn't look to Miguel like he was afraid. Rather he seemed to be waiting, as though he were expecting something to happen and shouldn't or couldn't move until it did.

At last the drumming stopped and the dancing Indian gave a leap toward the fire pit, stopping at its edge. The sound of small clods of dirt falling into the pit filled the sudden silence.

Or maybe it was the sound the snake made as it hissed. The Indian flung the snake at Esteban. Instead of falling to the ground, it seemed to glide through the air toward the man, curving around between him and Miguel. As it moved past Esteban, the snake struck at him. Esteban raised his sword and slashed at the snake. It drew back before the steel could touch it.

Esteban assumed a fighting stance, his sword held so he could parry or strike as needed. The snake continued moving in a circle, never rising or dropping. No snake could do that. No natural snake.

Miguel realized the Indian was a *brujo*. He knew that wasn't the actual word the Indians would use, but he couldn't think of what the correct word was. It didn't matter, though. What mattered was what the Indian could do that defied the laws of nature.

Such as the snake.

It struck at Esteban again, and for a second time Esteban tried to cut it with his sword. For a second time he missed.

The snake was not so slow to follow up. It struck again, and this time it was successful. Its fangs penetrated Esteban's sleeve and the cloth turned dark from the blood as it withdrew.

Esteban cried out in pain and staggered back. When he recovered his balance, he seemed to be a bit more uncertain in his footing.

Esteban was more successful when the snake struck again. This time the snake glided in low, changing its height above the ground for the first time. Esteban brought the sword down in a sweeping arc, letting gravity aid his arm. The snake spun away when the metal hit it, hissing as loud as the wind. Miguel watched in horror as the gash the sword had opened along the snake's side closed up.

The snake didn't hesitate to retaliate. It flew back toward Esteban and struck again, then a second time and a third. The first and third strikes found their mark, but the second caught Esteban's shirt under his arm, narrowly missing the flesh. Blood spots appeared where the fangs had left their poison.

Esteban was showing the effects the poison. Incredibly the snake's bites were aging him. Esteban's hair and beard were turning gray. His movements became slower. After the snake's third strike, liver spots appeared on Esteban's hands and face.

"My magic is more powerful than yours, conquistador," said the Indian who had thrown the snake.

"Don't be so sure," said Esteban. Instead of the strong, rich baritone Miguel was used to hearing, Esteban's voice was weak and quavered.

Miguel hated seeing his friend this way. Perhaps the rumors really were true and Esteban was a *brujo*. What of it? Esteban had always been kind to him.

Miguel wanted to help Esteban, but what could he do? He was still a boy. Then he realized there was one thing he might be able to do. He began to move away from the fight. He needed to move quickly if he was going to help Esteban, but if he moved too fast, the Indian might pay attention to him. Still, he had to take that chance.

Miguel's blanket had fallen from his shoulders when he'd stood at the beginning of the stampede. He took two steps toward it.

As he did, Esteban dropped to one knee.

The snake struck, but Esteban's move had been a feint. He lashed out with his sword in a vicious slash that caught the snake as it moved in. This time the cut in the snake's body took longer to heal. The snake screamed.

Esteban staggered to his feet. He was weakening. The snake's poison was still in his body, and it was taking a toll.

Esteban's hand shook as he raised his sword.

Miguel knew he would have to act now.

He reached down and snatched up his blanket with both hands and hurled it at the snake. His aim was good. The blanket covered the snake, and the extra weight bore it to the ground. Miguel didn't watch to see if his throw had hit his target. He turned as soon as the blanket left his fingers and grabbed the brand he had been fidgeting with earlier. Using both hands he brought it down on the blanket. The impact made a satisfying sound as it hit the snake underneath. He raised the brand and brought it down again.

Behind him both Indians screamed.

The snake's head protruded from under the edge of the blanket. The horns reminded Miguel of pictures he had seen of the devil in the chapel when he used to accompany his grandmother to mass. The glowing eyes turned to regard him as the body slithered out from beneath the blanket.

Fear coursed through Miguel. He had only thought he had been afraid earlier.

Then Esteban's sword flashed across his vision in a silver arc. The edge was sharp from where Esteban had run the whet stone along it earlier. This time the blade severed the head completely from the body.

As it did, a bolt of lightning struck the snake. Or perhaps the lightning leapt toward the sky from the snake's body. It happened so fast, Miguel was never sure afterward which way the lightning had moved. The flash of light blinded Miguel, and the sound was deafening. The shock wave from the blast threw Miguel back several feet. He lay stunned until he heard Esteban calling him.

"Miguel. *Muchacho*, I need your help, *por favor*."

Miguel sat up. A few small fires were burning from where the lightning had struck. The wind had died down entirely.

Esteban was lying on the ground. Miguel crawled over to him. The vaquero looked ancient, as though he had aged centuries in minutes.

"His magic wasn't so strong after all, eh, *muchacho*?"

Miguel shook his head.

"In my saddle bags, there is a water skin wrapped in a thick heavy blanket. Bring it to me. *Adelante!* I don't have much time left."

Esteban pointed to his saddle bags, lying next to his saddle. Miguel scurried over to them. Miraculously they seemed to be unharmed from the lightning strike. After a moment of searching, he found the water skin. It was large and full. Miguel estimated it held at least a gallon of water.

He brought it back to Esteban. The man was so weakened, Miguel had to help him sit up so he could drink. At first Miguel held the water skin, but as he drank, Esteban's grip on the skin grew stronger and soon he was holding it without any assistance.

Miguel watched as Esteban drained the skin. The more he drank, the younger he got. The liver spots faded from his hands and face, and the tremor in Esteban's hands subsided while desiccated muscles filled out along Esteban's body. The gray disappeared from his hair and beard.

When he'd finished, Esteban lowered the skin. "*Muchas gracias, amigo.*"

Esteban practically leapt to his feet. He put two fingers in his mouth and whistled. The whistle was answered by a whiny from somewhere in the darkness.

"Are you really a *brujo*?" asked Miguel.

"No, just an old conquistador."

"But how can you be a conquistador?"

Esteban didn't say anything, just smiled sadly as his horse trotted up.

"It's time for me to leave, Miguel."

He saddled his horse. Miguel watched in stunned silence.

"Why?" he asked when Esteban was finished.

"I need to replenish my supply." Esteban picked up his

water skin and put it in his saddlebag.

"Thank you again, *mi amigo*. I hope someday our paths cross once more."

"Wait," cried Miguel as Esteban started to ride away. "Take me with you!"

Esteban turned his horse back and sat facing Miguel.

"No," Esteban said slowly. "The Indians aren't dead. Merely defeated. I should have left the cattle drive when I first sensed them. They will come for me again. You are safer here."

"But I'm not," said Miguel. "The alcalde's men are searching for me. When they find me, they will either kill me or take me back to be killed."

"The alcalde?" asked Esteban.

"*Si*, from my village. I killed my father to protect my mother. He was *amigos* with the alcalde. Now his men are hunting me."

Esteban seemed to be considering Miguel's words.

"I can help you," continued Miguel. "I did tonight."

"*Si*, that you did."

"We can protect each other." Miguel had no idea what he could do to protect Esteban if the Indian *brujos* returned, but he knew he would try.

"*Muy bien.* Very well."

Esteban reached down. Miguel took his hand, and Esteban pulled him up. Miguel slid onto the back of the horse behind Esteban.

"Let's go find your horse, *amigo*."

~ *Keith West* ~

Keith West has been a fan of the science fiction, fantasy, mystery, horror, and historical adventure genres for more years than he's willing to admit. By day he teaches impressionable young people his bad habits (of which there are many) and by night he tells lies for fun and profit (more fun than profit). He commits dayjobbery in the field of Physics where in addition to teaching he occasionally writes cross-genre documents known as grant proposals, consisting of science fiction (the proposal), fantasy (the budget), and horror (the reviewers' comments). He and his wife make their home in West Texas with their son (adopted from Kazakhstan) and two dogs (adopted from the animal shelter). He denies having an addiction to using parentheses.

The Hungry Castle

by Liam Hogan

The knight stood in his stirrups, peering into the mist-shrouded evening. For two days the path had winded beneath thick woodland. This switchback, atop a rocky outcrop, offered a rare opportunity to spy the lie of the land, to seek some place more comfortable than the crook of an old oak for the approaching night.

What held his attention was the castle in the distance. It had a forlorn, deserted appearance. Nothing stirred except the lazy wings of a crow settling high in the half-ruined tower. No lights emerged as evening turned to dusk. No smoke betrayed fires lit to ward against the chill.

As the knight studied the bleak vision, a peasant, bent beneath his load of firewood, shuffled up the incline toward him, eyes fixed firmly on the dirt at his ill-formed, cloth bound feet.

"Ho!" called the knight while he was still a way off. "Who lives in the castle yonder?"

The peasant tilted his thinning head, revealing a worn, filthy face with cruel twisted lips and a disquieting milky cast to his left eye. "Yonder?" he echoed with weary impudence, before spitting heavily on the dusty road. "No one lives yonder."

"Then to whom does the castle belong?" The knight had a mind to beat the insolent fellow with the flat of his sword, but the blade would need a damned good cleaning afterward. And there was no one else around to answer his questions.

"Castle belongs to itself," the peasant said, lowering his burden and stretching his back. Even erect there was something crooked about the man. "It's empty." He paused as if in idle thought. "'Cept the princess."

"Princess? A princess lives there?" the knight asked.

The peasant shook his head, matted hair swinging in heavy clumps. "A princess *dies* there."

As the knight rasped his sword halfway clear of its scabbard, the peasant's one good eye widened. "Explain, rogue!" the knight demanded.

"Every seven years," the peasant said, cringing lower, "a princess is imprisoned in the castle. The castle feeds off her until there is nothing left but a withered husk."

"And the people in these parts, they let this abomination happen?"

The peasant shrugged. "It is only once every seven years."

"Seven years or seven days, I for one will not let this evil persist!"

The peasant took a moment, then shrugged once more. "Good luck."

"Have a care, peasant! I am a Knight of the Royal Court. An adherent to the Chivalric Code. A *proven* hero."

The peasant glanced up the road to wherever he was headed. The eye with the cast swiveled back until it fixed the knight in its baleful stare. "We've had heroes here before."

"And?"

"The castle makes short work of them." The peasant was grinning now. "*Very* short work."

The knight shuddered. In the thickening gloom, the peasant's smoke-filled eye appeared to glow. Fumbling in his purse, the knight withdrew the meanest coin.

"Is there a village nearby?" he asked. "One with an inn?"

"There is," the peasant said with a sneer. "A mile or two down the trail. But you're unlikely to find a welcome there."

"Why not?" the knight demanded.

"Because the castle's influence stretches far beyond its walls. If you are fool enough to tell them you intend to rescue the princess, they will surely try and stop you with their lies and their deceit and, should those fail, then by pitchfork and axe, hammer and torch."

With a snarl the knight tossed the coin. It fell short, leaving the peasant scratching in the dirt as the knight spurred his charger on.

Even in the dark, the village wasn't much to see, hardly worthy of a name, for all there were signs it had once been a thriving community. The inn and stables were the largest of the remaining buildings, a place to break a long journey, little more. There was a well, its roof half rotten, a pillory in rather better condition. A half dozen rough shacks clustered together for protection, the road between them churned to mud.

As the knight approached the inn, a lantern appeared and beneath it a pot-bellied landlord and his shrewish wife.

"Have you a room?" he asked, not much caring for the answer. It was the sort of place that made the crook of an oak look inviting.

"Why yes, good knight!" the innkeep beamed. "Nothing worthy of your high status, I fear, but the very best we have. Stables for your horse, hot food and imported wine."

The knight grunted. Prepared to dismount, until the shrew stepped forward, no smile on *her* lined face.

"Tell me, sir knight, what brings you to our humble village?"

The knight remembered the stooped peasant's warning. "Merely passing through," he said. "I'll be leaving in the morning."

"Then you are most welcome, sir knight." She coaxed a smile onto her face. It sat, awkward and fearful, staying there almost until she turned away.

In the smoky tavern, shorn of his armor, the knight picked at the remains of his meal. Inwardly, he seethed.

He kept expecting one of the garrulous villagers to mention the castle or the princess, to call on him for help, to champion good over evil, right over injustice. He could not in faith believe that they were all so heartless, so swayed by the dark malevolence of the brooding castle. But on and on the farmers and woodsmen rambled, asking questions about affairs in the rest of the kingdom, refusing to be drawn in return on local news, refusing to name the chivalrous deed.

The wine was sour, the bread musty, and the serving wench who tried to invite herself to his room was almost certainly poxed. This was a dark, soulless place, the inhabitants in jubilant mood, declaring it a good year, a very good year, while somewhere hard by an innocent lay imprisoned and dying.

The knight shrugged away a refilled flagon. Long journey ahead tomorrow, he claimed, the hostess quick to replace wine with candle, the noise in the inn briefly stilling then rising again as he made his way up creaking stairs.

In the narrow, uneven bed, he listened to the sound of drunken farmers arm wrestling the solidly-built blacksmith, and imagined bedbugs burrowing into his flesh. His dreams were haunted by tiny ruined castles with claws at the end of skeletal arms, eagerly trying to hop onto his bed. When one finally succeeded, it landed heavily on his chest. As he struggled to avoid the sharp, foul-smelling teeth, the tiny castle grew larger, heavier, the stones slowly squeezing the air from his lungs.

Waking with a start, a mangy cat hissed and leapt from the bed, leaving a bloody scratch from its unfurled claws. The knight reached for his dagger beneath the pillow, but the spiteful beast had already fled the room.

The Hungry Castle

"Leaving so early?" the innkeeper asked, rubbing reddened eyes.

The knight checked his saddle. He would not put it past the inhabitants of this hellhole to swap his tack for an inferior one. "Yes," he answered, mounting his charger with difficulty, the wooden step designed for shorter horses or less encumbered riders. The knight turned not along the muddy path toward the Royal Court, nor the border lands he had come from, but toward a third, overgrown trail, heading vaguely east. "Thought I might visit the castle on the way."

The reaction was dramatic. The innkeeper's jolly face transformed into an ugly mask. Or was the jolly face the mask, one that had finally slipped?

"Sir!" he whined, face contorted. "I implore you, stay well away from the castle! Please, continue on your way. No good comes from following *that* path."

The knight smiled. "And the princess?"

"Princess? What princess? There is no princess, sir! Good knight, believe me! There is nothing but despair and wickedness—"

"Enough!" the knight barked. "I go where I will." He wheeled the charger around, scattering the corpulent innkeeper and the yawning groom.

"Please, sir! I beg of you! Come back, let me explain!"

The knight spurred his horse until he was out of earshot. And then he dawdled, picking his way through the saplings that were trying to reclaim the path he hoped led to the castle.

The villagers were waiting. They'd chosen a spot where the trees were even denser than usual, the way narrowed. A chokepoint. Had they gone another route to get there before him, alerted by the innkeeper? Or had they been there already, just in case?

True to the peasant's words, the two farmers carried pitchfork and axe, the blacksmith held a long-handled hammer. Disappointingly, the fourth, a sallow man the knight did not recognize from the inn, gripped a stout cudgel rather than a torch.

"Halt, knight!" the blacksmith called out.

The knight steered a few steady steps toward them and then pulled on his reins. His charger, ever obedient, stopped immediately.

"I have no quarrel with you," the knight said, pleasantly enough for all it pained him to do so. "Stand aside, let me pass."

"We cannot allow you to interfere," the blacksmith said, shaking his bearded head. "To reawaken the slumbering evil."

"Lower your weapons and stand aside, I say, for the second time. I will not ask a third."

"Nay, we shall not," the blacksmith said, setting his stance squarely on the path. "Sir, you know not what you do. There is no honor on this path."

With a battle cry, the knight urged his charger forward.

The knight cursed as his mount stumbled, cursed as he glanced down at the splattered blood.

It did not belong to his horse, but to the villagers.

He had only meant to give them a beating, to ride heavily into them and force them from the path. That would have been enough to teach them a lesson, to send them running home. But the curs had not attacked *him*, they had attacked his horse.

If he and his charger had been in full battle armor, that would not have mattered. Travelling light, travelling alone, his charger had been unprotected other than a hardened leather breast plate. His charger had been vulnerable.

Angered, he slayed them all, though not before the blacksmith had swiped the charger's right foreleg with his hammer.

Only heavily bruised thankfully, not broken or cut, but

The Hungry Castle

the horse would need to rest for a day or two. And the village was no longer the place for that.

The knight forged on with a sense of foreboding. This quest was descending into nightmare beset by dark omens, by evil portents.

Finally the trees gave out onto scrub pasture. Perhaps it had previously been fields, now it was thick with nettle and thistle. The castle loomed over it all, somehow both smaller and more ominous than when the knight had seen it at a distance.

He dismounted his lame horse, led it through the tangled weeds.

The crows' throaty caws echoed off the ruined keep's walls. As he approached, more of them were flushed from the long grass, great black wings gliding effortlessly out of range. He stumbled onto the remains of a road, not part of the trail he had arrived by. The going was easier and he followed it toward a stone bridge across the moat.

The moat was dry, but not empty.

Half hidden among the grasses and bulrushes there were rusted suits of armor, the occasional piece still glinting in the thin light along with flashes of something white.

Bones. Human bones. Heroes' bones.

No wonder the crows looked well fed.

The knight rapped the front of his shield with his gauntleted hand, summoning courage from the crucifix emblazoned there. He took small comfort that none of the crows were down in the moat, fighting over the spoils.

These were not *fresh* corpses.

He lowered his visor, eyed the bridge. Was this some devilish trap? Was that why the bodies were gathered here?

Tying the reins of his charger to a crumbled pillar at the foot of the bridge, the knight unsheathed his sword, leaving the scabbard with his horse. He stepped out onto the stone walkway, wary for loose cobbles, for some hidden trigger.

The crows mocked him as he edged his way across.

In the castle courtyard, he took stock. He had crossed the bridge without incident, passed through the open gate to the other side. He'd expected to fight his way in, but the castle was silent, unwilling to pose a challenge.

No ancient thorn hedges, no beastly guardians, no hidden archers.

Just a moat full of those who had failed before him.

He tried to remember the peasant's words. "The castle makes short work of them," he'd said. Was it the castle and not the inhabitants that were the danger? If danger there was. If inhabitants there were.

The place seemed empty, dead.

It was not a large castle and had seen better days. The walls enclosed the small keep, a modest hall, and various outbuildings that had collapsed into ruins, trees reclaiming the ramparts.

If it weren't for the corpse-strewn moat, he'd have been easily convinced there was nothing here for him. Nothing here for anyone.

The ancient oak door to the keep refused to budge. Halfway up, the stones were blackened where a ruinous fire had escaped the lowest of the windows. Craning his neck, he glimpsed sky. The roof had gone, then. The door was probably blocked by rubble.

Closer up, the hall was a mix of styles and ages, a chapel at one end absorbed over time, stained-glass windows rising halfway along the tiled roof. At some point the hall's grand double doors had been barricaded, masonry and rotting timber piled high.

Further along its squat length, a smaller wooden door lay flat in the dirt, the opening inviting him in. The blackness opened onto what had once been the kitchens, the ovens gone long cold, oak tables scarred by knife and cleaver. Dust lay thick, though something had passed this way, whether

The Hungry Castle

beast or man it was hard to tell. Not footsteps, not like those he left, peering back toward the daylight. These crescent tracks were left by a serpent or wounded animal.

At the doorway, he had three choices, left, right, or up via rickety stairs. He chose left, assuming correctly it would lead to the great hall. A tapestry, ragged around the edges but still largely intact, obscured the view. With his sword, he brushed it aside.

Like the kitchens, the great hall had been abandoned in some haste many years ago. Heavy chairs surrounded the two tables, a candelabra devoid of candles rested on its side along with a half dozen pewter plates in seemingly random positions.

Something crunched underfoot, and in the rafters a bird took flight. The knight lifted his metal boot, saw fragile bones rendered into dust.

He scanned the gallery overlooking the hall, checking if anything had been alerted by his clumsiness. Nothing stirred and he almost wished it did. Would he have to search every room of this forsaken place just to prove there was nothing here?

He ignored the stairs for the second time, followed a twisting corridor past the larder—what had once been edible had long since turned to dust or been carried away by rodents—past the scullery, the sinks piled with dishes as though in the aftermath of a feast.

The corridor ended at a door with a cross carved into it. Taking this as an overdue good omen, he carefully entered.

He found himself in the vestry, the priest's rooms adjacent to the chapel. In the gloom he could make out a low bench, a dark robe lightened by fine dust, a heavy bible stand, empty.

Beyond, the chapel was dappled with light, wintry sun finally getting the better of the mist and slanting through the stained-glass windows above. After the dark of the vestry, it took him a moment to sort through what he saw.

A congregation was waiting for him.

The pews were occupied by skeletons wearing faded dresses and once elegant embroidery, tattered robes and expensive doublets. Skulls grinned and paid close attention to the front of the chapel. He followed their empty gaze to the chancel. On the stone slab of an ancient altar lay the shrouded form of a woman.

He had not come in vain! He leapt forward, then slowed as he caught a glimpse of her wizened hand beneath the white gown, lit by a mote-filled shaft from above. Her face…

While it was no skeleton, the face was that of the frail and impossibly aged: the flesh sunken, the skin parchment thin and ash gray. He'd been misled by the colors spilling from the painted glass above.

Too late, he was too late! All he had found was another corpse. The castle had done its evil work, had drained the life of another innocent victim. He tried to imagine the poor princess as she must have looked when she had become trapped in this evil place, this false house of God. Though the body was desiccated, a ruin, it was still somehow a noble one, tall of frame, slender of limb. It wasn't hard to see she must have once been a rare beauty.

As he stared down, he saw the faintest flutter of movement, heard the gentlest of rasps. The princess was still alive, still breathing! Though barely, her life force drained almost entirely.

He crossed himself and raised his sword. He could do nothing for her other than to commend her soul to the Lord, to put her out of her terrible misery. A thankless, heart-breaking task, but one he would not shirk from.

He muttered a prayer, the words thick and halting. Her eyelids flickered, opening to reveal luminous eyes that stared imploringly into his. A hand lifted from the cold, heartless stone and he bent forward to receive her dying words.

The Hungry Castle

Sitting on the altar, a young woman peered into a tarnished mirror, turning it this way and that, running translucent fingers over flawless flesh. Unseen, or perhaps ignored, something crept into the chapel: a man, stooped and groveling, one trailing foot leaving long crescent marks as he dragged it through the dust.

"Did I do right, my lady?" he whimpered, a ghostly white cast haunting his left eye. "Did I do well?"

"You did very well."

The servant stared dispassionately at the suit of armor lying on the steps of the chancel, the knight's shriveled face visible through the open visor, mouth stretched into an endless scream.

"The moat, m'lady?"

"The moat," she said with a nod. She would be strong now, strong and beautiful, for six wonderful years, her beauty and youth fading rapidly only in the seventh. A bargain for the many times she had cheated death. She ran a fingertip over the pagan runes carved deep into the blood-soaked stone, an ancient relic only a fool of a long-dead priest would think he and his impotent religion could tame.

He had paid the ultimate price, he and the rest of the castle. Why she alone had been spared—or cursed, as the villagers ignorantly claimed—she truly did not know.

Was it her beauty? Her innocence? The fact she had been the bride, that fateful day?

Or was it her youthful hunger? Some seed or flaw recognized and accepted by the dark gods?

Perhaps one day the villagers would succeed and her knight in shining armor would not arrive in time. She would finally perish on the hard surface of this sacrificial altar. Until then…

She plucked at the dusty white wedding gown, favored her faithful retainer with a smile. The son of the son of the…how many times? She had lost count. So many knights!

"Let's dress up, shall we? Put on our finery," she said, licking her lips as he nodded in eager assent. She turned her cold, cold gaze west. "Let's go into town."

~ *Liam Hogan* ~

Liam Hogan is an Oxford Physics graduate whose award-winning short story, "Ana," appears in *Best of British Science Fiction 2016* (NewCon Press). "The Dance of a Thousand Cuts" appears in *Best of British Fantasy 2018*. He lives and avoids work in London.

The Bull and the Djinn

by Logan Whitney

A ragged, giant of a man wearily tread his way across the endless desert wastes. Wind and sand had scoured his sun-bronzed skin and the salt of sweat streaked his night black mane. His mouth was as dry as the land that enveloped him, his lips cracked and worn. The arduous trek across a waterless expanse, the blistering heat of the sun, the frigid nights upon the sands, all would have all proven deadly to lesser men. But not to him. To the giant, death was but a distant dream, a gift he feared would long be denied no matter how long he searched for it.

The afterlife will greet you one day, my son, but not this day. There is still so much to do.

The words of his mother echoed through the cavern of his barren mind. The concept of death had never before weighed so heavily upon his heart. He had once roared through battlefields, cleaving a bloody path as he went, his clothes stained in crimson, both his enemies' and his own. Beasts, ancient and terrible, had fallen like ripe grain before his threshing hand. The very mention of his name had once sent kingdoms trembling for fear of his brutal wrath. None of that mattered any longer. The dire loss of a kindred soul had left his spirit broken and his body aching to rejoin his companion upon great battlefields, even if that meant he must first embrace the great beyond.

In his blood-soaked days of adventure, not once had he given thought to why death had not yet claimed him. Now that death was all he sought, it would not come.

A small, shadowed shape grew from the shifting sands with each ponderous step. From a distance it looked to be little more than a simple mirage, an illusion that's only purpose was to lead the lost and lonely even further astray. The edifice was no great monument, a simple construction of sandstone bricks and brittle cedar planks. Where once a bucket had hung above cool, refreshing water, only a fraying rope remained. Peering into the blackened maw of the empty well, the giant gave a grim smile, finding triumph where others in his situation would only see despair.

With a tired heave, the big man leapt over the lip of the pit and plunged into the darkness below. A long moment passed as the walls of the well sped by. With a lurching jolt, the man met the floor and sank to his knees in the damp sand, a shock of pain racing through his tired frame. Waterlogged sand slipped through his mallet fists as the heat of the world above washed away in the shadows of natural cavern, a thin shaft of light the only illumination.

"You," the word almost a serpent's hiss. "I know you."

With a groan, the giant rested himself from the grip of gravity and dusted himself off. He peered into the shade of the well bottom, letting his dark eyes adjust to the lack of light. The speaker's voice slithered from wall to wall, making the exact direction of the words indiscernible.

"If that is true, then you know I am not to be trifled with," the man's voice boomed within the depths. The only reply was a mirthless, ophidian laugh. "Show yourself!"

"Your reputation precedes you. You are quick to anger, mighty Bull." A slender form melted from the shadows, revealing an emaciated human shape draped in the black tatters of a desert nomad. What little exposed skin the Bull could see was drawn tight across strangely-shaped bones and elongated fingers. Whatever face the creature might have had was hidden beneath a shredded veil and a mask of black shadow. The speaker moved closer toward the newcomer, but never strayed too close to the column of sunlight at the center of it all.

"I have searched far and wide for you," said the Bull.

"And here I have been," the creature hissed, taking a step forward, but meeting an unseen resistance.

Eyes finally accustomed to the dim environs, the Bull made out the faint shape of a pedestal set neatly into a niche at the back of the well. Upon the pedestal rested a small, metallic object that gleamed dully in the darkness. A spout protruded from a flat bowl, a thin hooked handle on opposite side. The bronze of the simple oil lamp had long turned green from age and element, locked for countless ages in the gloom of the well.

"I have come to ask of you one wish," said the Bull. "Can you grant what I desire?" The creature leaned forward, struggling against its tether to move closer to the man. The Bull expressed no revulsion nor fear despite the rising urge to run and scream. From somewhere within the creature's veil, the Bull thought he saw a devious smile crawl across hideous, pointed teeth.

"I was not aware that someone such as you had wants unattainable."

"My reach does not extend to prizes such as this," growled the Bull. The shadow man leapt backward with a flutter, moving thin digits with excitement as it went.

"Tell me, great Bull, what wish could I grant that you could not grant yourself?"

"To be mortal," the Bull answered quickly. "To die."

"I must admit, this is a strange request."

"Is it within your power?" asked the Bull. There was a long pause as the creature turned inward, contemplating the costs and consequences of such a feat.

"Your gods. Would they not be angry at such a thing? Would they not interfere? Perhaps seek retribution?"

"Answer the question. Is my wish within your power to grant?"

"Yes."

"Then let it be done!" The shade drew back into the shadows at the sudden burst of rage.

"Great Bull," the dweller bowed. "Your wish is well within my power to grant. That is not the issue."

"What *is* the issue?" the Bull growled in blunt response.

"There is another," the creature hissed meekly. "You are not the first to seek me out"

"Then what must be done?" The creature laughed and needles pricked at the Bull's flesh.

"Bring me my master's head. Slay him and I will be free to grant all that you desire."

"Where, then, can I find this man?"

💀 💀 💀

"That cannot be a man," exclaimed the grizzled watchmen in disbelief. "Look at his size!" The youthful guard to which he spoke said no words, but his face told that he agreed with the assessment.

The city of Sabatu was less a true city and more a fortress hidden upon the jagged slopes of Dragon's Spine. High walls of sunbaked brick and sheer cliffs served to protect a ragtag conglomerate of daub-wattle huts and towers of cyclopean stone that served as a base of operations for every bandit and thief this side of the Desert of Souls, at least those who paid tribute to Damuzi, the King of Thieves.

In the wildlands beyond the gates of Ur, it took little more than a strong arm and cunning to claim oneself a king. Free from the shackles of formality, blood rights and heirs, a young robber had transformed himself into the ruler of a rogue state. Lords across the Twin River lands had long sought the assassination of the thief whose grasp had reached too far. It was not the walls, nor guards, nor parapets that repelled every attempt, but the bribes. Somewhere deep within Damuzi's makeshift palace was a horde of riches to rival all the ancient kings, or so it was said. Potential assassins who did not succumb to allure of riches, were killed.

"I wish audience with the King of Thieves," bellowed the Bull to the watchmen.

"And who are you to request such a thing?" inquired the older of the two.

"I bring tribute. I wish to enter the ranks of the brotherhood." The grizzled scout looked the man up and down, an incredulous grin across his pockmarked face.

"You're too big to be a thief," chuckled the guard. The Bull ignored the laugh and removed a leather purse from inside his travel stained robes. The man's laughter grew louder at the sight of such a small offer; his partner remained silent. "That is what you bring to our lord and master? There are men within these walls that have stolen more when they were but babes!"

The Bull turned to the silent youth and held out the bag. Hesitating, the boy took the purse and gingerly looked inside. His face turned pale and his eyes grew wide with what he saw within.

"Nergal's hand, you must see this, Mahud." The man called Mahud ceased his guffaw and snatched the purse from his counterpart. Silence stretched for some time as he peered at the contents.

"Urgan, open the gate," whispered Mahud. The boy did not respond, still in shock at the contents of the bag. "The gate! Open it!" Urgan jumped at the command and flung open the heavy, bronze door. The Bull reached out a hand and the purse was promptly placed upon open palm, quickly disappearing within the folds of the giant man's robe.

💀 💀 💀

The great Damuzi stood at the high arched window of his throne room and gazed absently down upon the bustle and clamor of commerce, thoughtfully stroking his curled black beard. Damuzi had rested control of Sabatu the Fortified when he was very young. Barely a man when he first became headmaster of his fledgling organization, his childhood was a blur of dream and memory. He had barely come of age when he found himself at the head of an illicit empire. It had been years since he had seen his home, and now he found himself unable to recall the names or faces of the other orphans and beggars he had once called his family.

"Do they resent me? Think ill of me for leaving them behind?" he asked of the wind.

Just then, there was a knock at the door to his chamber. He was not expecting anyone for quite some time. He sighed, expecting the worst, the toil of kingship a never-ending grind. As he paced to the doorway, he thought of what new issues or complaints would be brought to his attention. If not for splinter groups, shadowy rivals or royal assassins, he might have been able to find time to escape for a moment and relive the wild days of his youth that he had given up so thoughtlessly.

The massive, gilt-worked doors swung lazily open, revealing the stolid frame of a giant. Four men wrapped in the armor of Damuzi's elite surrounded the man. From behind the hulking figure slipped a sun-weathered rogue with a face full of scars, recognizable only vaguely as one of the city watch.

"What have you brought to me, watchmen?" asked the king, never taking his eyes from the massive newcomer.

"He comes to pay tribute to you," said the guard warily. "To join the ranks of our brotherhood."

"What is your name, giant?"

"He said to call him 'the Bull,'" interjected Mahud.

"Is he mute?" derided Damuzi. The watchman only shook his head.

"Then let him speak for himself. Besides, is there not a gate you should be watching?" Mahud took a sheepish bow and slunk away. "Come, Bull, let us sit and talk for a while," said Damuzi, without care.

The Bull walked into the gaudily-decorated chamber as the soldiers were waved away. He admired the place, the lapis lazuli and gold that caused the room to glitter in the light of the noonday sun, the high-backed throne hewn from exotic wood and the scent of jasmine that permeated the air. For not being a true king, Damuzi knew how to dress the part.

"Wine?" asked the King, pouring himself a goblet full.

"Yes. Please."

Damuzi filled another cup and gently passed it to the Bull. This giant man couldn't have been much older than Damuzi himself, but there was a weariness about him, a weight carried upon his broad shoulders that the king could not describe.

"Is something wrong, my friend? If I didn't know better, I'd think you a ruler yourself." The Bull chuckled and lifted the wine to his parched lips. Damuzi smiled and did the same, then wiped at his lips. "You wish to be a member of our brotherhood? If you made it this far, I assume you have brought us something to offer."

"Yes," said the Bull, removing the prize from his robes. "I admit, upon first glance it appears to be a treasure of little consequence, but I assure you, it is worth more than all the world."

Damuzi smiled grimly at the sight of the tiny oil lamp, wolfish eyes studying the alien symbols etched into its surface.

"You are a clever man." The king gently plucked the lamp from the Bull's palm. "How did you find this?"

"Everyone knows the story of the little orphan thief who wished himself king And a heist unimaginable to even the most daring of robbers."

"Of course they do. I made it so. Do you not think every wild-eyed rogue in this city has not dreamed of resting this treasure from my grasp? To wish themselves king in my stead? My followers must know that above all, I am more clever and cunning than they. That is the source of my power, more so than wishes from a magic lamp. But you have not answered my question, Bull. How did you find my secret?"

"I have my ways. A thief as cunning as yourself must know that some secrets must be kept."

Damuzi glowered at the Bull, teeth grinding together nervously as he contemplated what needed to be done. The Bull easily stood a full head above the king, had proven himself smart as a whip and was no doubt strong as his namesake suggested. This man was dangerous, there was no doubt. But he could also prove useful. The king's frown transformed into a smile and then to a laugh.

"Welcome to the Brotherhood, my friend. How can I deny entry to someone as bold as yourself? Come, sit with me and finish your wine. We shall celebrate!"

For hours, Damuzi and the Bull sat and talked of past adventures, enjoying wine pilfered from Kesmet caravans and succulent fruits from far off Harappa. The sun grew low and the moon began to rise, casting a silvered glow about the City of Thieves. Torches were lit and still the streets bustled, not with the sounds of trade, but of revelry.

"I have put off my kingly duties for long enough," said Damuzi. "I am afraid I must retire."

The Bull stood, teetering ever so slightly from the excess of drink, and bowed to his new master.

"Many thanks, great king."

With that, Damuzi escorted the giant to the door and watched him disappear into the shadows of the hall. Closing the door behind him, his mask of cheer vanished. The lamp sat silently atop a dais, drawing his attention. This was a dangerous situation to be in. If word spread that the lamp was within the walls of Sabatu, the natives would begin to grow restless.

"Irkalla, you may come out now."

As if by some sorcery, a lithe form emerged from a

hidden compartment in the wall.

"Seems you have made a new friend, my lord."

"Then you have heard everything?"

"Is that not what you pay me for?" Irkalla had once been an assassin sent from the east, disguised as a dancing girl, hired to kill Damuzi. The lure of the king's wealth had stayed her blade. Now, she acted as the king's eyes and ears, for a hefty sum. There was no one in the world that he trusted more, a trust well compensated.

"That Bull. He is hiding something. Find out for me his true name."

Irkalla's eyes darted to the lamp and then back to her master.

"Your wish is my command."

"How do you do it?" Damuzi asked in amazement. For the last several months, the Bull had proven himself a thief second to none. After each foray, the loot returned to Sabatu's vaults was unparalleled in extravagance. "And they said you were too big!" laughed the king as he cradled a golden idol, bedecked in shimmering jewels.

Outwardly, the King could not have been more elated to have such a steady stream of wealth. However, beneath the calm and carefree demeanor, there brooded an ever-darkening storm on the horizon. Keeping control of the largest band of cutthroats in the known world was a difficult thing. When all was said and done, there had only ever been three real threats upon his life from the kings of civilization. The stories of bribes and murder had been allowed to spread, only adding to the allure of his brotherhood. What really worried the great Damuzi, were his subjects.

There were many circumstances that could drive a man to steal. Perhaps he was hungry; no merchant would miss a single fruit. Maybe it was not the thief that was hungry, but the children who sat huddled together for warmth. Some thieves stole for love, for jealousy, for desperation or thrill. Damuzi remembered well the empty pit within him, the rumbling growl of hunger emanating from within the frail figure of his youth. However, none of these things truly made men thieves. Not until the greed set in. The first job was always the hardest, but just once was never enough. There was always another job, another score, and another after that. Damuzi knew all too well that greed was what made men thieves. And there he sat, surrounded on all sides.

Sabatu had always housed disgruntled men and challengers to Damuzi's throne, that was nothing new. It was not until the Bull had arrived in Sabatu that there had been anyone he thought could wrest the crown from his head. While the giant man never outwardly expressed interest in Damuzi's throne, there were many in the streets who would support him if he tried.

Yet, the Bull remained an enigma, even after months at Damuzi's side. Irkalla had been gone since the day the Bull had returned that cursed lamp. Damuzi knew that his servant was faithful and the best spymaster money could buy. Surely she was doing everything in her power to uncover the true nature of the man that sat across the table sharing his wine. But every minute that Irkalla did not return, Damuzi grew all the more restless, and each passing day more of his subjects turned their backs on him and defected to the Bull.

It had taken many restless nights, but finally the king had decided he was tired of waiting. He had to take matters into his own hands.

"How do you like the wine?" asked the king, as innocuous as he could. Indeed, as his namesake suggested, the Bull had consumed his weight in wine and yet he barely seemed drunk.

"I have not tasted better in all my travels," said the Bull, laughing and showing a rare glimpse of mirth. "I once had a friend, the very best of friends, and he could drink even I

The Bull & the Djinn

under a table." The Bull's eyes flickered as fond memories floated across the haze of his liquor-soaked mind.

"What happened to him? Where is he now?" inquired Damuzi. The Bull paused, smiling faintly into his empty cup. The king snapped a finger and suddenly a beautiful, dark-haired woman appeared with a pitcher, refilling the Bull's cup as if by magic.

"He is gone. Taken from this world to live with the gods." The Bull tossed back his head and downed the cup.

"I am sorry to hear that, my friend," said Damuzi as the Bull's cup slid from his fingers and crashed upon the floor. "But I am sure you will see him again one day."

"Yes. One day. If the gods allow it."

"That day may come sooner than you think, great Bull." Damuzi sneered as realization of the king's machinations finally donned on his guest. Where the king expected to see horror, sadness perhaps, he was shocked to find only a grim smile beneath the Bull's night-black beard.

"You are a true king," said the Bull with another laugh. "You reach for power that you may never attain. Tell me, with what did you poison my drinks?"

"Venom of the black adder," said Damuzi, doing his best to keep his composure. "There is no stronger poison in the Nine Kingdoms. And you drank the lot!"

"Ah, yes. I feel it now. It burns like fire in my veins." The Bull flexed his mighty hands, finding enjoyment in the feeling of approaching death, however brief that death might be.

The king motioned to the serving girl, sending her from the throne room in a panic. Soon after she fled, appeared a contingent of guards flooding in, swords drawn.

The Bull stood, a looming colossus above the cowering King of Thieves.

"What are you waiting for?" yelled the King to his men. "Slay him! Slay him now!"

The guards rushed in, curved swords rattling in the air, ready to slice bloody ribbons from bone.

The Bull took up a wooden table in two hands and tossed it as though it were a pebble. The table soared across the room, smashing headlong into two of the men. Bones snapped and splintered like dry twigs beneath the force.

The other men did not stop to look at the crumpled heaps of flesh that had once been their comrades. They were no longer driven by their king's commands, but the desperate need for survival. Eyes drawn wide in awe at the display of strength, each man knew that they must fight or die.

The first soldier swung downward in a rending arc, but was not fast enough. The Bull caught the plummeting sword arm mid swing. As though caught in a vice, the man's arm snapped in two. The Bull snatched up the blade from a quivering hand as the man screamed in agony.

His cries were cut short as the giant drove the sword home with a disemboweling thrust.

In an instant, the others were upon The Bull. Bronze blades clashed and rang with deadly life, each soldier fighting frantically to find an opening in the giant's guard.

The Bull pressed them mercilessly, his blade slicing through the air with unmatched speed. Bolts of flame arced through the night with each deflected blow.

The Bull did his best to keep the guards on the defensive, but he knew this dance must finish quickly. The venom tore through his flesh, setting his heart ablaze and scratching murderously at his mind. With each frantic sword stroke, the weight of the weapon seemed to grow. His arms withered and his vision began to swim. The world teetered as if it were balanced upon the edge of some cosmic precipice. He had not thought Damuzi so daring, had hoped the game would continue till just the right moment. The King of Thieves had forced his hand and caught him unaware. New sensations of pain lanced through his quaking frame as the soldiers began to draw blood. Sword strokes rained upon his flesh, scoring his skin and dousing the floor in crimson spatter. He was running out of time.

The Bull & the Djinn

The Bull roared and charged forward, battering the soldiers' blades with every drop of strength that remained. Like a titan of old, the Bull surged forward and beat the desperate guards to the ground. Given a mere instant to breathe, he turned and leapt toward Damuzi, who cowered in the corner of his throne room. In one hand, the king clutched at his crown, in the other was a slim dagger, jewels adorning the hilt.

Damuzi screamed as the giant towered over him, the thief-king thrusting the small dagger out of pure instinct.

The Bull stopped dead in his tracks. His limbs went limp and the sword crashed to floor. Looking downward, he saw the king's knife now protruding from his heart. Time slowed to a familiar crawl as life began to slip from his grasp. Another blade slid from between his ribs, followed shortly by another, but he felt no pain. He teetered, reaching vainly for something on which to lean, and then toppled to ground in a blood-drenched heap.

Suddenly, the throne room door burst open. Standing within the threshold was a lithe figure draped in black.

"Don't kill him!" Irkalla yelled. "Don't kill him! I know his name!"

Those words were the last thing the Bull heard before the world went black.

💀 💀 💀

The Bull opened his eyes to an ocean of stars. Countless pinpricks of brilliant white light blew without aim across vast infinity on unseen winds. Clouds of cosmic dust billowed with iridescent storms within an endless field of black. For a long breath, the Bull lie still, floating weightless in the empty space. His wounds were gone, not even a scar left upon his skin. Where the dagger had jutted from his chest, only a small pang of emptiness remained, the feeling that once something had been there. If this was what the

49

afterlife was like, silent, a place to rest for eternity in endless peace, he supposed it would not be half bad.

"Get up, my son. You are not dead yet."

The voice that rumbled through his very soul was at once hard and musical, like the ringing of a massive Bell. The Bull groaned and pulled himself upright on tired limbs.

"Yes. I know." This was not the first time the Bull had found himself washed upon the shores of time and space.

"How many times must we meet like this?" asked the voice.

"Until I may rejoin my kindred soul in the Great Beyond," the Bull said. A figure appeared from the black with a dream-laced song. The woman was taller than the Bull, and beautiful beyond comprehension. For a mortal man to look upon such divinity would surely drive them mad. Ribbons of stardust danced around the goddess' supple form, and the fire of a thousand suns burned within her dark eyes. "Ninsun."

The goddess drew close. The Bull closed his eyes as her soft touch caressed his cheek with motherly concern.

"You are so tired. Why must you continue on this path?" she asked.

"There is nothing left for me on Earth. The only friend I have ever had was taken from me."

"You know I did what I could. The others, they would not listen. Your cousin, she can be very persuasive. My vote was outnumbered."

The Bull dismissed her words with the wave of a hand.

"It's no matter, mother. I have found a way."

Ninsun sighed and the heavens shuddered.

"I was afraid that you would stay this course. I realize that I will never convince you to cease this foolish quest. But perhaps another can."

"There is no one in Heaven or on Earth that can persuade me otherwise."

"Not even I?" boomed another voice, jovially.

The Bull & the Djinn

The Bull turned to see a man who could only be described as his equal. At closer comparison, the subtle difference in the man began to show. Where the Bull was a product of civilization, the vibrant spirit of the wildlands left an undeniable mark upon the barbarian who now stood before him.

"This can't be. Is it truly you?" asked the Bull, stunned in disbelief.

"Aye. In the flesh."

The Bull embraced the man, tears welling in his eyes. "It has been so long, my friend."

"And it will be longer still."

"No, I have found a way," exclaimed the Bull. "Soon I will be able to join you in death. Then we will continue our adventures across the heavens."

"I wish it were that simple, sword brother. But it is not," the barbarian gripped his long-lost companion by the shoulders. "There is nothing here for you."

"What do you mean?"

"The gods, they have deceived us. There is no paradise in the next life, nor any life after that. There are no endless battlefields to revel in the glory of war. There are no fountains of milk and honey where beautiful women wait on you hand and foot. It is a gloomy place. Grim and gray, where the dead wander endlessly with only the memories of their past lives to keep them company for eternity."

The Bull turned to his mother, seeking confirmation. She turned away, a steam of crystalline meteors pouring from her eyes in shame.

"That cannot be. This is a ruse. A vain trick of the gods as they attempt to bind me to the yoke of their destiny."

"You lie to yourself, my friend. All that we can do is live life while we have the chance. I have no regrets and there is no need to mourn for me. I have lived like no man ever has. Much of that is thanks to you. The memories of our deeds will keep me until the very stars grown dim."

"You do not understand, Enkidu. I will never die. You will wander the void with your memory of a life lived. I will be damned to life with only the memory of loss."

Enkidu laughed like thunder at his friend's moaning.

"You have much to do. Much to learn, old friend." The barbarian gave the Bull a hearty slap on the back, and the Bull plummeted through space.

The Bull awoke face down in a spreading pool of his own blood, the sound of Damuzi and Irkalla locked in heated argument filling his ears.

"How was I to know who he was?" roared the King.

"You were supposed to wait for me! Let me do my job! You have gotten messy and complacent! No wonder the masses look to him for leadership," hissed the spy.

Damuzi growled and stomped on the floor in frustration.

"What do we do now?"

"Use your lamp. Call up the djinn and have him fix the mess you made. It changed your fate before, surely it can again."

"It has no power over life and death. That thing is a cheat and not to be trusted. I regret even seeking it out in the first place. Why do you think I kept it hidden all this time?"

"Then we run. We take what we can and leave this place."

"We have facilitated the death of the greatest king in all the world. Do you not think that armies will hunt us down for such a sin?"

"Why do you suppose he was here in the first place? Why would he stock your storerooms with his own treasure?" asked Irkalla.

"Who can guess the motive of a man three-quarters god?"

The Bull rose from the floor as his limbs slowly regained

The Bull & the Djinn

feeling. Rivulets of blood ran across his mighty arms. His legs were weak, but grew stronger with each new heartbeat. The Bull wiped blood from his eyes and stood, red-soaked rags hanging about his heaving chest. Damuzi met his lion eyes and froze, fear wrapping about him like a cold mountain breeze.

The two guards who had survived their last encounter with the King of Uruk had no desire for another tussle. Their swords dropped to the floor, their owners disappearing through the threshold. Only Damuzi, Irkalla, and the Bull remained.

"Gilgamesh," gasped the King of Thieves. "I did not know. I would not have been so bold had I known it was you." Damuzi fell to his knees, begging for an audience with the king of kings. Irkalla stood in silent awe of the living god. She placed a gentle hand upon her king's shoulder and whispered.

"Damuzi. We must go."

The king ignored her advice, drowning in fear at the consequences of his rash decisions.

"What is it you want, Great Bull? Just ask and I will provide."

Gilgamesh laughed mirthlessly at the prospect of a man offering up his own head. "No, I do not think you would."

"Please, my lord," begged Damuzi. "Give me a chance."

The King of Uruk sighed and smiled.

"There are two things in this world that I desire. One, you cannot give. The other, Damuzi, is your life."

With those words, the ruler of Sabatu began to tremble. "But why?"

"Because that is the cost of what I desire most."

Cogs began to turn in Damuzi's head, connecting lines of thought that had not surfaced before. With great effort, he wrenched his eyes from the looming figure and stared upon the lamp sitting silently in its place.

Madness overwhelmed Damuzi "What deal did you

make with that devil-thing? Do not listen to its lies!" He clutched at Gilgamesh's torn robes, foam frothing at the corners of the thief-king's mouth. "His wishes are lies. He promised me a kingdom and what did I get? A life of paranoia and deceit. Daggers in the hands of my own subjects thirsting for my blood. I am wealthy beyond belief, but I have not seen the outside world from anywhere but this window since I was but a boy!"

Gilgamesh looked down upon the orphan king with pity. He knew well the cost of kingship. He had been absent from his throne for so long, he doubted he even remembered how to rule. Regardless, he was in no shape to be a king. His head had not been able to focus on much beyond his ultimate goal since the passing of Enkidu.

"What are you going to do?" cooed Irkalla, refusing to meet the eyes of Uruk's king.

"I have no quarrel with you. Take your leave from this place. Take what you are owed and go."

Irkalla hesitated. She knew the fate of her employer had already been sealed. What did she care if he died? His death was what had sent her to Sabatu in the first place. Her own purse had grown fat in his service, and she had enough to live out her days with relative ease. If she ever needed money, there was always work for a spy in the courts of the shining kingdoms.

Damuzi watched in disbelief as his loyal assassin strode across the room and plucked up the golden idol he had been admiring not an hour before. There was a look of melancholy as she walked by him, stopping only briefly at his side.

"I am sorry, Damuzi. But there is not enough money in all the world worth dying for." With those last, parting words, Irkalla vanished from his side.

Gilgamesh knelt down and looked the King of Thieves in the eye with sincerity.

"In truth, there is nothing that you could have done. The gods have had our fates planned for countless ages. This was always going to be. A good friend once told me that you must cherish the life you lived. That is all you will ever have."

"Oh yes! Yes! You have done a great thing," the djinn shouted in a vile mockery of joy. The creature softly clapped his hands in celebration of Gilgamesh's success. Like a curious child, the wish master peered into the cold, dead eyes of the severed head that had once been its master.

Damuzi had put up no fight, accepting his destiny with relative grace. Still, Gilgamesh felt something akin to regret deep within his soul.

"My side of the bargain is complete. Now it is your turn."

"Tell me, Great Bull, did he cry? Was he surprised by your deceit?"

"That is of no consequence. What does it matter to you?"

The djinn seemed irritated at Gilgamesh's refusal to divulge the details of Damuzi's last moments on Earth. "I suppose it does not matter at all. Now. What was it you wanted, again?"

"To be mortal. So I can die on my own terms and not on those my family has lain out for me."

"Yes. That is right. Your family is indeed quite complex. To meddle in the affairs of men." The djinn let out a reptilian laugh. "The gods of my day would never have stooped so low."

Gilgamesh did not understand the creature's commentary, and dismissed it outright.

"Grant me my wish, demon."

"I wish that I could, King of Uruk. But that wish has already been granted to you. A gift of fate upon your birth."

"Of what do you speak?"

"Gilgamesh, you are a fool on a vain quest." The djinn's toothy grin grew wide, its yellow eyes glowing from beneath its veil with malevolent light. "You have always been fated to die. You have always been mortal. The gods have already inked your death upon the scrolls of time."

"These are lies spoken by a devil of the desert sands! Damuzi warned me of your treachery!" raged the Bull!

"Only a fool such as you would head the words of another fool."

The room grew dark as though a shadow was cast from high above, blotting out the sky. The demon thing appeared to grow from the size of a slender, emaciated form to a hulking giant, shrouded in writhing smoke. The serpentine noise that had comprised its speech had become a bestial roar, unheard on this planet for millennia. Gilgamesh stood tall against the display, despite the rising tide of horror surging within him.

"You have so much to learn, but your time is running short," the monster called out. "This is the day you die, Gilgamesh the King!"

With sudden speed, Gilgamesh leapt forward, scooping up a discarded sword.

The djinn moved to stay his headlong rush, but the giant dove beneath the swipe of a massive paw.

Rolling across the floor, Gilgamesh barely escaped the jagged claws of the monstrous djinn. He came to stop beside the dais where the magic lamp rested and raised his sword high.

The djinn halted its course, shrinking back down to its original size in the blink of an eye.

"No! Wait!" wailed the djinn. "You were right. I lie! I am a treacherous thing! Spare me, great king!"

"You have wasted my time, beast. Have denied me my right and made me the butt of a cosmic joke. If indeed I am mortal, that one day I will die when the gods deem it necessary, I still have so much to do."

The bronze blade crashed upon the pedestal, shattering the small bronze lamp. An unearthly scream thundered through the night.

~ Logan Whitney ~

Logan Whitney was born and raised upon the rolling plains of Nebraska, but has now adopted the deserts of the Southwest as his home. He is a teacher, an archaeologist, and avid explorer as well as co-host of the Rogues in the House podcast.

Just Add Holy Water

by Dawn Vogel

Imlee opened the door to the Hall of Heroes slowly. To an outside observer, it might seem she struggled with the heaviness of the door. In truth, she took her time because she was afraid of the outcome of this visit.

Inside, a tall woman with smooth black hair, dressed in crimson robes embroidered with the resplendent sun crest of Korrad, the god of the reborn, smiled broadly. "Welcome! My name is Chaplain Marta. How may I help you?"

Her fist tight around the small bag of gold she had, Imlee stammered. "I…please…need…"

Chaplain Marta nodded, her smile remaining even when she spoke. "You're here to hire a rebirth?"

Imlee nodded.

"Excellent. We can offer you the finest in reborn heroes to serve your needs. Can you tell me a little bit about what you're looking for in a hero?"

"My brother was kidnapped." Imlee stared at the toe of her worn shoe. "I need someone to help me get him back."

The chaplain cocked her head to the side. "Kidnapped?"

"By goblins."

"I see. Not the sort to ask for ransom, then?"

Imlee shook her head. "The ransom price is too high."

"How much?"

"Ten thousand."

Chaplain Marta gasped, a hand to her chest, though the expression seemed exaggerated. "Ah, yes, that is far too high. You can hire a group of adventurers in the tavern for half that and the promise that they can loot the bodies when they're through."

"I don't have half that," Imlee admitted.

"We can find you a reborn hero for less than half their price."

"Less than half?" Imlee choked out. "How much less?"

Chaplain Marta's gaze swept over Imlee, and Imlee squirmed under the scrutiny. She wasn't even sure how much a reborn hero might cost, but she'd done what she could. If that wasn't enough…

"Shall we talk about pricing?" the chaplain asked, stepping toward a desk.

"What can I get for one hundred gold?"

Chaplain Marta chuckled. "Oh, dear…I'm sorry, I didn't get your name?"

"Imlee."

"My dear Imlee, perhaps you should come back with your parents?"

Imlee bit her lip, holding back tears. "They're not around anymore. It's just me and Petyr, and no one at the Foundling's Home seems to care that he's gone."

Chaplain Marta frowned. "You and your brother are orphans? Then why do the goblins think they might get a ransom for him?"

With a sigh, Imlee said, "There was a wealthy family touring the Foundling's Home with their children when the goblins came. I think the goblins thought they were taking the wealthy child, not my brother. I went to the wealthy family's house to ask for their help, and they gave me—" She held up the pouch of gold. "So it's all I've got to get him back."

"Oh, I see." Chaplain Marta paused and glanced over Imlee again. "I'm afraid our offerings at that price are a bit slim. I do have one option available that might suit your needs."

Pulling back a nearby curtain, the chaplain revealed a

59

wall covered in small wooden boxes. As more of the wall was exposed, the boxes turned to cubby holes, each containing a small, plain pouch. And beyond the cubby holes, a large swath of wall had similar pouches simply pinned to the wall. Marta stopped at the last of these sections, running her fingers through the air row by row until she stopped at one of the bags.

"Yes, this will do just fine. Radis is known to have defeated a goblin incursion some time before his death. I'm certain he can help you recover your brother."

"And he only costs a hundred?" Imlee asked, the faintest bit of hope fluttering around her heart.

"Yes."

"All right." Imlee placed her bag of gold on the desk in front of Chaplain Marta. "Then I'd like to hire him."

"Excellent. I'll get started on his reconstruction immediately."

"Reconstruction?"

"Yes, his cause of death left him a little less than whole, but I'm sure it will be sufficient for your needs."

"Oh," Imlee said. "Should I wait here?"

"No, my dear. Come back in the morning, and Radis will be ready to enter your service."

💀 💀 💀

Imlee returned to the Hall of Heroes as the first rays of sun illuminated the sky. In addition to his role as the god of the reborn, Korrad also included such concepts as daybreak and light amongst his purviews. It stood to reason that this Radis would be ready for Imlee early in the morning.

Standing on the steps of the Hall of Heroes was a skeleton, draped in a length of tattered red fabric that crossed over its chest cavity and was held around its hips with a worn leather belt. Bones grinding audibly, its head swiveled to point in Imlee's direction, though it had only hollow sockets where its eyes should be. "You the one who hired me?" it asked, its voice deep, its words simple, and its projection literally impossible.

This was not what Imlee had hoped her hundred gold would buy. "Are you Radis?" she asked, hoping the skeleton was just a daylight guard for the Hall of Heroes.

The skeleton's skull bobbed. "That's me. You're Imlee, then. Right. Goblins to be slain. That's my specialty."

"Surely there's some mistake," Imlee said. "I need to speak with Chaplain Marta."

Radis's skeleton shook his skull. "No luck with that. She's popped off to bed. Takes a bit out of a priest to put me back together, it seems. But I'm ready to accompany you to rescue your brother, was it? Taken by the goblins?"

Imlee studied the skeleton. She didn't understand how he was mobile, nor how he could talk without lungs, tongue, or lips. If this was truly what she'd spent her last hundred gold on, she supposed she was going to have to make this work, somehow. "Yes, that's right. Chaplain Marta said you could help me get my brother, Petyr, back from the goblins without paying their ransom."

"The goblins have asked a ransom?" Radis shook his skull. "What's this world coming to?" A noise rattled from his jaw that might have sounded like a sigh if he'd had need to breathe. "Well, there's nothing for it, I suppose. Find the goblins who took him, slaughter them all, and get your brother back."

"Is slaughter necessary?" Imlee said, the blood draining from her face and her voice coming out as a squeak.

"What were you thinking? Ask them nicely?" Radis asked.

"There's no harm in starting there, is there?"

Radis's shoulders lifted and fell in a shrug. "Most goblins back in my day would eat you alive if you try to bargain. But if they're asking ransom, more things might have changed than I realized. Lead on."

"Lead on where?"

"To the goblin stronghold, of course."

Imlee blinked several times in response.

"You don't know where it is?"

"Out of town somewhere, I suppose?"

Radis made his sound like sighing again. "Well, we're off to a bang-up start."

Imlee crouched behind a hedgerow atop a hill overlooking the goblin stronghold, but Radis stood upright, his eyeless gaze sweeping across the entirety of the encampment surrounding the abandoned farmhouse.

"Don't you think we ought to hide?" she asked.

"They won't recognize me," Radis replied. "I've been dead a good long while."

"Of course they won't recognize you," Imlee said. "But they'll see you."

"They'll see a skull atop a hedgerow. They might send scouts, but we'll see them coming. Then I'll ambush the scouts and question them."

Imlee grimaced. His logic was sound. Perhaps attracting scouts was the best way to get the goblins in a position where she could ask for Petyr back. She hadn't heard him wailing or crying since they arrived, and she was worried. "So we want them to send scouts, then?"

Radis shrugged. "Well, if we walk down there, we'll be dead—or re-dead, in my case—before we make it to their front lines."

"What if we snuck around to the back?"

Radis shifted his gaze, his bones grinding as his head rotated. "Worth a shot."

Imlee and Radis made their way along the ridgetop. But while Imlee crouched low and moved quietly, Radis had difficulty doing the same. His bones clacked together whenever he moved, as they had outside of the temple, but now the sound seemed amplified. Imlee slowed her pace, glancing down at the goblin encampment every few steps.

It didn't take long before a handful of goblins started looking toward the ridge.

"Shhh," Imlee said. "They may have noticed us."

Radis stopped, peering over the top of the hedges. "Oh, yeah, they have." He looked back toward Imlee. "We should probably run before they come up here to investigate."

Imlee slumped against the side of a building on the outskirts of town, her breathing heavy. They'd run all the way from the abandoned farmhouse to town, sure the goblins were on their tail.

Radis stood guard, watching the path they'd taken. When Imlee's breathing finally slowed to its normal rate, he returned to her side. "It looks like we've lost them."

"That's good news," Imlee said, "but we're still no closer to rescuing my brother."

"They're going to be at a heightened state of alert," Radis said. "We may want to give it a few days to die down."

Imlee frowned. "No, that won't do at all! What do you suppose they'll do with him if I don't pay their ransom or rescue him?"

Radis opened his mouth, but no sound escaped it.

"Wait, how long are you reconstructed for?" Imlee's eyes widened. "Do you even have a few days?"

"I'm here until the job's done," Radis replied. "I suppose you're right about the need to move more quickly, though. I'm just not accustomed to goblins making ransom demands. It's unheard of."

"I can show you the note, if you'd like."

"Can't read."

Imlee sighed. "Well, we need to come up with some sort

of plan. Sneaking is out, and you've already said a frontal assault wouldn't work. Do you have any other ideas?"

"Burrowing underground isn't going to be easy for either of us, so I suppose that's not a good option. Unless you've got some friendly dragons or eagles on your side, an aerial assault is out too." Radis paused. "Though I suppose if you had help like that, you wouldn't need me."

Had Imlee not spent several hours with Radis, she might not have noticed the faint downturn in his voice. He lacked facial expressions, but the tone of his speech sometimes gave away his feelings. It was strange to think of a reconstructed skeleton as capable of emotion, but he truly seemed to be.

"I agree with you on the burrowing or the aerial assault." Imlee considered the other approaches again, a thought coming to her. She didn't like it, particularly, but it seemed viable. Taking a deep breath, she said, "Maybe we should look at it from a different perspective. How long do you think you would last in a frontal assault?"

"It's not a good idea. You'd likely be killed.

"But what if it was *just* you, by yourself?"

"By myself? Oh, I could hold off an army of goblins for at least twenty minutes."

Imlee nodded. She'd never been inside this farmhouse, but most of the homes in the area were fairly similar. There weren't too many places to hide a young child who likely wanted to be found. "Twenty minutes, and you think that would draw most of the goblins out?"

Radis nodded. "Especially if I tell them who they're facing. I'm sure they still tell stories of Radis the Goblin-Slayer."

"Then here's what I suggest," Imlee said. "You draw the goblins out, while I sneak down from the ridge and into the house. I'll find Petyr, and you'll get to slaughter goblins, like you wanted."

Radis stared at Imlee, reaching one skeletal hand up to stroke his lower jaw. "That might just do it."

Just Add Holy Water

Imlee remained nervous until she heard the clash of swords outside the goblin stronghold. As anticipated, the goblins watching the hillside turned their attention toward the obvious threat. None of them remained behind for long, as their curiosity drew them to the fracas.

She still moved quietly, even when she reached the door at the back of the house. Just beyond, she heard two distinct voices, both raised as though they were in disagreement.

This hadn't been part of the plan. She'd been certain all the goblins would move toward the fight. Why were these two lingering so long?

She tested the door with a gentle nudge, and it swung partially open without a sound. Though the hallway within was dimly lit, Imlee saw two goblins. One of them held up a hand to the other, shorter goblin, their gaze fixed on the now partially opened door.

Imlee choked back a gasp and moved away from the door, hunkering down by the building's foundation. There was nothing for her to hide behind. If the goblins came out the back door, they would see her.

Footsteps on the wooden step near the back door pulled her attention back in that direction. The taller goblin looked around the area behind the house, but his gaze was fixed at the height of a human adult, not at the level of a young girl crouched beside the house. Finally, he shook his head and pulled the door shut behind him.

Wood scraped on wood a moment later, and Imlee's heart sank. She was hesitant to try the door again anyway, but if it was barred, she'd have no chance of entering the house as she and Radis had planned.

A faint snuffling sound drew her attention in the opposite direction before she could bemoan her lack of progress. She looked to see a floppy eared dog sniffing at the corner of the house. Its eyes were milky white, but dogs hunted more by scent than by sight.

The dog moved closer to her, and Imlee tried to remain calm. Perhaps it would sniff her and move on, since she had no food with her.

Instead, the dog stopped when it reached Imlee, its nose pressing against the small leather pouch she had used to carry the money that had bought Radis's services. Empty now, it served no real purpose.

Unless it could serve as a distraction for the dog.

Her fingers fumbled at the knot that held the pouch on her belt. Once it was loose, she hurled it away, toward the hill that flanked the farmhouse.

The dog sniffed at her for a moment longer, then took the bait and ran off after her empty money pouch.

Imlee ran the opposite direction, toward where the dog had come from. She wasn't sure what she might find, but she didn't have time to play fetch with the dog if it tried to return the pouch to her.

As she rounded the corner of the house, she scrambled to a stop. A pair of goblins had just exited the house through a pair of doors set at an angle just above the ground surface. Neither of them looked in her direction as they whooped and ran toward the front of the house.

Imlee tiptoed toward the doors and peeked at stairs leading down to a cellar. The smell of freshly churned earth assaulted her nose, but she heard and saw nothing in the darkness.

Taking a deep breath, Imlee clenched her fists at her sides and descended.

Above, scattered running footsteps all seemed to be headed toward the front of the house. Imlee took a moment to wonder what Radis might have done to draw so many goblins, and she said a quick prayer to Korrad, asking him to look after Radis. Then she continued into the cellar, blinking to try to force her eyes to adapt to the dim light.

Once she reached the bottom of the stairs, she noticed a

doorway leading to an upward staircase, which she presumed led into the house. She scanned the cellar quickly to ensure Petyr wasn't tucked away in a cage in the corner, and then proceeded upstairs, her courage growing by the moment.

Imlee paused at the top of the stairs, listening again for any sound of the goblins. She heard only a faint sobbing, which she recognized at once. Checking both directions in the hallway first, she ran to rescue Petyr.

💀 💀 💀

Petyr was heavy for Imlee to carry, but she didn't want to risk him being grabbed by the goblins a second time. They'd gone back out the way she'd come in, and so far encountered no goblins. Shushing Petyr softly, Imlee snuck to the front corner of the house and peered out at the area in front of the goblin stronghold.

There were far fewer slaughtered goblins than she'd anticipated, but there weren't any goblins standing around, either. Perhaps Radis had only injured the goblins, and they'd run off rather than fall at his hand. That would be what she told Petyr, at least, when he was old enough to hear the story about how she and Radis had rescued him from goblins.

Radis.

The skeleton stood in the center of the yard, still gripping a sword with his right arm. His left arm had fallen off, though it still clutched a goblin sword in its fist. His right leg, too, looked as though it had seen better days, with large chunks missing from the bones there.

Imlee scanned the area once more for any remaining goblins and then moved to Radis's side. "Are you alright?" she asked.

Radis shrugged, then fixed his eyeless gaze on Petyr. "That's your brother, then?"

Imlee nodded.

"Good. The goblins took off into the hills."

"How? What did you do?" Imlee asked.

Radis shrugged. "I told them I could keep fighting like this all day, and they'd never take me alive. The latter was more true than the former, but it worked either way. My work here is done."

"No, wait, please don't go," Imlee cried out. "Thank you for your help. And—" She paused, searching for a way to keep Radis active. "I feel as though you ought to go back to the Hall of Heroes, don't you?"

Radis shifted his gaze toward Imlee, cocking his head to the side. "I suppose so. Not really sure how I got back the last time someone hired me, if I'm being honest."

"We'll help you. Wait a moment, Petyr," she said as she set Petyr down, picking up Radis's left arm in her right hand, and prying the sword from its grip. "This isn't yours, is it?"

Radis shook his head. "Nah, took it from a goblin. You'll probably want to get the town guard to come clean up later."

"Alright." Imlee dropped the sword and offered her left arm to Radis.

He stared at her for a moment longer before taking her arm.

Then she offered Radis's bony left hand to Petyr, while holding the skeletal arm at the elbow. "Hold on, Petyr."

Petyr reached up and took the skeleton's fingers in his grasp, toddling next to Imlee.

"Off to the Hall of Heroes, then," Imlee said, helping both Radis and Petyr to walk in the correct direction.

Imlee opened the door to the Hall of Heroes with her shoulder, still holding both of Radis's arms, with Petyr at the end of the detached arm.

Chaplain Marta quirked an eyebrow at the scene as the

three approached her. "My dear Imlee, you seem to have your brother back!"

Imlee nodded. "Yes, thank you for suggesting Radis. He fought valiantly. But I'd like to make a suggestion on his behalf."

"What?" Radis asked, his voice betraying his puzzlement.

"Radis is a brave and noble skeleton. I hope you'll be able to repair the damage he sustained, and I'd like to request that he be upgraded in the Hall of Heroes, rather than hidden away behind a curtain." Imlee smiled at Radis, then turned her attention back to Chaplain Marta. "He's worth far more than one hundred gold."

Chaplain Marta looked at Radis with an appraising gaze, then returned Imlee's smile. "I will make sure Radis's arm and leg are both repaired immediately, and we will add your recommendation to our files for future reconstructions."

Radis's bony fingers squeezed Imlee's hand. "Thank you, Imlee. It was good to get out again." He turned his attention to Chaplain Marta. "Can we make a note that any time Imlee needs help in the future, I want to be assigned to her at my current rate?"

"Yes, of course, I'll note that as well. Anything else?"

"If I have one hundred gold later on, can I have Radis animated just to visit?"

Chaplain Marta pursed her lips but nodded. "I suppose there's no rule against that."

"Good!" Imlee threw her arms around Radis, ignoring the rattling of his bones as she hugged him. After a moment passed, he patted her on the back, returning the hug in his awkward way.

She released him from the hug, wiping the tears from her face, and picked up Petyr. "See you later, Radis!"

Radis pointed at Petyr first. "You behave for your sister, young man." Then he looked at Imlee, his eye sockets somehow glistening in spite of him not being able to produce tears. "See you another time, Imlee."

~ Dawn Vogel ~

Dawn Vogel's academic background is in history, so it's not surprising that much of her fiction is set in earlier times. By day, she edits reports for historians and archaeologists. In her alleged spare time, she runs a craft business and tries to find time for writing. Her steampunk series, Brass and Glass, is available from DefCon One Publishing. She is a member of Broad Universe, SFWA, and Codex Writers. She lives in Seattle with her husband, author Jeremy Zimmerman, and their herd of cats. Follow her @historyneverwas.

To Walk on Worlds

by Matthew John

For years Maxus heard a voice calling from beyond the Black Rim. Through the haze of the flower, he studied the signs of the night sky and puzzled over its messages. So many words—all of them strange and unfamiliar—none that he could answer. But that was about to change.

He leaned back in his chair and pondered the heavy book in his hands. In the blackened depths of Gruundal he paid in blood to secure the dusty tome, and now he alone would exploit its secrets. What other fingers might have turned its yellowed pages, he mused. What other minds decrypted its riddles?

He ran a blood-stained hand over the pale leather cover and opened it, wincing as the spine cracked in protest. He scanned the contents with hungry eyes, and the pages promised power—sacred words of lost tongues, incantations of rebirth, of transmuting flesh to smoke, blood to dust. The Book of Thuul offered immortality and would allow him to walk the worlds of the Black Rim—to spread across the stars like mist over an endless lake.

The time drew near; soon *it* would come. He needed only to set the bait.

"Boy! Run and tell the court that Maxus would speak to the King." Artum, a gaunt, pock-faced lad, nearly jumped from his seat at the command.

"My lord!" He pulled a threadbare hood over his greasy head, strode across the chamber, and pulled open the door. For a moment, harsh daylight and birdsongs invaded the brooding murk. Then, Artum shut the door and was gone.

Maxus had purchased the youth from a starving family years previous. Their crops had failed, as had most that autumn, but none realized Maxus was the cause. A man can do whatever he wishes, if he decides which bellies are filled.

And even kings hear the call of hunger.

The shadows of dusk stretched across Maxus' chamber when a firm knock came at the door. He rubbed his eyes. The smoke of the flower must have lulled him to sleep, but the censer to his left yet smoldered.

So quickly you've come, my King.

Maxus didn't so much as raise an arm, for the lazy flick of a finger was all it took. The door swung inward, and the shadows of armored men spread across his chamber. General Playsus was the first to enter. Maxus could mark his visage from a hundred paces—his bright, arrogant eyes forever scanning for some perceived slight, his fingers ever a flutter over his sword, aching to right some injustice. Though the king himself and most of his court understood the secret hierarchy, Playsus remained the fool. Always resisting. Always challenging.

"I see you have been busy, Maxus," Playsus said with a sneer. The aging warrior towered above the instruments strewn across the floor and the markings inscribed in the stone. He kicked a pile of burned bones as he strode to the window and blocked out the dying sunlight, becoming a black, featureless silhouette. His men, five in total, fully armored and carrying shields, spread out after him. The chamber resounded with boot steps, the creak of leather, and the heavy breath of armored men who had climbed a steep road. But not Playsus; he gave no indication of any exhaustion. The general turned and fixed Maxus with sea-blue eyes that managed to shine even in the absence of light.

"I thought you would have heeded my letter," he continued. "It was quite clear, after all. The king won't be seeing you, *meddler*. Not today. Not again. You were instructed—

and clearly so—to request an audience with *me*. Only then—should I deem it necessary—will the king endure your mad musings."

Animals know when danger lurks. They can smell it in the air, feel it in their blood and bones. They can taste it. At that moment, so too could Maxus. Playsus was finally taking his stand. The other soldiers confirmed it: eyes wide and expectant, fists clenched, frames erect.

Beneath the book in his lap, Maxus pulled free a pouch from his belt. "You've made some wise moves. None would doubt your cunning," Playsus went on. Maxus snuck the pouch into his left sleeve and placed his arm in feigned laziness on the armrest. "And so, I've made the climb all the way to your vile little nest to further clarify matters." Playsus stepped from the window and the light poured into the room, causing Maxus to squint and turn away. "Your influence on this kingdom has ended. The poison you've poured in the king's ear has all dried up. And you," he paused, stabbing a gauntleted finger toward Maxus, "are *done*!" He stomped a heavy boot in succession with the last word.

A twang cut the air, followed by a hollow thud.

Maxus watched, bewildered, as a red stain spread from the arrow in his shoulder.

"Fool!" snarled Playsus.

The arrow had passed through flesh and muscles and pinned Maxus to the back of the chair. As the pain surged, panic threatened to addle his mind. But he snapped his fingers without a thought. The censer burst into flames.

"Your job is to shoot!" Playsus admonished the unseen archer. "To arms, men! Do not let him utter a word!"

Through watery eyes, Maxus saw the men draw swords and advance. Even the subtle movements it took to retrieve the pouch from his sleeve sent scorching waves through his shoulder.

Playsus and his men were just out of sword's reach when he managed to empty the contents of the pouch onto the flaming censer.

A flash. An explosion.

And darkness.

💀 💀 💀

A makeshift tourniquet encircled his shoulder, drooping and sodden with blood. In dumb fascination, Maxus watched as the red drops fell and flooded the tiny canals between the tiles. Never again would his arm function as it once had, and without proper supplies and treatment it would fester and rot and probably kill him. But soon that wouldn't matter.

Though he had learned many secrets during his preparations, none proved as useful as the tunnel leading from the king's quarters. Not even Playsus knew of its existence. And Maxus couldn't even be certain the king—drunkard that he was—had any memory of the cobwebbed passage.

Mere moments ago the smoke had brought him here, and since then his mind had become a swirling mess of logic and emotion. At present he burned with embarrassment. Why had he sent the boy? Even more than his wounded pride, he lamented wasting all of the precious powder to get here. So rare was the alien spore that he'd have to leave this world just to find more. After harvesting the contents from the last meteorite, he had rationed it, using only a pinch when necessity compelled him.

And because of an ambush—because of a virtuous fool—the most powerful substance in existence was gone.

But it had saved him, after all, and allowed him to shed the physical tethers of the world. Now in position, he had only to wait unti—

A door creaked open inside the chamber. From the tunnel, through a tiny aperture disguised in the brickwork, Maxus could see into the king's quarters. Lazy footsteps scuffed along the rich red carpets. An exhalation of breath. A belch. A stifled laugh.

The king returned, drunk and staggering, his hunched frame and doughy flesh inspiring pity even in Maxus' monomaniacal brain. *So weak. Such a sad sack of guts.* But Maxus brushed away this useless emotion and relished the King's vulnerable state. Since the queen perished months previous of an *unfortunate illness*, the King had taken to drink and, most nights, came alone to his chamber.

He shall not see me coming.

The thought made him reckless and he considered striding into the room without taking the proper precautions. His throbbing shoulder reminded him he was in no condition for a struggle, so he spoke The Words of the Void to silence the air around him. Then, he wiped the sweat from his brow and cleared his throat to confirm the spell had worked. Once satisfied, he pulled the lever and the door slid open without a sound.

The king lay on his back, his head lolling from side to side. He belched in short intervals but did not rise. Maxus slipped across the room like a snake, unheard, unseen, and stopped at the edge of the bed.

There he paused and recalled the necessary words. To prepare the spell, he spoke the first seven in his mind and kept the last cocked on his tongue like a quarrel in a crossbow.

Maxus listened as the king blew out rhythmic breaths, interrupted by random snorts and gasps. When he was sure the king slept, he made his move.

Approaching the right side of the bed where the king lay, he reached out with his wounded arm, ignoring the pain shooting from his shoulder, and placed a firm hand over the king's mouth. Just as the monarch's eyes snapped open, Maxus spoke the final word and slipped beneath his flesh, assuming control.

In an instant, King Nylan, was gone—his life essence tossed away like a corpse poached of its prize. Maxus felt the weight of the wine, the burning belly, the need to piss. A long forgotten, yet familiar euphoria—a numbness of the face and tingling of the prick—washed over. A smile tugged at his lips. His shoulder no longer pained him, but despite the warmth of the wine, the king's heavy frame was a new and unwelcome discomfort. As he rose to find the chamber pot, he glanced at his own expired corpse slumped on the bed. For so many years it had served him well.

But greater things await.

He stumbled over to the chamber pot on the bedside table, pulled open his new luxurious robe and relieved himself. As he quivered with satisfaction and mused over the golden etchings of the piss pot, a knock came at the door and cut off his stream.

Gods! Not now.

"Sire, forgive the intrusion, but the meddler, Maxus, has fled and I fea—

"One moment, Playsus. I'm draining my prick." Maxus knew the king to be a crass man. Sure, he could play the diplomat and deliver kingly speeches, but most often he spoke like a classless serf. Maxus squeezed out the last few drops of royal piss and stumbled over to his own corpse. He pulled loose a dagger he'd kept in his sleeve and, without hesitation, plunged it into the heart of his former body. A few scratches down his former face completed the ruse. Then he retrieved the Book of Thuul from his satchel and placed it in the drawer of the bedside table. The sensation of wearing this new skin, coupled with the alcohol, affected his balance and he almost tripped as he approached the door. He found the king had forgotten to draw the bolt, so he simply pulled it open.

Playsus stood on the other side, wearing a worried, timid expression. "Sire, we uncovered a plot and moved immediately to capture the meddler, but he used his tricks to slip away. We know not where he's gone, but one of our archers wounded him. He's likely desperate, and I fear he will be moving t—"

"Be silent, Playsus." Maxus was startled to hear his voice transformed into that of the king's, but he was careful not to show any outward sign of alarm. Playsus' blue eyes were blackened in the shadowy torch light, but the look of obedience on his face was clear.

My, how things have changed.

"I've taken care of it." Maxus pulled the door open and waved toward the bed where his former body bled out on the fine linens.

Playsus' jaw dropped and his blue eyes beamed as he stepped past Maxus and approached the grisly scene. "Gods," he whispered. "When? How? Si—Sire, forgive me. I should have come sooner bu—"

"Yes, you should have." Maxus cut him off. This new dynamic excited him, but he kept his composure. "The rogue, thinking me asleep, tried to put a knife in me, but I managed to plunge it through his own heart." Maxus watched carefully as Playsus inspected the scene. Would he be convinced? The man was cunning; there could be no doubt. But Maxus believed the corpse would allay his suspicions. "General, we know that Maxus worked alone. He was always a loner and, though he proved most useful on many matters, his intentions are now clear. Send for someone to clean this up and have them burn the corpse. It's bad luck to bury a meddler, I'm told."

Playsus' icy stare told no secrets. Maxus returned in kind and the two men locked eyes for an uncomfortable moment until Maxus broke the silence. "Now, I am beyond weary and must res—" a hiccup interrupted his speech, followed by an involuntary belch. This new body was gassy. *And so heavy.* "And you must rest as well; I have a mission for you and your men—one that begins at sunrise."

Playsus stood as a statue, arms folded, one hand rubbing his chin as he stared down at Maxus' former body. For several seconds he said nothing in reply. And then, as if suddenly waking, he said, "Of course, sire. We shall make the preparations. I'll send the servants at once to clean this mess and someone to retrieve the body."

"One more thing, Playsus." Maxus reached over and grabbed the full chamber pot. "Do dispose of this for me." Maxus thrust the spilling vessel at the general so that a few drops sloshed onto his armor. The tall knight recoiled and paused before accepting the stinking pot and fixed him with narrowed blue eyes. Maxus couldn't be sure, but just before he locked eyes with the general he thought he saw him glance at the back wall. From where Maxus stood, it seemed unlikely Playsus could have seen the slot leading to the tunnel. But Maxus *had* forgotten to close it, and couldn't be sure.

"Of course, sire. Good evening."

Playsus swung around and his cape flapped behind him. So perfect and elegant was the turn that Maxus was certain the general had practiced it. As he vanished in the dark hallway beyond, Maxus retrieved the Book of Thuul from the drawer and stashed it beneath his robe. Whether or not Playsus saw the tunnel was of no real consequence. Soon all would be as planned. He still had an hour's study before he'd be sure of the necessary spell. Looking out the window he saw stars winking faintly from a moon-brightened sky. Tonight *it* would enter this world, and Maxus would greet it at the door.

💀 💀 💀

It was the discovery of the Rim of Ancients that prompted the First Men of Pathra to settle here and build the grandest city on the continent. It had been chosen not only for its advantageous terrain—a narrow wedge of land surrounded on all sides by sheer ridges rising a hundred feet from the sea—but also for its alien infrastructure. Of course the average citizen was unaware these architects came from beyond the Black Rim. In their ignorance, most reckoned them deities. *Like savages glimpsing God in the sun.* But Maxus knew the truth. This site attracted the Others like a magnet. Though these beings could only enter at precise times, dictated by the movements of celestial bodies, there was one location in particular—a beacon wrought from lost technologies—that served as a doorway from their world to this one. And there it lay, at the very edge of the Rim, untouched and forbidden.

Using the secret passage, Maxus circumvented the usual routes and avoided all eyes when slipping away from the castle. A simple cloak marked him as a wayward beggar to any who might have seen him passing during this late hour. Reaching the Rim, he scanned for any signs of life and slipped among the ancient stones like a thief through a crowd. The breeze smelled of salt and sea and helped awaken his wine-addled senses. He had only to contend with this new bloated husk—the heavy steps and sour guts of a drunkard. *And not for much longer.*

The green stone walls of the maze rose slightly above his head, but he knew the way; he'd mapped it countless times in his mind's eye. He paid little heed to the markings etched into the smooth surface but couldn't help admiring the soft edges and strange angles of the structure. It was as if the walls had been sketched or painted rather than hewn.

Clearing the maze, he met a vast seascape. A long shimmering worm of moonlight stretched across the water, seemingly pointing at him. He began reciting the studied words so the final few could march from his tongue when the moment came—when the last stars faded and Gryzmahl took its first step onto the Rim of Ancients.

"Zevlala. Zevlala. Awulakin dez'luum dezva. Zevlala, Gryzmahl. Zev—"

"You snake." Playsus' voice cut the night wind like a poisoned blade. "Remove that cloak and face me. It matters not what you wear—fabric nor the king's flesh. I know it's you."

Maxus turned to see the smug general. His arms were crossed over his chest and ten men stood at his back. Quarrels were fitted in crossbows. Swords hissed from scabbards. And the crowd of armored men tossed a frail figure to the cobbles in front of Playsus.

Artum. His face was streaked with blood, his ratty clothes torn to ribbons. Maxus cared little for Artum's well-being, but the boy was his property, and he wouldn't abide its mistreatment.

"I'm sorry, m—my lord," said Artum.

Ignoring the boy, Maxus gazed at the general. "I admire your strength, Playsus. It shall soon be mine." He felt a thin smile part his lips.

"You'll have nothing, meddler. Not even a cold grave. Your corpse will feed the gulls and they'll shit you into the sea. And to think—your plan almost worked, but you came here, of all places, to this isolated quarter."

Maxus fought back curses as they tried to slip from his tongue. He eyed the stars impatiently.

"You know, of course, that without a queen and without an heir, the king's rule falls to me. I need only direct the blame to you, meddler." The general's blue eyes seemed to blacken in the predawn shade. "Men, cause him pain, but avoid his face, and use no blades. Soften him. Then we'll carry him back to some dark corner of the castle where a nefarious meddler shall cut his throat. Sadly, I shall arrive too late to save the king, but will drive my knife into the sorcerer's heart."

Maxus did his best to endure the beatings, all the while silently appealing to the fading stars above. As each steel fist struck his blubbery frame, he whispered another Word of Thuul. But as the pain overwhelmed him, hope faded. Years of plotting and preparation would be for naught. And worst of all, Playsus would win. As the first strip of pink cut across the eastern horizon, Maxus gave up. The words left him. Throbbing and bloody, all he could do was spit a final curse at the smirking general. "You've won the day, Playsus. But there are," he paused, spitting blood, "realities beyond this. And I sh—"

Maxus' words broke off as a pale light washed over the Rim of Ancients. The sky purpled dimly on the horizon, heralding the dawn, but an uncanny radiance beamed down from overheard. All eyes shot to the sky and mouths sagged open at the phenomenon—all eyes save those of Maxus. "Zevlala. Zevlala. Awulakin dez'luum dezva. Zevlala, Gryzmahl. Dusunda Gryzmahl und Wyrrl dum Zevlala." Above the meddler's words, came the roar of fierce wind. Louder and louder it grew, and within it sounded a thousand voices like a dissonant chorus bellowing from the depths of Hell. Most of the soldiers backed away from the blinding beam; the others stood petrified.

The chorus reached an awful crescendo before fading to silence. A whisper of sea breeze followed. The harsh light began to fade, but in the empty space between Maxus and the soldiers, a hulking silhouette remained. A figure of the deepest black seemed to consume all ambient light. It was man-like in its proportions, but stood taller than ten feet, its back half as wide. Yellow eyes beamed from a skeletal face that stretched backward into a talon-shaped head. When it craned its neck, Maxus could tell that it was composed of abyssal blue flesh and wasn't merely a strange trick of the light.

Gryzmahl had come.

"Zevlala zut duum," it said in a deep and phlegmy voice. None of the men spoke. None of them moved—not even Maxus. Ignoring the meddler and the prostrate boy at its feet, the creature took a single step toward the petrified soldiers and reached out an arm as thick and corded as a tree trunk. One of the men—a young, thin-bearded man—raised a sword in defense, but Gryzmahl swatted the blade and sent it clattering to the cobbles below. Despite its size, the creature moved quickly. Again the heavy arm shot forward clamping a massive, clawed hand over the soldier's head and hoisting him skyward. Its other hand gripped the man's feet and savagely wrenched his body in opposite directions. A muffled scream preceded a sickening snap as the fiend ripped him in two.

There was a collective gasp. Blood trickled on the cobbles. Gryzmahl's skeletal jaw parted into a maniacal grin as it brandished the two flopping portions of the soldier like clubs. The men broke from their stupor and backed away as the beast started swinging. But it was too late. With two mighty blows, four men were knocked from their feet and smashed against the green walls of the ruins. Pealing laughter followed and the alien hulk waded into the horrified assembly.

"Stand and fight, you dogs!" Playsus tried to maintain his steely composure, but there was panic in his voice. He was a veteran swordsman but had never beheld a thing like Gryzmahl. The general gave stern command, but he, like the rest of his men, stepped back and spread out, circling around the massive skull-faced figure.

Gryzmahl ceased his pursuit and dropped the dripping clubs to his sides. It craned its neck like a curious animal and seemed to be searching for something.

It seeks the king.

"Zevlala. Zevlala. Awulakin dez'luum dezva. Zevlala, Gryzmahl. Dusunda Gryzmahl und Wyrrl dum Zevlala." As Maxus recited the words, the creature turned to him. Its luminous yellow eyes bloomed from the black silhouette, widening as another grin split its jaw. It found its quarry—found what it traveled infinite gulfs to steal.

A king's power. A toy. A project with which to slake a gnawing boredom developed on its cold and desolate world. For years, it watched over this kingdom, marking its ruler and planting seeds. Posing as King Nylan, it would sew discord on this planet, savoring every war, every plague, and every conquest.

It would…but Maxus had plans of his own.

As Gryzmahl released its grip, the bloody makeshift clubs hit the cobbles with a wet smack. The ground shook as Gryzmahl stomped toward Maxus, gaining speed with each step. The meddler closed his eyes and escaped into his mind, whispering the final words and awaiting the creature's touch. As the claws made contact, he bellowed the final word, "Dumnak!" and slipped beneath the demon's flesh.

Inside, rage and panic coalesced as two beings shared one vessel, locked in a battle of wills. The Words of Thuul coursed through Maxus' thoughts as he cut the tethers of the demon's consciousness, stripping away the mind of Gryzmahl and replacing it with his own. Maxus felt the hot lash of claws as the demon struggled to hold its grip—felt the fierce blows as it tried to beat him back. But the words were older than even this ancient name. The words of Thuul were command.

It seemed he labored for weeks in the ethereal blackness of two minds. Only when the fight was over did he realize it took but a breath of time. An itch on his new leg brought him back to a world gone red through the eyes of the demon. Several feet below, Playsus was as a child, his sword jutting and swaying from the thickly muscled leg of Gryzmahl. Maxus laughed at the feeble blow, and the demon's acerbic cackle sounded over the Rim.

"Behold, general, your new master!" The demon's cruel timbre pleased him.

"Maxus? It cannot be!" Playsus' incredulous gaze fell from the demon and landed on the king's former body.

"Oh, but it *can*. And there's more."

Maxus used the might and speed of Gryzmahl to dispatch the remaining soldiers. Heads sprang from necks, arms snapped from shoulders, and a spreading pool of crimson shone in the early morning gloom. Playsus stood alone, gripping a puny dagger in his shaking fist. Impressively, he did not step back as Maxus closed in. The aging swordsman seemed resigned to his fate, a sad frown sinking his visage.

"It grieves me, general, that you won't be around to lick my boots and clean my piss pots, but I've another need of you." Maxus placed two massive claws around the general's shoulders and lifted him bodily. The creature's raw power was a welcome shift from the king's feeble strength. Playsus struggled in the steely grip, but was forced to endure the demon's gaze.

"Do not despair; with my mind and this creature's power, *Playsus* shall accomplish great things." The general's blue eyes widened at the implication. "Drezlun, drezlun, val, livraduk!" The Words of Seizure wove through the demon's essence, snaring the aspects of its power that Maxus desired. Then, the meddler spoke the Word of Passage once more: "Dumnak!"

As he slipped beneath Playsus'skin, he caught a lingering whiff of despair. He expected to feel a drastic shift from alien omnipotence to human frailty, but was pleasantly surprised at the strength he harvested from Gryzmahl.

The Rim had gone silent save for the whisper of sea breeze and the distant squawk of hunting gulls. The bright yolk of the sun crested the eastern horizon, casting an ironic glow over the grim scene. The demon was gone. With its essence seized, its dead husk would be left to rot somewhere in the fathomless depths of the universe. Perhaps, one day, Maxus would venture to its world, but for now there was still work to be on this one.

"My lord? Is it you?" A weak murmur came from among the crumbled bodies. *Artum.* Maxus had forgotten about the boy. As the meddler approached the skinny youth, an idea bloomed in his mind. Though he desired nothing more than to tread the worlds beyond the Black Rim, he was reluctant to lose control over the pieces and players of this one. But what if he did not have to choose?

He looked to the king's crumbled and bloody form. The mind of Nylan had been obliterated when Maxus invaded.

To Walk on Worlds

But the king's body yet lived. Next, he bent down and peered into Artum's eyes. The boy had been his servant for years and never questioned his actions nor challenged his authority. In the youth's haunted gaze, Maxus saw no resentment, nor animus, despite the years of cruelty; he saw only loyalty, devotion, and gratitude. He had broken the boy like a horse. The wretch would continue to serve, but he would serve in ways he could never have imagined.

"Boy, all your life you've been a beggar…a slave. Tell me, how would you like to be king?"

Matthew John is an English Language Arts teacher living in Nova Scotia, Canada. When his day job doesn't consume all his time, he likes to compose short fiction and waste away at the gaming table pretending to be someone he's not. His work has been published in *Skelos* (Skelos Press), *Weirdbook* (Wildside Press) and *Robert E. Howard's Conan* (the role-playing game by Modiphius Games).

The Immortal Contract

by D.K. Latta

Garanth woke with a grunt. It was pitch black in the dingy, rented room; coolness lingered in the air, a relief from the day's broiling heat. But nothing could dispel the stink of fish that clung to him from his day's work as a fishmonger's assistant.

What had roused him, he wondered? What had—

The door splintered inward. Garanth flung himself from his cot as robed figures spilled through the aperture. Limned indistinctly by moonlight, they formed a mass of shadows sprinkled with glints of steel. Instinctively he clawed the floor beside his cot in the darkness, groggily searching for a blade. Then he remembered: it had been a long time since he had kept weapons close at hand.

Fortunately, though, Garanth *was* a weapon.

He kicked out, sending one assailant crashing into a corner. He twisted, avoiding a bear hug, and chopped down with the edges of both hands, cracking that man's clavicle and knocking him to the floor. Two more came at him—he was surprised the meagre room could contain so many—and he leapt into the air, kicking out with both legs, snapping their heads back. He landed gracefully among their crumpled forms.

Four attackers—and not one seemed to be the leader.

Panting, legs braced, he waited for the true battle to begin. Suddenly the hairs on the back of his arms bristled as before a storm. Too late he knew he was facing no mortal adversary. Too late he looked to the yawning doorway and its promise of escape.

Ebony smoke bubbled from the ground before him, roiling and swirling, the stink of unnamable things scouring his nostrils. A long, sinewy arm stretched from the smoke, followed by a man swathed in a dark purple cloak that twitched and coiled about him as though a thing alive. Garanth tried dodging the clutching fingers, but the arm flicked out like a snake's tongue, grabbing his throat, hoisting him effortlessly from his feet.

Horrified he stared into black, soulless eyes.

"You are Garanth?" asked the man, though it seemed more statement than question. "Of the Night Vendors?"

"Not—not anymore," Garanth gasped, clawing at the hand about his throat. "I quit the assassin's guild."

The cloaked man flicked his wrist dismissively, sending Garanth sprawling across his cot. The eerie mantle undulating about him as though catching a wind that existed not on this plane, the newcomer casually said, "Leave us." For a moment Garanth was unsure who the man was addressing. But then the other men rose unsteadily and filed sullenly from the room. The stranger's dark, eerie eyes locked upon Garanth again. "Do you know who I am?"

Garanth started to say "no," then halted. There was something familiar about the robed men, about their manner of dress. Then he placed it: they were followers of the Cult of Aar! His lips grew tight as he inhaled sharply. "You…you are Aar, The Undying—The Living God."

"Aye, little mortal," purred the tall man, satisfied. "I am the God Who Walks the Earth, The Living God. And you…you are Garanth, formerly of the Night Vendors. But you left that exclusive establishment. No mean feat, I hear—as most who attempt to go their own way end up victims of their erstwhile colleagues."

"I was apprenticed to the guild as a naive boy. As a man, I grew a conscience," Garanth said, defiantly, still surreptitiously eyeing the freedom offered by the rectangle of moonlight cut from the darkness behind The Living God.

"I will employ you in your former profession," stated Aar, a being accustomed not to asking, but to instructing. "Failure will mean certain death…success will mean a suitable reward."

"And what would be suitable for me?" demanded Garanth, glancing around at his hovel. "I who want for nothing…because I've forsaken everything?"

From his cloak Aar drew a small vial and tossed it to the prone man. "Inside is merely water. But upon the completion of your task, it will instantly transform into a curative elixir."

Garanth stared wide eyed at the little vial, feeling a sudden tightening in his chest. "How would you know—?"

Aar laughed. "I know many things. I am a god, after all."

Garanth frowned, angry, and made to say that he was an assassin no more. His words, though, caught in his throat. One did not arouse the ire of a god impulsively. Instead he said, "You have a cult of followers eager to do your bidding, eager to die in your name, if need be. You have powers derived from the other realms. Who could you possibly want killed that you couldn't do the deed yourself?"

Aar smiled a thin, humorless, smile. "A most singular target…myself."

Garanth could only stare.

The Living God shrugged. "A thousand years is a long time—a very long time. And existence loses its luster." He glanced around at the dingy room, at the depths to which Garanth had allowed himself to sink. "As I'm sure you can understand. One becomes, not sullen, but simply…tired. Worn out. And desirous of the final sleep that true mortals are blessed to know. But I am immortal. Even I know of no way to end my existence. But you are the greatest assassin the Night Vendors ever produced. You say you have a conscience, perhaps that is why. The rest of your guild are too in love with death; they have made it banal. Only someone who appreciates the value of life, or at least the

The Immortal Contract

value others instill in it, can master the art of ending it."

"How do you know I was their greatest assassin?"

"Because they told me."

Garanth could only gawk again.

"You were not my first selection. I approached the guild first, and offered them terms as attractive to them as, I expect, are the ones I offer to you. They sent their best man. Alas, though I desire my end, my followers do not, and anyone who wishes to kill me must first pass through them. In this the guild's assassin failed." Garanth frowned, suddenly realizing why The Living God had sent his followers from the room: they were obviously being kept in ignorance as to the true nature of this meeting. They would not be happy to learn the very foundation of their faith was prone to suicidal impulses. "But when queried, the guild assassin revealed that you were the greatest of their number."

"He said that before he died?" asked Garanth, incredulous. He had heard that his name had been struck from the annals—that it was torture and death to any assassin who uttered it.

"No. He told me *after*." From out of his swirling black cloak, Aar hefted something in the dim light. Garanth squinted, then with a startled intake of breath recognized it as a severed, human head.

The wide-open eyes were blank, the jaw hanging slack, and from the yawning mouth burbled echoing words. "*Ssseeeek Garanth, grrreatesst of ouuur nuuumberrrssss. Innnn the ollld quarterrrr of the citeeeee.*" Dumbly, again and again, it repeated the words.

"Necromancy, speaking with the dead, is but the most meager of my skills," said Aar. He tossed the head at Garanth, who instinctively made to catch the repulsive thing. But it vanished just as his hands closed about it.

When he looked up, The Living God had disappeared as well.

Garanth stood knee deep in the moon-gilded river, scraping his hands searchingly upon the silt bottom, certain this was the place. A slight breeze rustled the reeds on shore so they rattled like old bones. The frogs remained silent, incensed at this nocturnal intruder into their domain.

His fingers closed about an old chain, tarnished after being submerged for two years. Straightening, he hauled upon the chain, straining against the thick sludge under foot that clung to what he sought like a miser to his last coin. Disturbed bubbles of trapped air pulsed to the surface and, at last, and with a *gollop!* of displaced silt and water, a narrow chest broke the surface. Garanth waded toward the shore, dragging the chest behind him.

Flopping down beside the chest, Garanth fingered the strangely unrusted lock. He thought for a moment, resurrecting the proper incantation buried deep in his memory. At last he muttered something under his breath, the words hard and bitter to his tongue—not a human language—and the lock popped open as though touched by an invisible key.

He hesitated, unsure if he truly wished to see what was inside—what he had discarded two years ago. Then he thought of the vial Aar had given him.

Feeling the bite of the chill night air upon his wet skin, he lifted the lid. Reflecting the glow of the moon like freshly formed ice, an array of weapons twinkled before him, carefully secured among tattered cloth. Weapons that had been his. When he had been a different man.

A man he was contemplating becoming once again.

The heavyset woman bustled slowly about her apothecary shop. The shutters were drawn against the night, but would be rolled back during the simmering heat of morning.

She was restless, her bed in the back room proving no hindrance to her gnawing insomnia. A stout candle flickered sullenly, and the shadows undulated in sheets as the flame sputtered, teased by the breeze of her pacing.

Suddenly the flame flared again, warningly, and she whirled, her features blanching. "Aar's Blood!" she cursed, invoking the local god. "Is it time? Have you come to kill me?"

Garanth grew out of the shadows that coiled in one corner. "Don't be ridiculous, Mhag. The Hand does not strike its Eyes and Ears."

Mhag relaxed, if only slightly. Then she shrugged. "It has been a long time since I was your Eyes and Ears," she said. Then, slowly, a grin teased the corners of her lips. "It is good to see you," she said.

They did not embrace, nor reach out. In their time among the guild, such familiarity between the formalized assassin pairs—the killer and the researcher—was discouraged. But he understood her sincerity. And he shared it. "Too long."

"Since we both fled the Vendors," she agreed. "Though why we are not dead, I do not know."

"The Vendors do nothing by half measures. Better not to undertake an assassination, than risk failure. And so they leave us alone, provided we do not draw undue attention."

"They may fear the humiliation of attempting to kill you, and failing. But I'm not so difficult a target."

"To kill the Eyes and Ears, and leave the Hand alone, is tantamount to admitting they fear the Hand. They will come for you only if and after they have come for me."

"Well…that's a comfort, I guess," she said wryly. "So why have you come?"

He hesitated. "You spoke the name 'Aar' when you saw me. Have you become a follower of the cult?"

She laughed. "No, but some of my customers are. I suppose I've picked up some of their expressions. Why?"

And he told her. When he was done, he said, "One last

time, the Hand calls upon the Eyes and Ears. One last time, I will kill, and I ask that you help me."

She stared mutely at the candle, settling in its pool of sallow wax. "Why?" she said at last. "I thought we left the guild to be away from the business of killing."

"Perhaps because this assignment is not so much a murder as a mercy killing. Or perhaps because I've allowed myself to sink into nothing. I have not left my old ways behind for something new…I have merely stopped. Mayhap this last kill will allow me to bring true closure to that part of my life. And perhaps because he offers me one thing as a reward…"

"And that thing is?"

"Can't you guess?"

She was again silent. She fidgeted with her belt, as though fascinated by its weaving. She ran a tongue over her lips. Then, as if half in a dream, she nodded to herself. "Find a way to kill the unkillable—to murder a god? It's a fascinating problem…"

The apothecary shop remained closed to customers all the next day as, inside, two old comrades poured over texts and potions, debating and discussing.

"Iron is too obvious," said Garanth, pacing back and forth. "It would have been tried before. Aar himself would certainly have thought of it."

"The enchantment of Boaranalth?" began Mhag. "But—no, it requires the blood sacrifice of one hundred virgins, and the employing of a star jewel."

"Some sort of cursed blade, perhaps?"

They were oblivious to the passage of time, barely noting as evening once more draped its cloak upon the streets…

More candles were lit, and two whole tables had been cleared of vials and powders. In their place were spread an array of scrolls and parchments, and even some of the more modern, bound volumes which folded open with a spine. Half remembered incantations and glamors were scrawled upon scraps of papyrus, then discarded as being inapplicable.

"Here is a reference to the Shiivar'talthwey—the war of gods that took place five hundred years ago," Mhag said, her fingers spreading open a scroll, revealing its pictographic writings. "I was taught of this as a young girl, by my teachers in the Night Vendors. Aar was one of only a handful of recorded gods to survive." She looked up dubiously. "If even *other* gods could not kill him…"

Garanth turned quickly, clearly having been listening more to his own thoughts than her words. "Aar said something odd to me: about 'a thousand years' being a long time. And about 'true mortals.' A strange choice of words for a god, yes? What other kind of mortal is there? A 'false' mortal?"

"Or…one who is a mortal—no longer!" Mhag said, the words spilling off her tongue even before they made sense in her brain. She and Garanth stared at each other for a moment. Then they pounced upon the piles of texts.

"I can find no reference in legend to Aar prior to a thousand years ago," said Garanth at last, settling back on a stool, and disdainfully tossing aside the scroll in his hands. "It is curious, but not—"

"Here!" exclaimed Mhag, straightening and proudly displaying a flaking old piece of animal skin, marked with a language Garanth did not recognize. "Here is written an ancient legend of a warrior name Eerah, and how he became a god. Eerah could be an early pronunciation of Aar—the time period is about right." She looked quite satisfied with herself. Then slowly, her grin of satisfaction sagged into a frown of vexation. "But how does that help us? We now know he was not always an immortal, but what matters is that he is now."

"Perhaps…perhaps not."

He pulled the black shirt over his head and tucked it into his black trousers. He cinched the knife belt about his waist, and coiled the garrote wire carefully around the steel band about his left wrist. He smeared dark paint upon his cheeks and brow. He had filed the nail of the little finger on his left hand till it approximated a point, then, very carefully, painted the nail with a black stain. He mounted his horse, its hooves carefully bundled with rags so as to mute the sound of its tread. He sat there a moment, barely visible against the ink-dark canopy, stars glimmering weakly through wisps of clouds.

Mhag stared at him from her doorway. "Will I see you again?" she asked.

"Doubtful," he said. "If I survive, I think I'll head east, or south. And if I fail…" He twitched the reins and the horse started away. "Good bye, Eyes and Ears."

"Goodbye, Hand," she said, formally.

Head downcast, but with nothing more to say, she turned and retreated to her shop, closing the door upon the night, and with finality upon this remnant of her past.

He was no longer Garanth, fishmonger's assistant; he was once again a Hand of the Night Vendors. From the saddle of his mount depended a series of gold and silver bells that tinkled with the breeze. It was part of the way, the ritual. The horse's hooves had been muffled for stealth, but the bells assured those he might pass that although he was out

The Immortal Contract

upon a hunt…he had not yet found his quarry. It was only when you did not hear the bells that a Night Vendor might be coming for you.

Despite this reassurance, the few late-night stragglers he passed pressed themselves fearfully into darkened doorways and held their breaths until he had disappeared into the darkness, and the jingling of his bells grew faint. Only then would they breathe again. And they would hurry home, whatever their plans might originally have been, and give thanks the Vendors were not seeking them.

He halted before the broad door of a convent and dismounted effortlessly, as quiet as the shadow he had become. With deft hands, he picked the lock in moments, and pushed the heavy door inward. In the courtyard a sister, perhaps returning from the latrine, spotted him and gasped, then ran fearfully to find a superior. He ignored her. Instead, he moved like a breath of wind across the grounds, instinctively sliding from one pool of moon cast shadow to another.

The mother superior found him in the infirmary, where the order tended to those no longer able to tend for themselves. His dark shape loomed over the bed of a sleeping girl. The young nun who had summoned the mother superior crouched by the doorway, white with terror.

"What do you want?" the mother superior hissed, approaching him boldly. "Your kind is not welcome here."

"No need to whisper," he said. "Your voice will not rouse her from her coma."

"I know that," she responded tartly. "For two years have we cared for her—ever since one of your guild killed her father, and poisoned her as well."

"That was unintentional," he said hollowly, staring at the pale cheeks of the girl, her features relaxed as though in blissful slumber. "Her father had been the contract. She merely got in the way. A stray drop was enough to do this to her."

"A poison for which there is no cure," said the mother,

her teeth tight. "Why do you come? To gloat? To finish your guild's work?"

"To make amends, if possible."

"Amends?!? *Pshaw!* How? There is no cure."

He held out a small vial. "Do nothing now, for it will be useless. But come morning, if all goes well, anoint her with what's inside and it will revive her."

The mother made as though to speak, then stopped, as if for the first time sensing something from him that she had not anticipated. Sincerity. "You speak of magic," she said doubtfully.

"Aye." Seeing she would not take the vial, he placed it upon the bed. He whirled and began melting into the shadows. "By morning she will wake…or I will have failed in my task, and I will be dead."

The mother sensed, rather than truly saw, him depart. And for a long time, she stared at the girl who had been in her charge for two years.

Outside, tiny bells jingled as they were cut from a saddle and discarded, and a silent mount was urged upon its silent way…

The acolyte's hand dropped to the kris dagger at his sash. He looked down the dimly lit corridor, occasional torches fluttering in the distance, causing the shadows to shift and seethe as though alive. The corridor walls were comprised of jade stones, so even the lit parts were cast in a weird, obscuring, verdant hue. Concrete ribs arched overhead, lending the passage the impression of being the inside of a snake's body. He studied the corridor, lips pursed, nostrils flared.

He thought he had heard something.

A shadow flickered down the hall, swelling out from the greater darkness as though a muscle flexing. Then it subsided again. A trick of the light, he wondered? His wavy dagger hissed free of his sash as his sandaled feet carried him forward, first briskly, then faster as he became more convinced he was not alone. He opened his mouth to shout the alarum…

A throwing star bit into his neck. He staggered, gurgled. One hand reached for his throat. But he was dead from poison before he could complete the action. He crumpled in a heap even as Garanth pulled away from the shadows hugging the wall, to stand in the verdant glow deep in the Temple of Aar. He moved to the dead man; from a pouch he drew a pinch of powder the color and texture of finely ground pepper. This he sprinkled on the body while muttering a minor incantation. Instantly the corpse grew indistinct—enough that someone unheeding could pass it unawares. The spell would only last until morning, but that was all he needed.

He wondered if the guild assassin had made it this far before being slain.

He slipped soundlessly down the corridor, all his old skills, his old ways, coming back to him in a flood. It was not entirely a welcome experience, being like a flood that causes a sewer to overflow its banks. But if it meant the girl would wake, then perhaps it would go some way—not to absolve him of his past sins, perhaps—but to help him sleep a little better.

Though even in this there was irony. He sought to make amends for a life of killing by killing. He could assure himself Aar wished to die. And as for any of Aar's followers he killed tonight, well, they were not without blood on their own hands given their many Holy Wars. And it was actually considered an honor among them to die in their god's name. Yes, he could certainly tell himself all that.

He slunk around a corner, and stopped. Ahead were three men positioned before an ornately-carved golden door. One was blind, his scarred eye sockets ritually marked; he was a seer, employed by the cult to perceive what eyes could not.

Garanth knew the man's tongue would also have been removed, as there was some superstition about such a man seeing more than mortals were permitted to learn, and so must not impart his knowledge to others.

Although Garanth was invisible in the shadows, the blind cultist instantly turned toward him, cocking his head as he attempted to discern whatever it was he sensed. The two men at his side noticed the action. Garanth knew he must strike before they all realized he was there. Forsaking the security of the shadows, Garanth burst from the darkness, rolling and coming up, a throwing star imbedding itself in one of the sighted acolytes. As the one man fell, the other drew a long blade and came at Garanth, screaming with fanatical zeal. Garanth's own sword flashed to hand, gleaming with a verdant fire, and the two blades clanged together.

Garanth parried and thrust, but the acolyte was skilled, deflecting the strike before thrusting himself. Garanth twisted, but not enough to avoid a bloody crease across his ribs. The acolyte swung again, and Garanth dropped to his knees, stabbing upward as he did, his sword erupting out between the man's shoulder blades. The acolyte fell, wrenching Garanth's sword from his grip. Momentarily unarmed, Garanth turned suddenly as the blind man fell on him, the tongueless mouth making grunting sounds as he bore Garanth to the floor.

The blind fanatic gripped a kris dagger in one hand, which he tried to drive into Garanth's throat; Garanth held his wrist at bay even as the blind man pinned the assassin's other wrist. Garanth strove to touch the acolyte's cheek with this other hand, the tapered, black-painted fingernail on his little finger seeking to prick the skin. Though blind, the acolyte sensed the poison on that nail, and redoubled his efforts. But panic taxed his nerves, and he tried too hard to stab Garanth with his knife. Garanth relaxed his grip on the man's knife hand, letting the blade dart forward, causing the eager acolyte to momentarily focus his energy on the killing stroke. Too late, the acolyte realized he had been lured into marginally relaxing his grip on Garanth's left hand.

The black fingernail scratched his cheek. The acolyte spasmed once, twice.

Gasping, bleeding from his side, Garanth shoved the corpse aside and rose to his feet. Dimly he was aware of bells jangling in the distance. The commotion had been heard. It would not be long before he was discovered.

He retrieved his sword, and stepping over the corpses thrust open the inner sanctum's door. He peered mutely into the room beyond, gold columns lining the walls. A swirl of black shadow—the seeming prehensile cloak—coiled about the jade throne at the far end of the chamber. And about the god seated there.

Sweat smearing the black paint on his face, Garanth deliberately closed the chamber portal behind him. Then he unspooled the wire about his left wrist and used it to tie the handles of the door, aware it would hold but a few minutes. Taking a deep breath, wincing slightly and putting a hand instinctively to his bloody side, he turned to his employer—and his victim.

"You made it this far," remarked Aar, The Living God. "You are truly talented. And are you equipped to do what you were asked? Can you kill a god?"

"I think so."

"More's the pity." Aar rose to his impressive height, his black cloak flexing impatiently about him. "For you see, I have changed my mind—such it is that capriciousness is the purview of gods. Strangely, I find that the longer I brood upon my initial plan, the more I fear death. Is that not odd? I have grown tired of life…but I suppose I've become accustomed to it in a way you true mortals will never appreciate."

Garanth waited, wincing from his injuries. "Will you still make good on the elixir?"

Aar stared at him blankly for a long moment. Garanth could hear the clatter of sandaled feet outside in the hall, the hollow thud of bodies being flung against the blocked door. "Regrettably, the vial will become a curative only upon my death. And as I explained: I no longer intend to die. Nor can I permit you to live. How would it appear, if their god," he nodded toward the door, "did not smite the killer of their brethren?"

"Or permit to live one who knows the secret of your death."

Aar narrowed his eyes. "In truth, I think you bluff in that respect. Better men than you have sought my end—gods even, and sorcerers, too. All have failed." Aar shrugged. "But why risk it?" he asked, as if of himself. Casually he flung his hand forward, black quills bursting from his cloak. Garanth leapt and arced his back in mid-air as the deadly missiles cut the air but inches from his body. He hit the ground hard, rolled unsteadily to his feet, then leapt again as another barrage thudded into the wall just behind him. Landing again, he spared a glance and saw that where the shafts quivered in the wall, the stone moldered and rotted, dropping away in gooey clumps. He shuddered and turned once more to The Living God. Garanth grinned wolfishly, half mad from the pain in his side, which burned fiercer every time he twisted to avoid an attack. "The others failed, o god, because they saw your death as a single problem. But I approached it as two separate ones. One, you are immortal…and two, I want to kill you. If I can deal with the former then, with but a simple blade, I can tackle the latter. I know you were not born a god, but became one a millennium ago." He drew from his pouch a golden sphere. "Are you familiar with Analthorsah's Crystals of Untrod Paths? I acquired this one at a friend's apothecary shop. With one of these, a man is allowed to glimpse an alternate destiny, a reality that might have been but was not. It lasts only seconds, but seconds is all I require." He hurled the ball upon the stones, smashing it. There was a blaze of colorless light, and a sound like a distant horn played off key. "And I wish to glimpse a world

The Immortal Contract

in which Eerah the Warrior did not become immortal!"

"No!" roared Aar, though even Garanth could not be sure if the spell had any effect.

Throwing caution to the wind, he leapt at the so-called Living God, sword raised. Aar must have sensed a change in his own nature, for he brought up his own sword to defend himself rather than arrogantly weathering the assault. Their swords sparked together, then again. Wryly, Garanth realized he had not anticipated the god also being a master swordsman, and he with a seeping wound in his side diminishing his own skill. Still, given time, he thought he could beat through Aar's defenses. But he did not have time. In seconds, the spell would dissolve; what was would restore itself, and Aar would once more be invulnerable.

Then even as he watched, Aar's face began to wrinkle, his limbs to wither, his hair to lengthen and gray. He moaned as his flesh began to molder, to peel away. And Garanth realized that, in a world where Eerah had not become immortal, Aar would have been dead a thousand years. Taking advantage of Aar's momentary shock at feeling his form crumble, Garanth thrust his sword deep into the man's withering breast.

Suddenly there was a second flash of light, and the distant, ethereal note ceased sounding. The spell had ended.

The Living God stood before him, once more strong, proud, impervious...save with Garanth's sword still piercing his heart from the fleeting moments when he had not been invulnerable. He looked at it dumbly for a moment, then reached for it clumsily. He took one step forward, then dropped to his knees. "Well...well played," said the once-living god before he pitched over upon his face.

Garanth had no time to revel in his victory, for he heard the door splintering at his back as the dead god's acolytes beat their way in.

Still, there were shadows aplenty in which to hide, and he was still the greatest assassin the Night Vendors ever trained.

With a confidence to his step, and a knife in each hand, he turned to face the on-coming fanatics. Although Aar had reneged in the end, the elixir he had given to Garanth had been enchanted prior to the god's change of heart.

And so Garanth faced whatever was to come, satisfied that, in a not too distant convent a girl would be waking from her long sleep at last…

~ D.K. Latta ~

D.K. Latta lives in Canada and has had dozens of short stories, mostly in the realms of fantasy and SF and (some) horror, appear in various magazines, webzines, and anthologies (the latter ranging from *The Best of Strange Horizons Vol. 1* to *Tesseracts Nineteen: Superhero Universe*). Raised in a haunted house (no, really!) and on a wildly unbalanced diet of old pulp stories, comic books, and speculative fiction, such influences continue to flavor his writings to this day. He has also written many reviews and pop culture essays about graphic novels, SF, and Canadian movies & TV. His interest in comic book superheroes, pulp fiction, and Canadiana, has led to him writing a two-volume short story collection imagining a Canadian superhero universe through the decades, *The Masques Chronicles*. He was born the same year Pierre Trudeau became prime minister of Canada—but that was probably just a coincidence. By day he toils in drudgery, but by night he dreams of other worlds…

Idol of the Valley

by Daniel Loring Keating

It was the beginning of the Month of Leaves when the peasant came upon Aemilius sitting under a tree, oiling his sword. The peasants of the valley thought the season beautiful. The leaves above turned from pale green to deep red and purple and fell, swollen and full of water, to the ground. To Aemilius, it was all just death. Trees dying, grass dying, animals that didn't horde enough dying. People dying. Always people dying, except him.

Perhaps it was the peasant's grim expression, a change from the jovial grinning permeating the valley's peasantry, that endeared Aemilius to the man enough to hear him out. When the man called to him to ask if his was a sword for hire, Aemilius glanced down at the steel in his hands, thirty-eight inches of death. "Aye," he said. "That I am."

The man approached. He was tall and heavy, qualities one didn't see often in a peasant. Otherwise, he was unremarkable, from his yellow dunlap shirt and trousers to brown leather slippers instead of shoes, to the fact he wore no sword. Instead he carried an old iron rake, its bristles sharp but brittle looking. "I have need of a man talented with both blade and mind. If you be both those things, sir, then do me the honor of avenging my daughter, whose cruel death was a heinous crime that has thus far gone unpunished."

Aemilius pushed himself to his feet. He was a scant two inches taller than the peasant, who nonetheless shrank back from him. Aemilius slid his sword into the scabbard that leaned against the tree. The dirk concealed in the folds of his loose leather tunic would be enough should the peasant be stupid enough to attack him. "I do no man's honor but my own, and precious little of that. As you observed to start, my sword is for hire. Honor buys little in return when given as payment."

The peasant reached into his tunic. Aemilius tensed, preparing for the man to attack; instead, he withdrew a purse, which he tossed to Aemilius. Aemilius caught it in mid-air, heard the jangle of coins inside. With a curious glance at the dour peasant's eyes, he pulled on the drawstring until it slid open. Inside was a small pile of gold, more money than ten peasants earned in a lifetime. "Clearly you are not a man accustomed to the possession of money. You would not have given me my payment up front. Who did you steal this coin from? He may yet have more that might be mine."

The peasant shook his head. "I have stolen nothing. I mortgaged my farm to Lord Maldon, who rules a third of the valley."

Aemilius laughed, a low, biting sound. "Lord Maldon already owned your farm. It is the labor of it you mortgaged, and that is provided by you and yours. You've sold your soul, old man." Aemilius tightened the straps on the bag. "Are the lives of the rest of your family worth so little you'd trade their future for your vengeance?"

The peasant spat. "There is no 'rest of my family.' My dear Tatiana was all I had, since the winter drought three years past took her mother." He clenched his fist, his eyes red and bloodshot. "If I die a slave, so be it, so long as the men who did this to my sweet girl die screaming first."

Aemilius studied the man in front of him. In nine centuries he'd seen conviction written across the faces of thousands. All died eventually, their convictions with them. If death rarely had a point, Aemilius once mused, then life never did. Choosing a purpose, if for only a short time, helped alleviate the boredom of time. Aemilius tightened his fist around the peasant's coin purse. "Very well. I'll set out forthwith. The men responsible will be dead in a week, two at most. What do you know of them?"

The peasant spat again, as though the saliva he hurled

Idol of the Valley

from his mouth were a spear thrust into the hearts of those who'd wronged him. "Precious little. My farm is successful. With success comes complications. The lord's steward requested my presence at Ducende Aire, at which I have just obtained that purse, to work out a problem of tax figures. I was gone three days. Upon my return, I found my larder half eaten, my ale gone entirely, my cottage turned inside out, and my precious girl, broken and bleeding." He swallowed a lump in his throat, his eyes rapidly oscillating between abject sadness and fiery hate. "They dragged her into the field and had sport of her. Then they pierced her knees through with their swords and left her to crawl. She was halfway to the cottage when I found her. She never uttered another word and died that night from fever and blood loss."

Aemilius took up his sword and buckled it to his belt, facing away from the peasant. "You wish for me to find men whose identities you do not know?" He sounded bemused.

The peasant noticed this. When he spoke, it was sharp as Aemilius' sword. "If I could accomplish this task, I would. It is beyond me. There is no shortage of evil men in this valley, but men boast and brag about these things. You can find the men who did this as assuredly as you can kill them."

Aemilius nodded. "Aye. I suppose I can." He scanned the horizon. Nothing but yellow hills in all directions, and two paths, the one on which the peasant had approached and which would lead back to Ducende Aire, and the other, on which Aemilius himself had been travelling, which lead to the Semyon, the fortress guarding the mouth of the valley. "Where should I bring their heads when the deed is done?"

"My name is Artem." The peasant turned and pointed in the direction from which he'd come. "My farm lies sixteen miles hence, beyond Ducende Aire. The cottage is framed by an enormous oak. My grandfather cut the image of a rabbit into it when I was a boy; it survives to this day. Bring their heads, their hands, their manhoods. Bring anything you believe they used to offend my daughter. Make them *feel* it."

Aemilius waited for Artem to disappear over a hill before he walked off the road into a copse of thick fir trees which still had their leaves. He didn't need privacy to begin the search. What he was to do, he had done in front of scores of people over the centuries. It'd never been his choice in those instances. When given his preference, he preferred to do it alone.

Once thoroughly surrounded by trees, Aemilius drew his sword, pressed the tip to his chest, and drove it into his heart.

Instant, white-hot pain seared him as the sword tore through skin and bone and muscle. Almost as soon as he'd registered the pain, it began to fade. He sank to his knees. Somehow, he always forgot to lie down, a mistake that had almost become ritual. He closed his eyes as his senses shut down. Gradually, the chirping of birds in the trees, the smell of fir needles around his legs, and the sight of all that beautiful death faded, until he was wrapped in nothingness more absolute than could be explained to men who'd never experienced death.

Not that he was, strictly speaking, dead. Aemilius had pondered for centuries the nature of his 'deaths.' He concluded that wherever he went when 'killed,' it was not the 'afterlife.' Not the same one the vast majority of people went to, anyway. On that plane of the dead, Aemilius could not see, could not hear, could not smell or touch or taste. His senses were blank, numb. All Aemilius had were his thoughts and the vague sensation that he existed. He could stay as long as he wished: for the time it took to recite a children's nursery rhyme, or to recollect every step from the Giant's Causeway to the Great Thirst. No matter how long he stayed, he always awoke mere moments after his 'death,' his wounds healed, his strength returning.

Many times he'd gone into the void, hoping to lose himself and never return. Never had he been successful. Some part of his mind always remained aware, eventually pulling him back to the world of the living. He learned to use the void. Even though he could not see nor smell nor hear nor taste nor touch, he could *sense*. Through this *sense* he could commune with the dead. It was not a literal communion. The true fate of the dead was beyond him. Rather, if he willed himself to move through the world of the dead, he would encounter echoes of the people they'd once been: a man's recollection of eating pie, a woman's bittersweet memory of childbirth, a stillborn's precious few seconds of consciousness, a soldier's terror as the enemy charged.

Aemelius searched for Tatiana. Just as time's meaning grew blurry in the void, so did distance. It might have been a few feet or a thousand miles that Aemilius walked until he encountered what remained of the murdered girl.

He saw those memories that she chose to see first. Memories of her parents when she was a child, memories of the farm on a cool spring day. A memory of a special boy whose family spent a season working with her father, to whom she'd given a special and secret gift. These Aemilius pushed aside.

He then saw those memories she would have sooner forgotten. Watching their herd of cattle be set upon by wolves. Watching her father worry during times of drought over papers she didn't understand—and hunger she did. Watching her mother waste away, longer than was necessary because her father stubbornly kept feeding her, kept mopping away sweat from her brow, kept washing her clothes and changing her bed.

He was getting closer, but these were still not what he needed. Tatiana had healed from those. They'd found a place within her. The memories of how she died never had the chance to become a part of her. This may have been a kindness of sorts. Those were the memories he needed, and so he pushed toward them. There was no conscious resistance from Tatiana. If the dead possessed any consciousness at all, he was unaware of it, and had no idea if she was aware of him.

He found the memories and immersed himself in them.

Her father was gone a mere hour before they came. At first she thought she heard him returning. He forgot his favorite hat. She picked it up off the hook it sat upon to carry it out to him. When she looked through the open door of the cottage, she saw not her gentle father, cool like iron from age and loss, but instead a pack of five ruffians.

Aemilius studied that image. It was frozen in her memory: the moment she'd realized that not only would she die, but she would die soon, and badly. She had been a smart girl, Aemilius thought. It hadn't saved her and neither could he. He could only study the men he meant to kill to avenge her death.

Two were short, one of medium height, the other two tall, one uncommonly so. The top third of the giant's head was obscured by the upper edge of the door frame. All wore mismatched leather armors, stitched and sewn together inexpertly, probably by their own hands. All were of medium build. Three carried the slightly curved sabers favored by imperial officers, one a stout short sword, perhaps three quarters the size of Aemilius' own one-handed blade, and the last, the giant, carried a massive broadsword, eighty inches in length if it was a foot. They had pale complexions, like men of the Causeway Shore. Two of them were a bit darker, their skin leathery from spending many years under an unforgiving sun.

There was nothing striking about them. Their faces were unknown and their weapons weren't famous enough to be known to him. He had hoped there would be some clue to their identities that would scream from Tatiana's first and least private memory of them. He was going to have to watch it all.

They'd thought the farm was empty, but she wasn't an unwelcome surprise. She tried to run, but the cottage had only one door. One of the shorter men leveled her with a punch to the jaw as she tried to run past. She saw stars but didn't lose consciousness, not from the punch nor the kicks, not even when one of them broke one of her ribs. When her skin was purple from the beating, they dragged her into the field, tore her clothes, and took her, each at least twice, the giant three times and one of the short ones four. They spared none of their appetites. All through the beatings and the rapes, she clutched her father's favorite hat. A small part of her, locked far from her conscious mind, wanted to live to see him wear it and smile at her again.

They finished. They bound her hands and feet. It wasn't necessary. She was too exhausted to move, let alone escape or attack them. They feasted, going through a week's provisions in a night, and drank until they were all stupid with it. They drifted to sleep without setting a watch while she lay in the field, covered in her own blood, and she prayed they'd simply move on in the morning.

When they woke they were upset at how sick the drink had made them. The one who'd had her four times pulled down his breeches for another go. When he wasn't able to sharpen his sword for the deed, he kicked her in the stomach, sneering that she'd have no bastard of his. The medium-height one stopped him, told him it was enough, they had to get moving. Hope flared again. Then he drew his sword.

It would have been merciful if he'd just cut her throat. She was a farm girl, had been raised putting animals out of their misery. As much as it had hurt to watch her mother die, Tatiana was bothered by her father's unwillingness to put her out of her suffering. In that moment, had she the strength to speak, were not half her teeth smashed in and her tongue pierced with their fragments, she would have asked for a quick death, and thought it possible they might give it her. Instead, she felt a new, searing pain as a blade slid into the back of her right knee. A second later, the same was done to her left.

They did not sever her legs, but her kneecaps were shattered, and arteries running through her legs were nicked, causing her to bleed freely. The man with the sword spit on her, sheathed his weapon, and left. Tatiana crawled. She remembered every quarter inch of the journey back toward the cottage. It couldn't provide any help except to allow her to die somewhere she'd once felt safe. That was how her father found her.

Aemilius stepped back out of the memory. He had no need to see the girl's final moments with her father. He could leave her that much. During the hours of torment, he'd overheard the short man, the one who kept coming back for more, say to the giant:

"Think we'll make August Trident before sundown tomorrow?"

In an age gone by, when Aemilius first learned to use his cursed gift, he'd thanked the spirits of the dead from whom he'd learned, a useless affectation. Not so here with Tatiana. There were no thanks as Aemilius withdrew from her memories, no parting words to the spirit of a girl who would never be more than fifteen years old, no closure. Death, as far as he knew, was closure for Tatiana. His business was closure for her father, who had to struggle on.

Aemilius woke in the copse of fir trees, sword by his side. He climbed to his feet. It would take a moment for his full strength to return to him. With the loose folds of his tunic he dabbed at the trickle of blood his killing blow had left on his chest. He looked east. They were going to the forest temple of August Trident. His ambivalence about the inhabitants of the valley aside, Aemilius had travelled it well over his long years. August Trident was at least a three-day journey from where he stood, and he wasn't a hungover barbarian. Aemelius knelt, picked up his sword, and wiped his blood off it. Soon there would be blood not his own coating the blade. When he straightened up, his fist clenching the blade was as strong as ever it was.

The hunt was on.

💀 💀 💀

It took a day of hard travel for Aemilius to find the outlaws. Nearing sunset, he spotted their campfire set off from the road by a half mile. They were camped in a clearing surrounded by large trees, purple leaves gleaming in the golden-red sunset. He could creep within one hundred feet without them having any idea of his presence.

Aemilius crept close through the woods, careful to avoid twigs and leaves. His boots were soft-soled, making it easy for him to walk silently. He caught snatches of conversation, mainly comparisons of their time with Tatiana. Aemilius' eyes narrowed. None would miss these men.

Aemilius reached the tree line and crouched, his left hand pressed against the bark to keep himself steady, his right hand clutching his sword. They'd brought Artem's ale. Three were already drunk, the other two not far behind. He'd wait for them to drink themselves out of their wits, cut their hamstrings, then sever their hands and set to work on making them suffer.

Before he could act, the one with the libido announced he needed to piss a bloody river, and tottered into the treeline, missing Aemilius by a few feet. Aemilius glanced at the still-drinking circle of outlaws before pushing off to follow.

The drunk stopped in front of a tree, fumbling with his breeches. Aemilius pounced, wrapping his left hand around the man's mouth, muffling his shout. Aemilius's elbow brushed something hard under the man's leather armor. Rather than draw his sword across the man's throat, Aemilius pushed the point of it into his back until he stopped struggling. Still ready to strike at the slightest sign of treachery, Aemilius reached into the man's tunic and withdrew a small piece of iron that changed the entire situation.

After a moment of hurried thought, Aemilius spoke, directly into the short man's ear, his voice low and dangerous. "Walk. Back to camp."

The man nodded and they turned. He shuffled back to camp, his breeches around his ankles, his limp little cock still dripping. They broke the tree line and came into the light of the campfire. The barbarians were slow to realize the danger. The giant was first, crashing to his feet, pulling his enormous broadsword free of its scabbard. The other three followed. Aemilius faced four armed men.

He prodded the short man in the back with his blade tip, his left hand still wrapped around his mouth. "I had thought only to rob this drunken fool." He lifted the iron item he'd taken from the man's tunic. "But I find the sigil of safe conduct of Lord Maldon of the valley on him." With a quick sleight of hand, the sigil disappeared into his tunic sleeve. "Stolen from a rightful bearer? Perhaps, but unlikely. You carry no spoils, and any band lucky or stupid enough to set upon travelers with Lord Maldon's protection would surely have carried off more than just sigils, which would become worthless the minute the crime became known."

The man of medium build was the least drunk of the four. He held his imperial saber steady. Up close, Aemilius saw the jewels studding the hilt. An officer's blade. "You have thought much of us, brigand. What are we to make of you, a thoughtful thief?"

"You are to recognize my value." Aemilius pressed the point of his sword into the little man's cheek, who shrieked into Aemilius' hand. "This fool does not think. He drinks and brags of his ability to rape a defenseless girl. If you truly prefer his company, then after I have cut his worthless pig throat, I'll cut my way through all of you, take whatever I find of value, and be done with you. If, however, you recognize the value of one holding the blade instead of one about to be cut, we'll be disposed of him and I'll call you companions, until our journey is through."

Idol of the Valley

Three of the men in front of him looked to the man of medium-build. He himself watched Aemlius through slitted eyes, his fingers playing softly on the hilt of his saber. Aemilius had seen that look before, the look of a true predator, a man who enjoyed pain above all things except his sense of value, the sense to which Aemilius appealed.

The leader lowered his officer's saber. "Kill him, then. He is of no great use."

The little man choked out a single word through Aemilius' fingers. "Matvey—!"

The leader glanced down at the small man's tiny swinging penis before rolling his eyes and turning away. "Try to die with some dignity."

Aemilius let go and swung his sword downward, severing the little man's hamstrings. Blood spurted from the backs of his legs as he fell forward, crying out. Aemilius stalked to his side and flipped him over onto his back. Pupils dilated with terror, the little man tried to squirm away, cringing with pain every time Aemilius put pressure on his bleeding legs. He put his hands up to defend himself, so Aemilius sliced them off, sending further torrents of blood spilling from his body, covering his mouth and torso.

Aemilius watched as the man's eyes began to flutter before driving his sword down into his crotch. Those eyes flew back open in one last terror-fueled gasp of agony. Then the rapist slumped back, dead. The man's blood finished flowing out before Aemilus reached down and severed his head in a single swing. He pulled his knapsack from his back, opened it, and slipped the severed head, hands, and penis inside.

The leader watched this out of the corner of his eye. "There is little empathy in you, my new friend. If I didn't know better, I'd say you bore him some grudge."

Aemilius retied his knapsack and slung it over his shoulder. "There are those in the West who pay for such oddities, and I do not let opportunities for profit go to waste."

The leader studied the dismembered corpse just outside the circle of their fire. "Clearly." He sheathed his sword and offered his hand to Aemilius. "I'm Matvey. You're welcome to join us on our quest."

Aemilius shook the hand, getting the dead man's blood all over it. "Quest?"

Matvey's handshake was firm and confident. "Quite so. You were right. We did not rob the lord's treasure seekers. We are the treasure seekers."

Aemilius watched as the other three men put their swords away. "What treasure do we seek?"

Matvey smiled. "All in time, my very new friend. Why don't you come sit by the fire with us?" He let go of Aemilius' hand and spared a last glance for the headless, handless, cockless corpse. "Would you like to know the name of the man you killed?"

"No."

💀 💀 💀

Aemilius shared their fire and consented to a swig of ale. In spite of his general coldness, he learned that the others were Vikenty, Varfol, and Yura. Yura, the giant, was a consummate follower who'd never raped a teenage girl had his companions not done it first. Varfol, the other of the short men, greatly loved ale, drinking twice as much as the others. Vikenty, the other taller man, was quiet, preferring to sharpen his sword. He went about it wrong and was doing more harm than good. Only Matvey held any real interest for Aemilius. Those with a predator's eyes were usually adept in combat.

It took three days for the group to reach their destination. Matvey lead them well. Aemilius did not give away that he knew the land, but had to concede that Matvey knew it as well as he. Were the other three not drunken fools, they'd have arrived in only two days, possibly one.

Idol of the Valley

When they came into view of August Trident, Vikenty and Varfol both gasped. The temple was forty feet high, carved from a single gigantic root. Of the tree that had produced it, no fate was known. It had been cut, its stump chipped away, many years before even Aemilius' time. The enormous root remained, and had been hollowed out to serve as a temple by the ancient forest-worshipping people of the valley. There was an undeniable majesty about the ancient place.

The party strolled up to the temple's twenty-foot double doors. "I do not know what you expect to find here, Matvey," Aemilius said. The clearing in front of the temple was deserted. "August Trident has been abandoned for an age. Its treasures were plundered long before you came out of your father's balls."

Matvey smiled at the casual obscenity. "So say the thieves. A true plunderer must unlearn the lessons of common thievery. Common thieves work quickly, to avoid detection. Look around!" He kicked at a pebble. "There is no one here to hide from. Yet the common thief can never fully unlearn his lessons, so he overlooks something. In this case, he overlooks the greatest prize."

Aemilius stopped walking, folding his arms in front of him. "And you are no common thief?"

Matvey also stopped walking. "Aye. If you doubt it, you're free to leave."

Aemilius grunted. "Your brilliance is a beacon for us in this bleak world."

Matvey continued walking. "Perhaps you will have more faith when your purse fills with gold."

The five of them pushed their way through the doors of the temple. Inside was a single room. In its heyday, light streamed in from dozens of square windows thirty feet up, ringing the temple. Benches throughout gave worshippers places to sit while they prayed. Now, the windows were clogged with moss, giving the air in the temple an eerie green glow. Those few remaining benches were rotten, split in two. If the tables or shelves lining the walls ever held treasures, they were long since gone. The temple held nothing but dust and the foreboding air of a place, once important, now long dead.

Aemilius turned to Matvey. "Nothing."

Matvey shook his head. "You disappoint me. Perhaps you shouldn't brag so much." He bent next to the largest bench, which had sagged and bowed under the weight of time. For a moment, he rooted around on the floor. His face lit up. He pulled on a chain set into the floor and, with a rumble, a trap door in the rotten wooden floor receded, showing a set of stone steps.

Aemilius felt the hair on the back of his head stand on end. Whatever was down those steps was old and powerful in a way he had not encountered for centuries, the kind of power he tasted in the back of his mouth and saw in the shadows of his nightmares. The only thing he'd encountered as powerful had been nine centuries previous.

Aemilius drew his sword. Matvey shot a smug look at the others before descending the steps, Aemilius close on his heels.

The dark green haze of the temple gradually gave way to a soft gray glow given off by the surroundings as the wood and earth gave way to stonework. It was not stonework to which any of them was accustomed. Whatever was beneath August Trident was carved out of a single massive piece of gray stone. Aemilius gripped his sword tighter. The further down they went, the more his stomach churned.

The walls gave way to an enormous cavern. The temple above was a regal if dilapidated corpse. What lay below was a monstrosity. Every cathedral Aemilius had ever set eyes upon could have fit inside the cavern with extra room for a city or two. It was impossible to guess its full size. It stretched far beyond the scope of the dull light, which didn't seem to come from any particular source.

Idol of the Valley

"My stars in the sky…" Yarfol breathed out.

Aemilius, despite his growing feeling of dread, regained his composure first, turning to Matvey. "This cavern must run beneath all of the valley. It would take years for a party ten times our size to search it. How do you mean to find the treasure we seek?"

Matvey grinned. "A pertinent question, if still lacking in faith." He reached into his tunic and pulled out a folded scrap of parchment. It was ancient, greyed and crinkled. "Our benefactor has supplied us with a map." As Matvey finished pulling out the parchment, it lit up, its gray glow matching that of the cavern but many times the intensity. "Well, my word." Its light momentarily shone brightly, then winked out.

Before any could react, they were set upon.

Aemilius expected the attack. He hadn't known what shape the attackers would take: stone monoliths to match the rock of the cavern; skeletons buried millennia ago and forgotten by all but whatever fell force inhabited this forbidden place; enormous rats, each the size of a man, their claws and teeth razor sharp, their appetite for flesh insatiable.

It was none of those things. The temple above was constructed from a single root from a tree that had been removed in ages past. None had given much thought to the tree in centuries. None at all had given thought to its other roots. Roots slithered out of cracks in the stone above. Before those below knew what was happening, one root cracked through the air, slicing off Yarfol's right arm above the elbow. Both arm and sword clattered to the stone steps and he dropped, screaming, clutching at the stump of his now-abbreviated arm.

Yura and Matvey drew their weapons. Aemilius and Yakenty were already armed. Matvey glanced at Aemilius, the predator's gleam bright in his eyes. "Let's dance."

Aemilius' eyes narrowed. "Let's not." More loudly, he yelled, "Watch out, Matvey!" and gave the leader of the

117

group a tremendous shove. There were no roots anywhere near him. He tumbled off the steps and down the remaining thirty feet to the bare stone below.

The others didn't have time to question Aemilius, as the roots were all over them. Yakenty hacked at one as it swung toward him, but his blunted sword failed to slice through the slick wood of the root. The force of his blow prevented the root from hitting him. Instead, the root wrapped around his sword and, with a tug, pulled it from his hands. Hastily, he bent and picked up Yarfol's sword, prying the dying man's stiff hand off it and swinging it wildly over his head.

Yura's enormous broadsword was better sharpened. Though he could only swing it slowly, he was able to catch each root as it attacked. Within a minute, a small pile of cut roots lay at his feet. Aemilius, for his part, did the same, hacking and slashing with strength and finesse as the roots attacked. As the minutes piled on, the three men began to tire, and Aemilius realized their doom. For every root they sliced off, another took its place, each as fast and deadly as the last.

When one finally got through Yakenty's wild defense, it ripped the man's face half off, leaving bare flesh and bone from his nose down. His eyes wide, as though to escape the destruction of his face, he collapsed to the stone steps and, bleeding profusely, began crawling up them. The roots continued to whip at him, drawing red gashes along his back. He collapsed after only a few seconds, blood pouring from a thousand cuts and gory remains of his face.

Each of Yura's swings was a little slower than the last, each root a little closer to landing a blow that even the giant wouldn't be able to shrug off. Though Aemilius had yet to find any true challenge from the roots, he recognized that, unaided, he had little hope of carrying the day.

Below the stairs, Matvey was stirring weakly. The roots weren't reaching him there. Struggling as he hacked and slashed, Aemilius made his way to Yura. "Yura! Down!" he shouted to the giant. As Aemilius sliced his way through root after swinging root, Yura began to follow him down the steps. After a very long minute and a close call with a root that managed to wrap itself around Yura's right arm, the two made the bottom. The roots stretched and whipped and cracked, but couldn't reach them, extending to a few feet above Yura's head.

"You bastard."

Aemilius looked around. Matvey lay in a heap, his body destroyed, blood pooling slowly around him. His left leg was broken in two places. His right leg was entirely pulverized, having taken the brunt of the landing. The bone, shattered in at least six places, was poking through in at least four. Even if the man was to somehow survive the wound, he would never walk again.

"Come again?" Aemilius asked.

Matvey, his eyes bloodshot and full of hate, tried to drag himself closer to Aemilius. He choked off a scream when he jostled his obliterated right leg. "They weren't anywhere near me. You pushed me down here on purpose!"

"Did I?"

"You did!" Matvey turned his attention to Yura. "Yura, kill him!"

"Too late." Aemilius' sword cleaved through the backs of Yura's knees. Unlike Tatiana, whose legs were not amputated, Aemilius sliced both Yura's legs off under the knees. He toppled to the ground, screaming in pain as blood flowed from the wounds. He tried to grasp his greatsword to ward Aemilius, but he was slow and clumsy from panic, blood loss, and exhaustion from the fight. Aemilius pressed a foot to Yura's hand trying to raise his sword. Bones snapped in the giant's hand under his weight. Yura tried to swing at him with his other fist, but Aemilius sliced it off, then plunged his sword into Yura's neck. The giant's neck was twice the thickness of Aemilius' blade, but it was enough that soon the giant gargled out his last blood-choked breath.

Behind him, Aemilius heard Matvey collapse. "Stupid." Matvey grunted with pain. "Why?"

Aemilius wiped the giant's blood off on the enormous corpse's leather breeches. "A job. The girl's father hired me to kill all of you."

Matvey barked out a laugh. "The girl's father! We left nothing of value at his cottage. Even she wasn't worth much by the time we took our leave. What could he have paid you with, cabbage?"

Aemilius walked over to crouch just out of reach of Matvey. "He mortgaged his farm to Lord Maldon."

Matvey laughed again, but this time it was lower and less surprised. "Then he's sold himself to the man who sent us to his farm in the first place."

Aemilius rang a finger down the length of his sword, making sure Matvey watched the whole way. "You will tell me of this, Matvey the Uncommon Thief."

Matvey turned away as best he could. "That's all I'm telling you, traitor."

Aemilius smiled, despite the fact that Matvey couldn't see him. "I doubt that."

Matvey passed out three times, once for every two bones Aemilius cut free of his body, before he talked. He told Aemilius many things: about the object they'd been sent to retrieve; about how he'd never understood why people felt for other people; about how his little sister had been his first rape when he was thirteen and she was nine; about how much he hurt and how he was looking forward to it being over. He begged to die. When Aemilius made it clear the only way he'd end Matvey's suffering was if he begged for the torture to continue, he begged for it until his throat was raw with it. Soon after that he left this world to join the dead. For the first time in an age, Aemilius hoped those on the other side knew consciousness. It felt a great pity that so wretched a soul as Matvey could escape further torment.

Once Matvey was dead, Aemilius took the parchment

that started the roots flailing. On it, he found a riddle, written in an arcane dialect he'd spoken before the language died. It read:

> *Sheath your sword, noble hero, lest that*
> *　usually below kill you from above.*
> *Sheath your sword, noble hero, in that old*
> *　home from which it comes.*
> *Sheath your sword, noble hero, lest you wish*
> *　to writhe and scream*
> *Sheath your sword, noble hero, and come the*
> *　Idol of the Queen.*

Aemilius looked closely at his sword. The second line was clearly the key. Matvey and Yura had been unarmed when the roots had attacked, so simply sheathing his sword wouldn't do the trick by itself. Due to the circumstances of who and what he was, he could not remember his home, and in any event couldn't get his sword there, not with the roots ready to dismember him as soon as he set foot on the stairs. Even though he'd wake up again in a minute, it'd be the same thing again and again for millennia.

That old home from which it comes… The entire cavern was made of stone. The iron used to make the steel that was then fashioned into his sword had to have come from the ground originally. He was to sheath his sword in the stone. He looked about for a crevice or fissure he could stick his sword into, but found none. Giving up, he drew his sword over his head and drove it straight down into the ground.

Rather than glancing off the stone and permanently dulling the blade, the sword of Aemilius bit deep. The cave started to shake. The roots above stopped whipping and snapping at him and receded into the shaking ceiling. Rocks above shook loose from the ceiling and fell to smash upon the floor. Directly in front of Aemilius, the floor split open and a pedestal rose up slowly. On it sat a statue, barely a foot tall, of a woman brandishing a woodcutter's axe as a weapon. Aemilius reached out and touched it and felt not just *a* power, but *the* power…It was precisely what he thought it was.

One task remained, a confrontation with Lord Maldon, whose machinations were responsible for the brutalization and death of Tatiana. Matvey knew little of Maldon's plan. He was hired through a steward who explained little beyond the lord's desire for the idol, which he'd called the Statue of Perpetual Sleep. His knapsack soaking through with the blood of all those bits of the outlaws he'd saved for Artem, Aemilius set out from August Trident for Ducende Aire, the seat of Lord Maldon.

In two days he reached the fortress. Ducende Aire lacked the looming hostility of the Semyon or the splendor of Bujnybasen, the seats of the other lords of the valley. Ducende Aire was a simple castle, set into a sheer cliff on the side of the valley. Its curtain walls only extended around three quarters of the perimeter. Three towers rose behind those walls.

Though the valley had known no significant military conflicts in twice the lifetime of a mortal man, the walls of Ducende Aire were well patrolled. Aemilius buried his knapsack under a bush away from the road. The guards at the gate told him that, without express permission of the lord or a member of the lord's staff, he would not be admitted.

Aemilius observed the fortress from afar for a day and a night. A few caravans entered and exited. These were searched before being given entry, the guards' swords driven through the wooden slats of the carts. The guards did not bother looking under the cart, even when their swords stuck on the slats.

When Aemilius spotted a farmer leading his cart toward the gate, he darted from his bush and slipped underneath.

Idol of the Valley

The sole peasant leading the cart never saw him. Aemilius lashed himself to the cart's underside with a rope dangling from the back. He'd need to be fast and lucky. If this didn't work, his body would be dumped outside the walls, the farmer would die unjustly, and Aemilius would have to find a different way into the fortress.

When a guard drove his sword into the cart, the blade missed Aemilius' head by inches. The next two blows also missed him. He breathed out silently. The fourth blow took him in the chest.

Moving fast, he twisted his body, despite the pain. When the soldier tried to pull his sword back, it caught. "Damn old carts," the soldier muttered. Reaching up with a hand shaking with pain, Aemilius wrapped the sword in a torn bit of cloth, then twisted back. The soldier yanked on his sword, which pulled free. Aemilius' cloth dragged along it, wiping it clean.

"That's enough," he heard. His senses started to dim. "Go on in."

By the time the cart was through the gate, Aemilius was dead.

He did not linger except briefly to seek out the shade of Matvey. He examined it as best he could. He'd hoped to gain some intelligence on the spirit's present disposition. Aemilius deeply desired that Matvey continue suffering. Instead he saw flashes of the outlaw's life: jobs he'd completed, jobs he'd failed, a war he'd fought, what he'd done to men, what he'd done to women. Aemilius turned away. No use. Whether Matvey truly suffered or not would remain a mystery until the day Aemilius joined him. If he ever joined him.

Aemilius woke still lashed to the underside of the cart as it was being unloaded. His tunic had absorbed most of the blood from the stab wound. Soon, the servants finished unloading the cart. When he felt the cart jolt, he untied the rope holding him and dropped to the ground. The cart rolled on, its master oblivious to the extra cargo he'd dropped off.

Aemilius was in an alcove of one of the towers. In front of him was the courtyard where a number of men-at-arms milled about. Behind him was a door. Aemilius pushed his way through it. The door led to a staircase. Down the staircase, he could hear the sounds of a kitchen—pots being stirred, flames crackling, the swish of a knife moving through food. Above he could hear nothing. No lord he'd ever heard of would take residence below his own kitchen. Aemilius went up.

The walls were barren but for iron braziers placed every few feet. Only half were lit. Each apartment to which he came was empty, dust covered. He was beginning to think the tower was unused and that he would have to devise a way to get to one of the other towers to continue his search when he realized there were two guards ahead, each bearing the seal of Lord Maldon on their armor and sturdy steel from the castle forge.

Aemilius had climbed many stories to reach the two guards. If he attacked, there was a chance noise from the battle wouldn't carry to the kitchen below. Then again, if he attacked and it turned out they were guarding something useless, it would limit his time in the castle. Eventually, two corpses would be discovered.

Aemilius didn't consider long. Gripping his sword, he charged from the shadows.

Both guards were leaning against the wall, relaxed and unaware, when Aemilius charged. The first died quickly. Aemilius' sword found the gap between his half-helm and his gorget, slashing his neck open. Aemilius slashed at the second guard, but that fellow put up his sword in defense. The blade of Aemilius clashed with the other, the steel ringing. Aemilius slashed once more and the guard parried before Aemilius backed off.

Then Aemilius lunged forward, stabbing at the guard's chest. The guard swept his sword in front of him to turn

Aemilius' aside. Unfortunately for the guard, he wasn't quick enough. Aemilius' sword connected with the breast plate. It did not penetrate, but it did dent. The guard staggered back, coughing, the steel of his breastplate pushing on his chest. The guard pushed himself off the wall into a lunge, his sword in both hands, driving it down toward Aemilius' head with as much force as he could muster. Instead of dodging the blow, as most prudent men would have done, Aemilius parried. The parry caught the guard off balance and Aemilius whirled, slashing for his throat. He connected with the side of the guard's helm, denting it. A bit of caved-in steel lanced the guard's left eye, which began to bleed profusely.

Again, Aemilius backed off. "Surrender," he offered. "I'll bind your mouth and your limbs. You need not die for a lord who sends brigands to murder little girls."

"Liar!" The guard reached up to dab at the blood flowing from his wounded eye. "My lord would never commit such an atrocity, even if he were able."

"Even if he were…" Aemilius started, but was cut off. The guard lunged again. Aemilius sidestepped the blow. The guard stumbled, his eyes full of blood. Aemilius elbowed him in the caved-in side of his helm, dropping him to a knee. With a precise swipe, he severed the leather strap on the guard's gorget, and then drove his sword to the hilt into his chest. The guard blinked wide, twice, then fell as Aemilius pulled his sword free, blood bubbling from his mouth. The man was dead before he hit the floor.

His sword dripping with the blood of the fallen guards, Aemilius pushed on the door the two dead men had been guarding. It didn't budge. With a sigh, Aemilius backed up and kicked. The door splintered and swung open. Aemilius walked in, sword at the ready, expecting to find Lord Maldon prepared to defend himself.

Instead, he found the lord abed, his eyes closed, his chest barely moving.

It was definitely Lord Maldon. Aemilius had seen the man before, once when the lord had been a boy, once only a few years previous. While there were more lines than he remembered, Aemilius had grown talented in the art of anticipating age on others. It never shocked him when a face he'd last seen youthful reappeared aged and worn. Lord Maldon wasn't just aged. He was sickly, his breaths ragged, his eyes drawn up, his skin a deathly yellow in pallor.

"Please, sir. End his suffering."

Aemilius turned. A woman wearing a gown of red and purple stood in the doorway. She was old, at least into her fifties. "Who are you?"

"Lady Malora. There lies my husband." She pointed to the dais. "Will you kill him? It would be a kindness to him, and to me."

Aemilius took out a piece of cloth and wiped the blood from his own blade, sheathing it. "My lady. I do not understand."

Lady Malora stepped further into the room. "It is my lord's steward's fault." She wiped at her eyes, which were red with tears she'd cried for some time. "My lord fell ill two years past. The sickness ought have carried him from this world, but the steward managed to arrange his survival. My lord has been like that ever since." She sniffled. "My Maldon would never have consented to being made to just...linger, like this."

Aemilius shivered. "Few would."

Lady Malora clutched at the necklace she wore. On a silver chain was a marital ring, gold infused with purple, an old style in the valley. "While my lord husband still lives, the steward rules. When he dies, my son, who serves the emperor, will be recalled to take his place. I haven't been able to get close to my husband. These guards have been told I'm mad." She stopped stroking her necklace. "You don't think I'm mad, do you?"

Aemilius shook his head, sadly. "No, my lady." Aemilius

pulled his dirk from inside his tunic. "Best you look away." Walking over to the dais on which lay Lord Maldon, a still-breathing corpse, he struck a single blow into the lord's heart. Maldon took two more ragged breaths, then lay still. To her credit, when Aemilius turned back to Lady Malora, he found she had watched the whole thing.

"Tell me where I might find this steward," Aemilius said.

💀 💀 💀

Two days later, Aemilius turned off the road and headed up the path toward Artem's cottage. Slung over his right shoulder was his knapsack, dirt-covered and stained red from the blood of the heads and other parts collected therein. Slung over his left shoulder was a larger sack, which squirmed and squeaked as he walked. Artem the farmer appeared at the door of the cottage. "Well? Does my daughter have vengeance?"

Aemilius nodded. "Aye, but not entirely." He upended his knapsack, spilling heads and other parts out onto the grass. "The men who tortured and killed her are dead." He upended the other bag and a little man wearing expensive silk robes rolled out, his robes catching on his forehead. His hands and feet were bound. "This man, though, is ultimately responsible."

Artem looked down, and then back up at Aemilius. "I don't understand. This is the lord's steward, he who summoned me to court."

The little man's eyes were bulging and he was trying to wriggle away, but he couldn't budge more than an inch or two. "Aye, that's true. He brought you to court so that his group of thugs could raid your farm for supplies to outfit their expedition."

"Expedition? What expedition?"

"To retrieve this." Aemilius pulled the Idol of the Queen out of his knapsack. At the sight of it, the steward's eyes bulged. "This steward has gotten used to running things. He hired Matvey's group to steal the Idol of the Queen from under August Trident. He believed the idol could keep Lord Maldon alive and in his coma indefinitely. He couldn't provision them at any of the lord's holdings, for their mission needed be secret, so he lured you away from your farm and promised them all of your food and drink for their journey." Aemilius set the statue down on Artem's chopping block. "This fool saw only a means to a very limited end. This artifact is capable of so much more." He looked down on it, sadness tingeing his eyes and his words. "It is one of perhaps a dozen like it. It was an artifact of this same power that made me what I am. When I learned of their quest, the traditions of my people dictated I complete their quest, to give to you, my employer, what they sought. The idol is yours."

Artem's eyes narrowed. "I have not heard of such traditions. Who are your people?"

Aemilius met the peasant's gaze. "You would not know them. The last died hundreds of years ago. I am all that remains. I've spent much of nine hundred years piecing together what I can of who they were, what they were like." Aemilius couldn't read the range of emotions passing over Artem's face. "Do you doubt me?"

Slowly, Artem shook his head in the negative. "All have heard tales of a traveler who has visited this valley many times over the centuries, a warrior who wears no armor and swears no allegiance. They say he defeated Pozhiratel Ognya in single combat five hundred years ago, that he stole the legendary sword Dreamshatter, that he dwelled for years in the Harem of Sokrushat and lived to tell tales no other man could tell. Do I believe you are this warrior?" Artem spat. "Perhaps. You have gone farther than any other man would to deliver me my justice."

Aemilius delivered a kick to the steward, to be sure he knew this information was not for his ears. "Then know this: the statue can bring back from death any who has died, and

Idol of the Valley

that person, having shunned death, shall dwell forever in the realm of men." Artem's eyes widened. The implications of what he could do with the idol swept over him like the tide. "But know this, before you attempt to bring back your sweet daughter. She would not remember who she was in death, let alone who she was in life. She would have no connection to this world, save that she must always dwell within it." Tears welled in Aretm's eyes, tracing the lines of his weathered face as they fell. "If you would take a bit of advice: to walk forever in a world to which one cannot truly belong is not a condemnation you should ever visit upon one you love."

Artem wiped the tears from his face. "You leave me with an impossible decision, immortal."

Aemilius hitched up his two sacks. "I do." He looked down at the sniveling steward. "Do what must be done to *this*, and when you are finished, decide whether this is a world you would have your daughter live in forever."

Aemilius turned his back on the cottage of the peasant Artem, walking slowly toward the road. As he went, he listened to the steward's cries of "noo, noo, noooo," which gradually dissolved into full-throated screams of pain and terror. It was the sweetest music Aemilius had heard in an age, or would for some time again.

~ Daniel Loring Keating ~

Daniel Loring Keating grew up in post-Industrial New England, where he earned a BA in Creative Writing from Chester College of New England. He has an MFA in Creative Writing at the California College of the Arts, where he was the Managing Editor of *Eleven Eleven Journal*. His speculative work has appeared in

Strange Fictions 'Zine, the Transmundane Press anthology *Transcendent*, and the Hawk & Cleaver horror podcast, The Other Stories.

A Thousand Deaths

by Kate Runnels

The witches curse didn't bother me at first. Why should it? "May you never know the peace of the grave, the quiet of death's sleep, the silence of the crypt, but feel the pain of a thousand deaths."

I was young then, a happy-go-lucky sellsword looking for a quick profit to then booze and carouse the nights away. She uttered the curse right before I chopped her head off with my trusty ax.

I soon learned what she meant by those words.

That first death—

I knew death would come—

Just not for me—

—not that soon. And it wasn't even death in battle.

I rode away from the witch's abode in the countryside, not far from a town and the bounty. I banged on the door with a fist that didn't clutch the bag at my side. It opened and the bounty issuer stood staring at me with a crooked nose that had been broken long ago and improperly set. Her eyes squinted at the sight of me. "Yes."

"I'm here to collect the bounty."

She pulled me inside before looking both ways as the door closed. She counted out the coins from her frock pocket into my palm, suspicion clear on her crooked face. "You sure she's dead?"

"Oh yeah." Pulling the head from the bag, for how else could you prove the deed done, I left it with her.

The rest of the coins clinked into my hands, a satisfying

sound. Smiling, I hurriedly left before the biddy could say anything. I needed to find a tavern. I strode across the dirt road to my tied horse patiently waiting. The town wasn't overly large, but consisted of more than one market and more than one tavern. I'd find one of them now.

The coin rang on the bar top. "Ale."

The woman who came up to me later that night wasn't better looking than the one I'd left the head with, but much better than the head of the witch herself. But, oh, she made up for it in other ways.

I rolled over in the rented bed, happy.

The sharp pain in my back had me leaping from the bed. I felt the blood trickling down. The slut was on her knees in the bed facing me, bloody dagger in her hand. I swung at her. The dagger darted out and caught me on the forearm, a small cut.

Growling, I charged at her. She leaped off backward and I tangled in the bed sheets. She stabbed again, getting my side. I swung a wild backhand swing, missed and tripped. On the ground, tangled up and bleeding out, the stabbing continued.

I lost count somewhere, and finally the world went black—the pain eased—

Until I woke up gasping.

"Godsdammit!" I clapped a hand over my mouth. Did my voice just squeak? I glanced around. Not in my tavern room, the slut nowhere in sight, and it seemed to be morning outside. What was going on?

I sat up and swung my legs off the bed and stopped. Those were not my legs, all white and pale and skinny. Where were my muscular bronzed thews? And my hands were skinny, small, weak.

"What in all the hells is going on?" my voice squeaked again, and I reached for my crotch. I was still a guy, but what kind of a guy?

The door to the room opened and an older man and

women rushed in. Mouths open, eyes wide, their hands outreached for me.

"Oh, my Barthemo!" The woman still came, intending to touch me, to hug me.

"What?" I held out a hand to stop her, but she grabbed it, pulling me toward her with thick arms in a squat body. She was much stronger.

I twisted my hand out of her grip in a move I'd mastered years ago. Even stronger than I, she was not a fighter. She looked like a baker in her apron and squat body. "Stay away from me," I told them. "I don't know you."

"Son." The man stepped up to the woman. He was tall and skinny and pale complexioned. "That knock on your head, you've been asleep a week now. Even the physician priests had given you over to the specter to take to the afterlife."

I narrowed my eyes. No, not my eyes, this couple's boy's eyes. The boy they'd given over to the dead.

"I don't remember," I said to give myself time.

The woman sobbed and covered her mouth with thick hands. I noticed flour dusting the nails. The sounds of birdsong increasing outside.

The man put his own hands on her shoulders. They were as skinny as the boy's, with no scars or calluses. "Remember Alron's brother? He had no memory of the event either. But he survived, Boleva."

She nodded, patting his hands.

I decided to stay. The couple weren't rich, but they were well off, and I needed time to figure things out. Where I was, how I got there, how to get back. Plus, this boy was only about fourteen winters and not nearly strong enough for my liking. I was a man, for land's sake, not some kid growing into his body! This was ridiculous.

One second I was being stabbed to death by a sweet-talking, sweet-laying slut, and the next moment I woke up in the boy's mind. Oh, I would find that murderous, thieving bitch!

I scared the couple, my parents—his parents. His body I now found myself within had changed so much since my miraculous, remarkable recovery. I trained out in their courtyard. Always training and eating more than the kid ever had. Because I didn't like feeling weak.

I tolerated their ministrations, those of the couple and those physician priests they paid, all the while trying to gather information on where I was.

It turned out far from where I had been.

"The gods have dammed me!" I explained when I saw the map in the father's study. The sting of a slap across my left cheek came suddenly after.

"I have tolerated lots of changes in you since you woke, Barthemo," said the mother, "but there will be no cursing in this house." She took my opened maw as acceptance and stumped her squat body off to the kitchen.

Curse! Of course. I almost slapped myself then. That witch's curse. Could that really be it?

I spent the next couple of days in the city's library. Which relieved the parents about the boy until they learned from the curator what I'd been studying. Witchcraft. That limited my time out of the house.

So I started readying for my escape, journey, whatever. I pocketed little items of value I could resell later. I'd need to buy a weapon as I missed my ax. One night after dinner, I filled the travel bag with essentials and climbed out the window, heading for the stables. There were four horses to pull the business cart. I saddled one and used a second as a pack horse.

I led them from the stables and out into the night without a glance back.

I was a long way from the tavern and the witch's abode where all this started—and hopefully along the way I might find a different witch, someone who might help for enough coin.

A month passed to no avail. Two. My body kept growing, but my voice didn't crack as much when I spoke, which was good. I bulked up with the training I put myself through, but not nearly as much as I had before I'd died.

I had all the training of my past life in a boy's body. Even with all that, I couldn't prevent the horse from spooking in the woods. From a shadow, or the wind, I didn't know. It bucked me off. The fall was quick. The end was not. I landed on rocks. Large rocks, almost boulders. I couldn't move my legs, could hardly breathe, and I felt the bones grating against each other with each breath. I gurgled. Blood spat out.

I woke to a priest cowled in red standing in front of me, mumbling words.

My wrists were bound and tied to a hook above my head. I looked up at those scrawny arms as I struggled. Blood dripped down from numerous cuts to each arm, not deep, but many. This was so not good. I glanced down—and there were the breasts.

"Godsdammit all!" I yelled. Much higher pitched than even the boy's. Piercing even.

The mumbling stopped and I looked at an old face as the priest in front of me glared. There were others behind him, similarly dressed, though not as fancy along the trimmings. Torches flickered and I didn't know if we were deep inside a building or deep in the earth, but most everything from walls to ceiling to floors was stone.

"You will be silent for the incantation. You volunteered, remember, or your family will die, excruciatingly."

"I'm going to die, you sick cultist freak!"

"Yes. Now be quiet." He stepped forward, intending to slap me or something. I kicked him between the legs. Even with weak womanly legs, it connected just right. He doubled over and I used his head as a step to lift myself and yank my bonds free from the hook above me.

I landed on the cold stone floor, semi freed, but surrounded. I laughed. That was not what they expected. Each held out, in some cases fumbled with, a ceremonial dagger toward me. I knew they intended to be frightening, but it was comical to a trained fighter. Old men and priests who knew nothing of fighting, only of torture, had me laughing again. Oh, this would be fun.

A brave, foolish, younger cultist lunged forward in a thrusting stab. I twisted the lithe female body away. This body wasn't strong, but she was quick. At the apex of his lunge, I grabbed above his wrist and pulled forward. He fell face-first to the ground. I slammed a knee on his elbow and took the knife from numb fingers.

I cut backward with the confiscated knife, slicing through his throat before standing back up. The old man I'd kicked was stumbling to his feet behind me, so I kicked backward and connected. Planting another foot, I spun around him, wrapping my free arm around his neck and lifted him up to be a shield.

"Now we're going to walk out of here," I told the cultists.

"No! Even if I die, the work will continue." With that statement, the old man gripped my arm with his own and held me in place as he cut his own throat.

I let the body drop.

I smiled up at the others, bloody knife still in hand. "So, who's next?"

Later, tired, cut it seemed in a thousand places, I sagged to the cool stone floor, surrounded by many, many dead cultists. I died smiling.

💀 💀 💀

I woke with a gasp. Sucked in water, buffeted around,

turbulent, dark. Lungs searing as if on fire. I searched for a surface, but water surrounded me. Vision began to fade. Then all went black.

I woke again.

Only to die again.

To wake once more.

I don't know how many times. I lost count. Sometimes I would live for a while, other times not. Old-age deaths. Young deaths. Sometimes surrounded by loved ones. Sometimes not. One thing remained constant. Dying was painful.

💀 💀 💀

I woke. This one was different. I wasn't alone. Someone held me in the candlelight, I could feel their warmth along one side. We were in a bed, in a room. I heard distant sounds of a city outside. But muted, as it seemed to be night.

The arms around me relaxed their hold and the body shifted so the person could look at me. "Are you all right?"

I stared. Taking a long moment. She had long, dark hair, bronzed skin, a sensuous mouth, strong nose, with sparkling light brown eyes. "Beautiful," I whispered.

Her head relaxed on my shoulder. "You always say the nicest things, my love."

A long moment of silence as I adjusted to this new body, a woman's again, but with more muscles and less breasts. The woman beside me breathed in.

"That was a nasty one this time." Even her voice was beautiful, melodic and accented from someplace I'd never been.

"What happened?" My voice was slightly deeper and harsher, but not raspy or unpleasant.

"You had another seizure." Her hand stroked my cheek. "I was so scared."

I frowned and swallowed. For some reason, I didn't want to lie to her as I had so many times, to so many others, in so many lives before. I shifted out from under her and out of the bed. There were some clothes and I started dressing.

I heard her rustling behind me and wasn't surprised when she came up and held onto my hands. Those beautiful eyes, concerned for me. No, not for me, for whom this had been. I wanted her to look at me like that. "What's wrong? What is it, Saskia?"

"I'm not Saskia."

"What?"

I struggled to explain. Along the way, she released my hands and went to sit on the bed, listening. Somewhere along the way, I'd convinced her. I really don't know how. Finally I stopped talking. Silence stretched in the room. I'm not sure how much time had passed when she sighed and stood.

"So, what should I call you?"

"Saskia's a nice name."

"It was hers."

"It still is hers. And mine now, too, I guess. It's better than Barthemo."

She pursed her lips together trying not to smile and failing. "Barthemo? Really?"

I relaxed a little. "Yes, Barthemo." I paused, thinking about my first transference. It seemed like a very long time ago.

"You say you've been cursed and body hopping. Why?"

"I was cursed by a witch to die a thousand deaths."

She breathed in and crossed her arms. Staring me down. She then uncrossed her arms and snapped her fingers to bring my focus back up. "I know you were cursed. Why?"

"I'd gone to kill the witch."

"Why?"

"For the bounty."

"You're a bounty hunter."

I shrugged. "A sell sword. Yes, I was."

She closed her eyes before saying, "You sound so like her. And not just the voice. How you say it. But there is a difference. So, can we bring Saskia back?"

Shaking my head, I saw the hope in her eyes. "I don't know. And I don't know why I'm even telling you all of this. I never have before." The room seemed so big before, but it felt cramped now, so I started pacing to burn off energy. "I don't understand why now."

"Why not now?"

That stopped me. "What?"

"How many times have you died?"

I strode to the opposite wall and turned to pace back across the room. "I don't know. I lost count."

"Ten? Fifty?"

I shrugged. "I don't know."

She stood, stepping forward as I approached. I had to stop or I'd run into her. "A hundred?" she asked.

"Maybe more."

She reached down, taking one of my hands in each of hers. "No one deserves that."

I ripped my hands from hers. "Why are you so nice? I just told you your lover is gone and not coming back!"

"I know." She swallowed and looked close to tears. "And I'll process that, but you are here now. It's given me more time with Saskia, even if it's not exactly her but you.

"And you trusted me, someone you don't know, with a great secret, your burden. You've carried that around for years? A hundred deaths? I'm humbled. I'm honored. And if you think about it, maybe you told me so that *we* can try to fix this!"

I stared. All trace of softness had left her on that last statement. All that remained was steel determination. I'd been entranced by her beauty, awed by her kindness, but after that demonstration, "I think I love you."

She laughed, the steel melting. "Come on, get dressed. I'll make breakfast and we can get to know one another."

I smiled back.

Tilly cooked breakfast and talked. Talked about what

work they did in the city for the king's regional government—she as a courier and Saskia as her guard. She had a little magic ability, so the messages were magically encoded and transported. The two traveled mainly within the kingdom of Ilor.

It turned out I knew of this kingdom. I'd never been in my first life. Too peaceful and little call for sellswords. The king controlled many aspects of life here, from state-sponsored schooling to magic users being forced to work for the kingdom or be declared outlaw. But there were always witches and warlocks who didn't conform. Many deep in the countryside far from government control.

"So maybe it's possible to get Saskia back."

I didn't know. I kept my eyes on the plate with eggs, slices of bread and bacon. Tilly pulled out a chair and sat across from me, setting down her own plate.

"What do you think?" she asked.

I looked into those entrancing eyes, light brown with streaks of gold. I breathed in for a long moment, the bacon filling the senses, before answering. "I really don't know."

"Even after all this time?"

"Sometimes there wasn't much time between one death and another."

"That's horrible."

"I try not to think about it."

"But you can't not." Then she nodded. "Well, I know of a witch not too far from here that might help. She owes us."

I didn't ask how.

"If there's any chance of getting Saskia back and saving you, we have to take it."

I nodded, still wondering how lucky I'd been to wake up next to this amazing woman.

Soon Tilly made arrangements to leave town, taking a few personal days, she told the mage at the courier station. I stood in the background saying nothing. That seemed to be normal.

A Thousand Deaths

As we wandered the streets heading out of town, we passed a small square. Barging their way through was a solid mass of a dozen or so people cloaked in red and heading out the same city gates as us. People stayed far out of their way.

"Who are they?" I asked Tilly, trying to keep the anger out of my voice. She again held my hand as we walked, giving it a squeeze.

"They must have killed you in a previous life. They are the red cloaks. They have a name, but everyone just refers to them as red cloaks."

"Cultists." I spat the word.

"You've heard the term, 'life is pain?'" I nodded. "That's pretty much their motto. They don't serve a death god or goddess. No. Pain and torment and a god from the dark times, the name lost to the ages, and with each torment they believe their god will be awakened to bring about everlasting torment to the unbelievers and power to those of the cult."

I snorted. "Right."

I kept my eyes on the red cloaks, not trusting them, as we followed them out of the city. But we soon took a different path and left them going in a different direction. It made me relax knowing they were not going our way.

As I relaxed, though, I felt my latest body tensing. A sharp pain entered my brain and I gasped.

Tilly reached for me. "What is it?"

"I don't know." I put a hand to my head. "This headache."

"Just breathe. And relax." She took a deep breath in and I matched her actions. "Ride it out. Breathe in and out."

I listened to her voice. And the pain slowly subsided, but was still there though subdued and I could stand again. I hadn't realized I'd gone to my knees. "This is normal?"

Tilly nodded. "Yes, unfortunately. I'm just glad you didn't have a seizure."

"Fuck me. Me, too."

She glanced out of the corner of her eye at me, looking

me up and down. "Maybe later."

I shook my head at her and kept walking. I didn't want to say it, but I did anyway. "I'm not her."

"I know." She gave my shoulder a little shove, and I relaxed more, smiling at her.

It wasn't until the next day and we were deep into the forest that we came upon this witch's abode. She was sitting outside in front of a fire pit on a split round of wood. She was whittling away on a walking stick. Not too old, not too young. She seemed to know us, but for some reason I took an instant dislike to her. For the sake of Tilly, I kept my dislike at bay and kept my mouth shut.

"Tilly, Saskia. What brings you all the way out here?"

Tilly gave her a brief hug as the witch stood. I shook my head when she came my way. She narrowed her eyes, but stopped and looked at Tilly.

"We need your help, Kerzel," Tilly said.

"Very well, straight to business." She rolled out two more rounds, cut from the same tree it looked like, and put a flat side down for us to sit on. Then she stared straight at me. I kept my silence and stared back. "You're not Saskia."

"I told you we needed your help." Tilly leaned forward and told the witch what I'd told her. At the end, she asked, "Can we get Saskia back?"

The witch shook her head, long shaggy hair shaking like a dog getting rid of a fly. "I'm truly sorry, my dear. I've heard of spells like this. It doesn't displace a soul already residing in a body, but fills a void left by a departing soul."

"No." I barely heard the word as Tilly seemed to fold in on herself. She'd held out hope, and the witch had snuffed it out.

I let Tilly grieve. She hadn't since she found out about me. I leaned forward, gaining the witch's attention. "If you've heard of the curse, or spell or whatever, can you dispel it?" I asked.

She leaned back and narrowed her eyes once more at me,

still holding the staff she'd been carving on. "Might. Tell me, as Tilly didn't, how were you cursed?"

"I came to kill the witch for a bounty. She cursed me before I cut her head off."

She spat at my feet. I didn't move as she spun on Tilly. "And you brought this filth here, Tilly?"

"Please, Kerzel. Don't forsake us, don't forsake me."

"I cannot help you." The witch stood.

I stood. "You could. You just don't want to."

"So, what are you going to do about it, bounty hunter?"

I shook my head. "Nothing." I held out my hand for Tilly. "Come on. We should get you home—"

"Wait," the witch said. "Fine. I'll help. But it is complicated. After the spell, you will have to right a wrong."

I looked to Tilly who nodded. "Alright," I said.

The witch turned and headed into her wooden abode. "Wait there."

We waited. Many hours passed. As the forest darkened, she came out just as I threw a log on her outside fire, sparks flying up. She carried a great deal of things in her arms. And she started placing them around me. I really didn't like this. Tilly's eyes reflected the fires light, and seeing me looking at her, she smiled at me as the witch began chanting. I refused to watch what the witch did, instead keeping my gaze on Tilly.

Then it was over. Without the witch's chanting, quiet descended on the forest The fire hissed and crackled. "It's done?" I asked.

"Almost," said the witch. "Lastly, you must right a wrong."

I stepped out of the ring of stuff she'd put around me. "Alright. What?"

"You know right from wrong," she snapped. "Go fix a wrong."

I stared into the flames of the fire. The smoldering red embers. I knew what I would do.

We headed back to the city the next day and I told Tilly what I was thinking. I told her that she didn't have to come, but she agreed on the plan and wouldn't let me go alone. It took a week, but when the red cloaks returned, we followed them.

Now, we stared down from an opposite hillside as they entered an encampment. Wooden walls surrounded the flat area they'd set up as camp. The far side of which gaped a cave mouth. There were some tents set up, a few sturdier structures, and many cages. Almost half of which were empty.

That's the wrong I would right. To free the captives from torture at those sick freaks' hands. I studied the layout. It was a basic set up and had one entrance. But that didn't mean much. I could probably scale the walls. They might be sturdy, but not overly tall. And the red cloaks were not fighters themselves. Though I did spy a few burly individuals, wearing red, though not cloaks, prowling around the cages. And every captive I freed was one more that could fight their captives.

I knelt beside Tilly as she tried to study what I saw. I put my hand on her sun-warmed shoulder. "Are you sure about this?"

She nodded. "I've learned some things from Saskia, and protective spells all couriers learn."

"Useful."

"How do we go about this?"

I pointed. "That back area is less used, hidden by tents. I boost you over and we start opening cages to free those people."

"That's it?" She raised her eyebrows in disbelief.

"Keep it simple." I shrugged. "You open the cages and I kill anyone who tries to stop us."

"Simple it is, then."

"We'll wait for night."

It went well. Until the third prisoner we released, shrieked, drawing attention to him and us, and he charged at Tilly. He now lay dead with several red cloaks who'd come to investigate. More poured out of the cave entrance and not all of them were priests.

Two of those were facing me as several red cloaks surrounded Tilly and the other two prisoners we'd managed to free. But this wasn't tactical battle. It was hack and slash. Something I knew very well.

One of the brutes overreached and I darted in, the sword blade flicking out, cutting his knee. He crumbled as the knee could no longer bear his weight. I spun to the side, and as I came around, my blade in a flat arc lopped his head off.

He was replaced by another brute. I backed up, being pushed into joining Tilly and the others. But there were some priests in between.

I faked an attack forward, then jumped backward, spinning in midair. Landing, I stabbed left, connected, pulled out the blade and stabbed right. One last slash connected and then I was in the ring of red, standing in front of Tilly. My three companions having done a respectable job themselves.

Now we were surrounded by the red cloaks, and not all of them were priests, those useless things, and they outnumbered us. I spun as one of the prisoners screamed, and watched as she was pulled into the mass of cultists. Tilly at my side, a man on her other side the last prisoner. Each of us breathing heavily.

"I'm sorry, Til," I said.

"Don't be."

A voice yelled out from beyond the throng. "Kill the warrior, capture the others."

They surged and I slashed left and right, but they pushed forward. I stumbled from a slash and watched Tilly go down as a priestess tackled her. I struggled to stand, but there was a dead weight on my legs. I reached out a hand to her. I could almost reach. She struggled to reach for me.

"I will find you!" I yelled to her. "I will!"

"Not if you're dead," the brute who'd cut me said. Again, I was surrounded by dead red cloaks, and I smiled.

Tilly tried to smile, but winced as the blade descended upon me.

I woke with a gasp, shivering and cold. It was night in a forest, though I lay at the bottom of a craggy steep-sided ravine. If the gods were at all kind, I was close to where I needed to be, close to where I'd last died.

But I had to figure out my own situation before I could find Tilly. I shivered, staring up at the stars. I stood and paced the narrow bottom while looking for the easiest way up and out. I had a slight limp in one leg, but it didn't hurt, so it must have come from an old injury. Maybe this person had been an adventurer once before taking an arrow to the knee.

The limp didn't hobble me much. And I scrambled over the lip of the ravine with powerful arms. Many scrapes and bruises followed along each arm as I climbed, and I felt small pains down my chest and back, but thankfully nothing was broken and no cracked ribs.

As I regained my feet, I smelled wood smoke on the breeze. Looking, I could just make out a fire's orange glow. It was a cold fall night and I knew I needed the warmth.

Soon I hailed the fire.

Two men jumped to their feet as I came into the light. "Nilko!" one exclaimed, glancing between the other man and me. "We saw you fall."

I watched as his Adam's apple bobbed and he swallowed with another furtive glance to the other man. These men were older, hair tinted gray, worry lines and full beards. But the first man had a thinness to him that meant a nervous nature. I stepped forward and the one took a half step back. Like I said, nervous. I picked up a splitting ax. It wasn't my old weapon, nor was it a conventional weapon, but it would do. "You mean, when you pushed me."

"We didn't have a choice."

I spun the haft within the circle of my left hand. It was head-heavy with a sturdy wooden shaft. "You always have a choice," I said.

"He has our families. If we didn't kill you…" He trailed off as I nodded.

"Who and where?"

"Big Vince in Westbank."

Westbank was at the farthest point in the Kingdom of Ilor. I was close, still within the kingdom at least. I could make it back to Tilly in a few days. I sat down on one of the rocks situated around the fire. The two watched me closely, but I was getting warm and didn't care. "Where's my stuff?"

One of them brought a pack and I started rifling through it. I put on the jacket I found within. The shivering abated, and I scrounged around the fire for the food and drinks there.

"What are you doing, Nilko?" the nervous one asked.

"Leaving. Tell Big Vince I'm dead. Get your families back."

"But—"

"But what?" I asked, slinging the pack across my back. I carried the ax in my left hand and left them, heading south. I'd come to a road soon enough. Thankfully there was a half-moon still high up to give enough light to see.

The limp didn't seem to hinder me and I made good time. Until I grew tired and made a rough camp for the rest of the night. I'd take the limp over the headaches any day, any life.

💀 💀 💀

I strode out into the clearing of the witch's house and she

came out looking me up and down. "You!" She spat.

"Yes. Me." I stepped forward, ax held loosely in my left hand. "You said this would end the curse. It hasn't."

"Why would I help you when you killed one of us, when you were cursed by one of us? You deserve your fate."

"And what about Tilly."

"That is on you. Whatever right you tried to wrong, it got her killed, if she was foolish enough to go with you."

I swung the ax up into my right hand, holding it across my body. She started cackling as I advanced. "If you kill me now, may the curse last for another thousand painful deaths."

I turned and strode from the witch's abode. Cackling laughter still ringing in his ears. I'd promised to find Tilly and I would.

~ *Kate Runnels* ~

Kate writes primarily science fiction, dabbles in fantasy, even rarer are the articles on roller skating and roller derby. At one time or another she has been a tax preparer, legal assistant, golf instructor, roller derby coach and ranked in the top 30 in the world for hardball roller hockey while with the US National Team. You can find more of her work with *The New Accelerator*, *SciFan Magazine*, *The Fifth Dimension*, *Antimatter Magazine*, and *Ripples in Space* to name a few.

The Death of Sleeping Beauty

by Brandie June

The old woman wasn't a witch. That's a lie told for so long it's now believed to be truth. Probably because it's easier to believe. People would rather think there was a villain behind it all; that an evil and spurned witch decided to wreak havoc on the kingdom and take revenge upon a young princess.

But that's not how it happened.

The old woman was immune to the plague, but that wasn't her fault. She didn't even know that she carried it. All she knew was she had gotten a spinning wheel from a traveling merchant. She didn't know who he was, and she didn't care. Merchants like him came and went all the time. They came with their collections of goods and strange tales of the faraway places they had acquired their wares. She didn't care for tales. She only cared what she could hold in her hand and see with her eyes, even if her eyesight wasn't as good as it used to be.

But when she saw this merchant at the market, she knew luck was with her. Amongst his wares, half used candles, dented pots, rusted horseshoes and the like, was an ancient spinning wheel. The old woman had never owned a spinning wheel, always having to pay for the privilege of using one in the bigger weaving shops. This might change all that. Though her joints were slow with age, she forced herself to walk briskly to the merchant.

"How much?" she asked without preamble, pointing to the wheel. She was too old for pleasantries.

"A beauty, isn't it?" the merchant said with false admiration.

"No, it's ugly and old, but it looks like it will work," the woman said. "It's like me in that way." She laughed. The merchant didn't.

But he did give her a price she could afford. It would cost her all her savings, but it was still far less than a new wheel. And after testing out the wheel, the pedal, and the point of the spindle, so sharp that it drew a drop of her blood at the slightest touch, she knew it would serve her well.

She never saw the merchant again. Soon after he left the kingdom, he came down with a terrible sickness that led to an even more terrible hunger.

The wheel and the woman lived in the small cottage for many years until her son, a grown man with a family of his own, got a position as a castle guard and took his old mother to live with his family in the castle. The old woman insisted they take the spinning wheel, to which her son obliged.

And life continued for the old woman. She lived with her son and his family and she spun wool. She never knew the danger she carried on the point of her spindle. The kingdom would pay the price for her ignorance.

💀 💀 💀

The princess was not the only child of the king and queen. She was their fourth child, their youngest, and as such, given more freedom than her siblings. Without the future responsibilities of ruling, she was often allowed to do as she pleased. She was not a spoiled or selfish child, not as far as royal children went, but she was very inquisitive. At fourteen, she would wander the halls of the castle and the surrounding village in hopes of learning something interesting and new.

She loved to learn. From the archers, she had learned to shoot arrows, though her aim was poor. She could make simple breads from spending time in the kitchens. And she had even mastered juggling from the court jester. The villagers loved their strange little princess who wanted to learn everything, even if she had no need of such skills. Amused and a bit confused, they taught the girl.

In one of her wanderings, she came across the sound of a spinning wheel, somewhere in the servants' quarters. It was a difficult sound to miss as this particular spinning wheel creaked loudly as it worked.

Intrigued, she padded down the stone corridor until she reached the apartment the noise was issuing from. She peeked her head inside, not accustomed to knocking, as she was a princess of the realm. There, she saw an old woman sitting at a spinning wheel.

The princess stared for a while, transfixed. It was a hypnotizing sight, the rhythmic movement of the wheel and the almost magical transformation of fluffy wool into a smooth and practical yarn. She suddenly very much wanted to learn how to create such a transformation.

"Old woman," the princess said, in awe. "I wish of you to teach me how to spin."

The princess had to repeat herself loudly to get the old woman's attention, as the old woman was partially deaf. But once the woman did hear the princess, she turned and smiled at the girl.

"You wish to learn how to spin wool? That's delightful of you. Not even my daughter-in-law wants to learn to spin. Of course, I shall teach you, princess."

There are moments when the world changes. But neither of them knew this was one of them.

The princess carefully came into the room, in reverence of the spinning wheel. The old woman slowly got off the stool and gestured for the princess to sit. The girl carefully sat and adjusted her red velvet gown as she faced the contraption.

"What do I do?"

"It's easy, once you learn," the old woman responded. She gently placed her gnarled fingers on the princess' soft white hands and guided them in the right direction. Soon, the princess was spinning wool into yarn. She giggled with delight and it warmed the old woman's heart. The woman stepped back to let the little princess create yarn all on her own.

As if in a trance, the little princess spun. She remembered a story of a merchant's daughter who had been tasked by a king to spin straw into gold. A strange man had helped her, and the princess wondered if it looked like this. The gold must have been a prettier sight than the plain, undyed yarn, but the transformation just as great. The princess imagined spinning straw into gold, and that the yarn wrapping itself around the spindle was actually glimmering gold. In her mind, it was a beautiful sight and she squinted her eyes to better imagine the spun gold.

The little princess was so entranced in her imaginings of liquid gold that for a moment she stopped paying attention to what she was doing. Her hand slipped and was caught up on the wheel. In a desperate attempt to free herself, she jumped off the stool and flung her hands out. The little wooden stool clattered as it fell. The princess yelled, more from surprise than fear, but when she moved her hand, she saw a small puncture on her right pointer finger with a tiny ruby of blood.

"Oh, dear princess," the old woman cried, "you have pricked your finger on the spindle. Oh, I am so sorry, please forgive me. I should have instructed you more carefully." The old woman wrung her hands in worry, dreading the punishment she and her family might receive.

For a moment, the princess stood in shock and didn't say anything. The drop of blood rolled off her finger and onto her dress, where it was lost in the red of the velvet. After a moment, the princess collected herself.

"Fear not, old woman, it's just a tiny prick of my finger.

The Death of Sleeping Beauty

Look, it isn't even bleeding anymore," she said as she looked at her own finger. And indeed, the tiny wound had closed. There was a very small black dot where she had stabbed her finger, but she would not notice that until it was too late.

That night she dreamed she was spinning wool into gold, and it was the most beautiful thing she had ever seen. But suddenly, the spindle became a sword, sharp and deadly. The old woman, with not her face, but that of a demon, pushed the princess onto the sword. The princess screamed as she fell onto the sharp blade. The cold steel cut into her chest and her heart and she saw her blood mixing with the golden yarn, staining it copper.

She awoke in a cold sweat. It took her long minutes to catch her breath and realize she was safe. It was such a strange dream, a strange nightmare, and she was not one prone to wild dreams. Most nights, she dreamt of nothing, or at least did not remember the dreams after waking. This one she couldn't get out of her head. When she had calmed enough to stand, she retrieved a cup and pitcher of water on the side of her bed and filled the cup. She drank gratefully and deeply of the cold water.

Even after she drank the icy water and then another cupful, she felt terribly warm. She was feeling hot, but also shivering. She felt a stabbing pain in her finger and looked down to her right pointer finger. Bringing it close to the candle by her bed, she saw there was a black spot where the spindle had pricked it. Radiating out from the spot were streaks of dark green and darker red. Immediately, she began to panic that the tiny prick of her finger had somehow become infected.

She had the physicians summoned immediately. They did what they could, but they had never seen anything like that infection. Her tiny hand turned green, streaked with red, and she burned up with fever while shivering violently and complaining of chills. In short order, she was leeched, bled, had a variety of herbal poultices applied to her hand and given all manner of elixirs and concoctions to cure the bad humors in her that were causing the infection.

After mere hours, it was decided there would unfortunately have to be an amputation of the limb, as the infection was spreading so quickly. A few hours earlier, the princess would have been horrified to even consider such a possibility. Now, she was delusional during the brief periods she was even conscious. She talked of spindles and gold. She said she was hungry, but no broth would appease her.

Her parents, roused in the early hours of the morning, sat with their youngest daughter throughout the entire ordeal They could not understand how their beautiful little girl had so quickly fallen victim to this mysterious infection. At first, they balked at the slightest mention of amputation, but as their daughter's health sharply declined, they reluctantly agreed. A daughter with one arm was far better than a dead daughter, they assured each other. The queen, feeling sick at the very idea, stepped out of her daughter's room when it was time for the surgery. Her father, the king, felt just as ill at the idea of mutilating his youngest daughter, but believed it his responsibility to put on a braver face and stayed in the room.

A surgeon was summoned. He had a very sharp blade that would do the job. He tried to numb whatever the young princess would feel by giving her sips of a very strong alcohol. He only got a few drops in her, as she retched up the rest.

The surgeon decided he would have to go ahead with the procedure. He tried to reassure himself that the princess was too far delusional to even notice. As he was sharpening his blade, the young girl let out a terrible scream. It was a death wail, and her high-pitched, searing voice broke through the somber mood and transformed it to one of terror. She gave a gasp after that, convulsed and fell back on the bed.

Everyone saw her die.

The kingdom went into mourning. Unlike the story you might have heard, there was not a magical curse put on the

The Death of Sleeping Beauty

entire kingdom. Instead, it was the mundane curse of sadness and incredible loss that overtook the kingdom. The king and queen were devastated to lose their young daughter. The king became stoic and talked little. The queen locked herself away in her chambers and talked less. The villagers and servants of the castle had fond memories of the little princess trying to learn their different skills, and they took her loss with difficulty.

As was custom, the body was placed in the chapel for a fortnight for anyone to pay their final respects. The dead princess was displayed in her finest gown, a velvet dress of blood red. Her golden hair had been carefully brushed and braided and woven in with tiny, glittering rubies. Her hands were crossed over her chest with her non-injured hand on top.

Flowers and sweet-smelling herbs were placed around the body and throughout the chapel to hide the smell of death. Had they not been there, the people of the village might have noticed there was no smell of death, not even after the princess' body had been on display for days. She showed no signs of decay, but looked like she was simply in a deep and peaceful sleep. Everyone knew better, but sometimes it helped to pretend.

Villagers would come and offer small tributes to the dead princess—a few apples, some freshly made candles, bouquets of wildflowers—whatever they could spare. Soon, there was a tall mound of offerings to the dead girl. When the old woman heard of the princess' demise, she told herself it was a terrible coincidence. But in the back of her mind lingered a fear that kept her silent. She placed a golden ribbon on the memorial pile, but never spoke a word of what happened with the spinning wheel.

News of the princess' death spread quickly to the neighboring kingdom. The king and queen of the kingdom to the south sent their son, the prince, to pay respects on behalf of their lands. He was a dutiful son and left immediately on the fastest horse in the royal stables to reach the neighboring kingdom. He thought about how he would feel if one of his younger sisters had died painfully. He shuddered at the thought and rode on.

It had been five days, not a hundred years like the stories tell, by the time the prince reached the kingdom. Everyone wore black and thought sadly of their little princess. She lay in death in an open casket in the chapel. Her skin was still soft and white and only up close could one notice she wasn't breathing or that her fingernails were growing sharp and pointed.

The prince arrived at the castle and paid his respects to the king and queen. He told them how sorry his family was to hear of the loss of the princess. There had even been talk of uniting the two kingdoms by a marriage between him and the princess, but that was no longer to be. After paying respects to the family, he went to the chapel to pay final respects to the princess.

He had braced himself for the smell of decay, for the look of rot on a young body. He had hardened himself to such an outcome. He had not prepared himself to see her looking perfect and beautiful. The green of her hand had receded into a deathly white, and she looked at peace with the world. The prince thought about how he had almost wed this girl, and his heart felt a strange longing. He knelt by the altar to which the princess had been laid and prayed throughout the day and very late into the night.

Sometime late that night the prince drifted off to sleep. He dreamed of bloody spindles and sharp teeth that could crack through bones. He almost fell over where he had been kneeling and the movement jolted him awake. His skin was slick with a cold sheen of sweat, and after a moment of terror he was relieved to realize his dream had been just that, a nightmare with no substance. Or so he thought. He tried to resume his prayers, having promised to sit vigil over the dead princess until morning, and it was still over an hour till dawn.

And then he heard it. The entire castle was asleep, and in the silence the prince heard a soft moaning. At first he thought it was merely the wind, but when he stepped outside, he realized there was no wind. He went back to the altar and knelt again before the princess. After a few moments, he heard the moaning again. It was soft, almost a whisper. The prince stood and realized the moaning seemed to be coming from the princess.

That is crazy. The princess is dead. I must be hearing things. The prince went back to praying for the soul of the princess. But after a few minutes, he heard it again. It was so soft, like the sound of air through lips. It sounded like a whispered cry for help.

The prince stood over the corpse of the princess. He half expected to see her move, but of course, she did not. She lay in the casket, pale and beautiful and looking so helpless. The prince was entranced with the body and examined it closely. There was not the slightest sign of decay. He looked around and saw he was alone with the body. He leaned close to her face, wondering if he would again hear the soft moan or see a slight movement of breath.

He did not detect any breath when he looked closely at her lips, the same red as her velvet gown. He leaned in closer and closed his eyes, focusing on feeling even the tiniest of breaths. He could swear he heard the soft murmur. He felt no air as he leaned his cheek toward the girl's mouth, but he heard a soft moan, he was sure of it. She was calling for help, she had to be.

He knew he had to do something. He was as chivalrous as any story prince, and had a bright moment of imagining himself the hero. If he could wake the princess, he would save the day. The kingdom would rejoice and he would be the happy cause. Perhaps that is why he didn't call for a physician. Instead, he leaned in even closer until he was almost on top of the dead princess. Not sure what to do, he looked intensely at her red lips. They were slightly parted, and he was sure she was moaning. He gently blew into her mouth, hoping the air would revive the girl. Nothing happened.

He blew into her mouth again with the same lack of response. Perhaps he was not getting enough air to her. He had heard a story once of a princess who had appeared dead until a kiss by a prince had removed a piece of poisoned fruit from her mouth. He let his lips close over hers and blew again, stronger this time. Her lips were soft and cold, but not frozen. She made no move. He imagined there was a stuck piece of poisoned fruit, and let his tongue search her mouth. He knew he shouldn't be doing what he was doing, no matter how noble his intentions. He should be horrified and disgusted. Instead, he felt a tingling sensation in his mouth, and lower. He tried to ignore it.

He was kissing her, deeply, and desperately hoping for something to happen, if only to prove he was doing this for a purpose. After a moment with his warm lips on hers, his hot tongue searching her cold mouth, something did change in the princess. As if in reaction, her mouth came alive and she kissed him back. She had not even opened her eyes, but her mouth accepted him and drew him in closer.

The prince was so shocked, he almost drew back. He was right, and he reveled in that thought as he kissed the princess. He was saving her. He had not found any fruit, but she was clearly alive. She would recover and they would marry and unite the kingdoms and always remember their first kiss as the one that had brought her back to life. It was a miracle. His worry about actions vanished and he knew he was not a pervert but a savior.

Had he been paying attention, he might have noticed she wasn't breathing. Then again, he might not have.

After a few more moments of passionate kissing, the princess started to suck violently at his tongue. He was shocked and tried to pull away. At that provocation, the

The Death of Sleeping Beauty

princess bit his tongue. She probably would have bitten the entire thing clean off had the prince not been pulling back already. As it was, she still got a chunk of flesh in her mouth. The prince jerked back, swearing and screaming and bleeding. He didn't know what to think. His mouth was on fire.

He stood back, panting and staring at the princess. Her eyes were still closed and the only part of her moving was her mouth. For a brief moment, the prince hoped it was an accident. Instead, he saw that her mouth, her tiny, beautiful lips and shiny white teeth were moving. She was actually chewing on the flesh she had cleaved from his tongue. The pain in his mouth was suddenly forgotten as a new sensation flooded him—horror. Blood oozed down the white cheeks of the princess and though her eyes were still closed, she seemed to relish the taste of his flesh.

She moaned again, this time in pleasure. Her tiny pink tongue protruded from her lips and licked them vigorously, as if afraid she would miss consuming some of the blood. The prince took another step back, terrified of what he had just witnessed. His mouth was filling with blood and he spit it out. With the sound of his blood hitting the stone by his feet, the princess' eyes snapped opened. They were no longer the soft brown they had been in life. They were a deep red, the color of clotted blood. She sat up and the prince took another step back.

The princess moaned again, louder. Stiffly, she pulled herself out of her casket. It was as though she had forgotten how to use her limbs and they had stiffened in death. Moaning, she dragged herself to the floor and crawling, she leaned over the glob of blood the prince had spit out and started to lap it up, like a hungry animal.

The prince had seen enough. He turned and fled. The princess needed a physician, or more likely, a priest. The girl, roused by hearing him run, started to crawl after him. Despite her awkward limbs, she was fast, driven by a demonic need for blood and flesh. The prince tripped over a pew and fell hard on the stone floor. The impact jarred him, and he spit more blood, this time on himself. The gash on his tongue was bleeding profusely. The princess clawed her way to him, moaning louder. She looked so hungry.

As she came closer, the prince tried to back away while getting to his feet. She was so much faster than he thought possible. She grabbed onto his foot. Before he could get away, she had bitten down on it, her sharp incisors cutting through the soft leather and into the flesh of his foot. He screamed in pain and kicked out. His boot connected with her head and he heard a loud crunch. Afraid of the damage he might have done, he stared at the princess. Her face, once lovely, but now terrifying with its red eyes and blood-stained mouth, was tilted at an unnatural angle from her neck. Her soft curls bobbed around her face.

For a moment, the prince was sure he had broken her neck. But the princess, even with her bent neck, continued to crawl toward the prince. Her moans turned angry. The prince stood as the princess crawled toward him. He kicked her again, putting all his strength into it. He heard several things in her crack, but he didn't spare the time to look at the damage. He raced to the door before she could find a way to reach him.

Outside the chapel, he closed the heavy wooden doors and moved a nearby cart to block the entrance. He ran to the main part of the castle and yelled loud enough to wake everyone. Half delusional from pain and shock, he concentrated on getting out his story to the priests and physicians. He refused to look at the king or queen, both of whom had been woken by the commotion and stood off to the side as he relayed what he could of the night's events. He had to talk slowly, as his tongue burned him even after the wound stopped bleeding. Having told his story, he passed out.

As the prince was carried to his quarters with a physician

to watch over him, the priests and the rest of the physicians went to the chapel. None of them returned. After an hour, the king sent guards to the chapel.

When the guards did not return, the king became very anxious. He went to stand outside the chapel, but did not dare to open the door. He heard moaning coming from inside. He did not hear the screams, because he had arrived too late. It broke his heart, thinking of his youngest daughter, but he had the doors barricaded. He commanded the holy building be set on fire and archers stood by to ensure no one escaped the flames. The king watched, tears streaming from his eyes, as the building was consumed in red fire and black smoke. Soon, nothing remained but gray ash.

💀 💀 💀

As soon as the last flame of the chapel died out, a gentle snow started to fall. The prince awoke in his chambers. His eyes were red and he moaned.

💀

~ *Brandie June* ~

Brandie June loves storytelling in all sorts of formats and spends her days marketing animated movies and her lunch breaks writing fantasy novels in coffee shops. Most of her early life she was on stage or at least as close to the front row as she could get. Initially an actor, she got her B.A. in Theatre from UCLA and branched out into costume design and playwriting, eventually getting her M.B.A. from UCLA in Entertainment Marketing. Her first standalone play, a dark comedy about

~ Brandie June ~

Oscar Wilde, premiered at the Hollywood Fringe Festival to a sold-out run and won the Encore Producers Award. As a writer, she has a passion for fantasy, receiving two Honorable Mentions from The Writers And Illustrators of the Future. Her first novel, one involving a cursed toad and creatures of mythology, is currently being submitted to publishers by her agent, Steven Hutson of WordWise Media Services. Follow her @brandiejune.

The Soldier

by KT Morley

Pater drove the butt of the pike into the mud of the flooded riverbank and stepped on it with his right foot. He'd fought this battle before. Literally. Sometimes as a pikeman, sometimes as the cavalry. He always died, though. Nothing he tried ever pried him free of the curse.

Pivoting his body forward, holding the twelve-foot pike at a precise angle with the rest of his troop as the cavalry bore down on them, Pater prepared as best a man could. Around him, men screamed and cursed at the charging horde. Not all; some remained stoically quiet, resigned to their purpose—focused on the onrushing wave of death.

They wouldn't stop the charge. There were only about two hundred left to even make an effort. No two-hundred pikemen alive could stop a heavy cavalry charge of over a thousand upon an open field. Pater figured his flagging band would kill maybe fifty of the armored wave. With a little luck, they might get twice that many horses. Still, upward of 2,500 pounds apiece of animal and man and steel traveled toward them at speed.

The commander of the cavalry was shrewd and decisive, too. He struck when the pikes were confused or disoriented. He had inventive ways of creating such confusion as well. Rumor said their harasser was all of fifteen. Everyone called the young warrior Sir Stygge.

Pater hated him. On many levels.

Stygge had cast the curse—a blood curse uttered as the damnable Stygge died—dictating Pater's life. A cyclic life, starting here. Always this battle.

They were out of room to run. Methodical Stygge had corralled them into a twist of the river. Their peninsula was just big enough to die in. They couldn't ford the river, either; Stygge had the other shore crawling with mounted horseman cutting down any riders sent for aide or reinforcements. It was a marvel the boy could command so precise a use of force.

Still, Pater slanted his pike, tensed his forearm, and weathered the thundering of the ground through the soles of his feet. Next to him, a boulder crashed into the ground, squashing half a dozen men in the tightly-packed formation. Pater had forgotten about the catapults. Another lamentable effect of the curse lay in his fogged memory of the lives he championed toward death.

Around him, the sound of screaming changed from anger at the gods and little lord Stygge to cries for mothers and loved ones. All of the noise joined the angry war cry. Clearly, Stygge would not let them meet a charge unmolested. *Sound discipline for a commander.*

It left Pater with little doubt, too. When the wave of mounted men hit the forward edge of their disheveled formation, the pike wall would break, and he would die.

Again.

Pater's pike slid through an entire horse, the animal sliding down to ram him off his feet. His left arm snapped under the weight of the horse on the pike. He tumbled backward, awash in blood and offal from the eviscerated animal, and fell in the crush of men busy about dying. The pain of the injury barely touched the surface of his mind. Fear had too hard a hold on everything else. Even after all of this time, the life in the bodies he sheltered in screamed for survival.

Pater lay on the ground staring into the bright blue morning, struggling for a bit of air as death and carnage collided around him. He levered himself to his feet and pulled the short sword he carried from his hip. Pikemen weren't the best of swordsmen, but he wasn't a normal pikeman, either. One arm or not, he could still fight. He would still fight.

The armored knight whose mount Pater had killed

The Soldier

climbed off the broken horse. The man ripped the dented helmet from his head, screaming at the audacity of a lowborn peasant to gainsay him. Pater killed the man, ramming the short sword through the angry brute's jaw before the man could arm himself. Pater twisted his blade savagely, opening a cavity for blood and brain to leak through.

He turned in time to parry a sword thrust from another mounted man. A second horseman joined the first, and Pater parried his first swipe, too. That was all he could do. The first man snapped a backhanded sword stroke that cleaved Pater's right arm just below the shoulder. The rider also spun his horse, slamming its flank into Pater and breaking Pater's fighting stance. Pater lost his head to one of them before he could utter a curse at fate.

He hated this part the most.

💀 💀 💀

Pater woke with a start and the sense he was falling. Dreams sometimes did that. He had often felt his transition from one life to the next to be a dream state. Possibly, it was the only euphoric sense in life he had.

He opened his eyes, the rushing of the air through his hair and the sound of the wind screaming in his ears, breathing life and vitality into his new world. The sky held a marvelous blue color, and the sun shone so brightly he thought he might go blind. His leather riding harness chaffed, and he scratched his chest, the wind dragging at his arm and the form-fitting cloth of his shirt.

A scream startled him. Pater turned his head to face the scream. His mind spun crazily. From below, a cloud hurtled up to embrace him. Cold droplets gathered on his face and hands. They streamed away from his clothing's fabric. *How unique?*

Then reality hit him as he dropped out of the bottom of the cloud. He wasn't dreaming.

"Aaaaarrrrrgggggghhhh!"

Out of the corner of his eye, he saw a dragon bank and dive, its rider waving furiously in his direction. Sunlight gleamed off the bluish hue of the behemoth and sparkled off the rider's matching uniform. The picture, a flashpoint now in his memory, took his breath away. A second dragon hovered, wings beating and voice screeching into the brisk morning. The saddle on its back was empty, and Pater had the sinking suspicion he had fallen from it moments ago.

Pieces of dragon-flying safety and protocol began flitting through his mind. Of course, recollection after the fact rarely proved useful. The ground rose to meet him, too. It moved with alacrity.

The dragon rider swooped underneath him and rolled her dragon. The beast folded its wings and extended a clawed talon. As their two speeds matched, the dragon plucked him neatly from the air and rolled back over. The world spun crazily, dragging another scream from him. His savior extended its blue wings and caught the air. Pater's plight evened out into a gliding descent.

His dragon flew in circles around the one holding him, chortling in dragon tongue he barely recognized. The rider of the beast in whose grasp he found himself spoke a dialect he understood clearly. Her language tended to the profane and included lengthy descriptions of Pater's heritage and various degrees of a pain-wracked future imminently approaching.

"You ungrateful and cocky bastard! You nearly got killed performing aerobatics on Bromenen like some drunken monkey. I—"

He lost the rest of her chastisement in the roar of wind. Indeed, most of her curses were ripped away by the wind, and Pater had to fill in the blanks. He had heard swearing before. He understood the gist.

The dragon carrying him banked sharply for the last hundred feet and pounded the air with its wings, slowing the

The Soldier

descent further. It hovered for a brief moment before lowering itself to a small hilltop. Pater's feet had hardly touched the ground, the idea of dropping and kissing it only half-formed, before his left cheek exploded in pain so sharp he thought his left eye might relocate to the other side of his nose. The sting of the blow evaporated thought. He struggled to catch his breath. Then the other rider was on top of him, cursing him, kissing him, and tearing at his clothing.

"You stubborn, stupid, man. How could you do that?"

The raging of his heart, the ecstasy of survival, and the not-so-subtle ardor of the dragons (a mated pair, he recalled) had stolen his soul and driven his libido to the heights from which he had recently fallen. Whoever the woman was on the other dragon, she had stamina and an intoxicating, insatiable desire for him.

By the time he came to his senses, she had dressed and was rubbing oil into the scales of her dragon. Both dragons cooed—cooed—at her. Pater stood and searched for his clothing, which had gotten twisted and turned inside out.

"Don't ever do that again." Her voice fell on his ears like a gentle rain. The change from the profanity-laden cursing she had laced him with earlier dragged a smile from him.

"I'm serious," she said, stopping the rub-down of her dragon and fixing him with an icy stare.

He held up his hands in mock surrender, one arm in a sleeve, and the other not quite started. "Sorry. I lost focus for a moment and—"

"Lost focus my ass." She pointed directly at him. "You set your stirrups and saddle warrior-fashion and then tried to pretend you're something you're not."

Pater bristled. "Oh, I'm a warrior. Make no mistake. I—"

"I don't think so," she said, slashing the air with her hand. "Challenging gravity to a one-on-one and living to talk about it later is not bravery or bravado. It's foolish." She pointed emphatically. "Wear your harness!"

Her uniform flashed again, and he saw the pin

responsible. Walking over, he picked her up, holding her aloft to see the brooch more clearly. She kicked, but not overmuch. The cobalt eyes of the coiled dragon in the brooch matched those of the dragon she rode.

"That's a nice piece of craftsmanship."

"Put me down, fool."

Pater obliged, her name finally worming its way to the surface of his mind. "Who made the brooch, Tamia?"

She looked at him as if he had addled his brain. "I did. I told you this morning. The dragon for me. The unicorn for my father. Stygges have blue eyes. In my case, the blue is also for Mralki." She patted the dragon in front of her.

Something stirred in Pater, but he ignored it. "You have talent."

"Some," she said, shrugging her shoulders. "It might—might—make my father like you better if you listened more astutely to my teaching."

Pater held up his hands in contrition and backed away. "I did everything you asked once we landed."

She swatted him. "Go rub-down Bromenen, imp."

With that, she turned back to her dragon and continued rubbing. Her dragon, yellow eyes gleaming, chirped at Pater. He looked at his dragon, every bit as resplendent. Pater fixed his shirt, grabbed a rag from his saddlebag, and a can of the oil the dragons favored. He began to rub it into the hide of his mount, scouring between the palm-wide scales where he could and evicting the detritus and occasional scale worm he found.

He gave up talking to Tamia. Her fear at losing him and joy at saving him oscillated, and he wasn't sure enough of her moods to risk inviting the negative one out for another round of insult-the-young-dragon-rider. Instead, he focused on learning his dragon and trying to remember the muscle coordination required to stay on its back.

After an hour, he decided to try a different angle with Tamia. "Why are we on patrol out here, Tamia? What are we looking for?"

She poked her head around the bulk of her dragon, "Lord Stygge expects a counterattack through the pass, an attempt to reopen the spice route." Tamia shook her head, disapprovingly, "We should tame the seas and bring them under our control. I would like to fly over the water." Her eyes took on a faraway look for a moment before continuing. "Anyway, we are here to find the head of whatever relief column they sent. Catch it out in the open and then burn it down. We won't be any use in the pass. The dragons won't have room to fly."

"Sounds simple enough." Pater figured it was probably time to apologize. He didn't think the *I'm sorry, your lover is gone, and I am a cursed, nomadic soul inhabiting bodies bound for death* was the right approach, though.

While he mulled it over, she continued. "Our forward elements are faring quite well, though some resistance is beginning to slow them. If the counterattack we search for is already in the pass or other elements have dealt with it, we may find ourselves retasked to the front." She shrugged her shoulders. Expecting such variety seemed a normal part of her life.

"How will we know where to go?"

"Are you sure you're okay?"

Tamia's face scrunched adorably in concern. Pater shrugged his shoulders.

"Magic, Damian. Magic."

Pater knew better than to comment on magic or mages. Blood-magic powered his spiritual sojourn. His immortality. Brashness, ignorance, and arrogance also warred with magic for the top cause of his inglorious romp through fields of war, but they lost, finishing distantly by comparison. Pater had broken parlay once—only the once—and slaughtered an aging king suing for peace. That king, the king, King Stygge, was at least three times older than the dragon rider's body Pater now rode. Probably four.

Breaking parlay had been easy. King Mikel had arranged it with Pater before the meeting, and Pater had carried out the assassination. The king had worn a brooch, too. A unicorn, as Tamia had just said, fondled endlessly during the brief parlay. He even held onto the jewel as he lay dying, muttering what turned out to be Pater's curse. Pater's wanderings began soon after when he'd taken a filleting sword stroke while trying to route Stygge's men. He died and then woke up carrying a pike.

The king's curse made Pater live forever, inhabiting bodies near a battlefield. Pater had lost count of how many bodies he'd been in and how they had all died. If a thousand people died in a battle, it seemed likely Pater would experience each of those deaths personally. He probably couldn't wander forward in time until he had experienced some ending set-piece. Pater had no idea what that might be or how to trigger it.

And now, as a dragon rider, he fought on the Stygge side of the war. He'd given up fighting for causes the third or fourth time through the cycle. His temporal wandering gave him time to ponder his curse. It seemed a strange form of immortality. The only benefit he'd found, however, linked to an overdeveloped and intimate knowledge of all angles and depravities of war. The memory of the king's death haunted him often, but there was no changing the past. Even if it now lay in the future. He'd given up sorting out time's twisting.

"I don't know why I lost touch and fell, Tamia. I'm sorry." It was rushed and clumsy, but he had to say it somehow.

"You have to be careful, Damian. You are a gifted flyer, but you take shortcuts. Shortcuts kill. There are no old, brave dragon riders."

Tamia snapped the leather riding strap holding the saddle snug and then continued rubbing the oil on its other side. She looked at him and smiled, her crooked grin and playful eyes measuring him. He hadn't noticed how blue they were

The Soldier

earlier. Stunning, actually. Perfectly matched by the pin she wore. He had never seen the dragon pin before and had only the curse-earning glimpse of the unicorn.

Two hours later, they were airborne again and heading to their assigned sector. The mountains grew closer, and as they did, the litter and debris of an army on the march became obvious. At the mouth of the pass, bodies dotted the plain. Crows and forest beasts feasted on the dead.

Tamia reined her dragon and sped westward, her orders received through some act of wizardry. The sun crested midday, and all of a sudden, she seemed hell-bent on being somewhere else. Pater urged his dragon faster in following her. They flew all afternoon and picked up others on their way. When they charged out of the clouds, their ground forces were in tatters. Enemy infantry had dislodged one flank and was rolling the whole of the line toward the river.

Lightning flashed in front of Pater, and Tamia disappeared in a blinding bolt of energy. He screamed, as much in shock at the brilliant bolt as the death it caused so suddenly and brutally. Bromenen roared in soul-seared pain, his body shaking in torment. Pater banked for attack as the remains of Tamia and her blue fell from the sky. He saw the mages responsible. He saw the markings on the earth feeding their magic. He aimed Bromenen and coaxed him into a fiery rage.

It only took a few seconds to arrow through the sky. When he reached the mages, Bromenen roasted them into eternity. The sand beneath their feet melted into glass as horses screamed and died along with everything else caught in the tumultuous tunnel of flame. The dead, dying, and anything resting on the transmuting sand began to sink into the sticky, gooey glass.

He turned the dragon's head, steering it with his knees to wash the kiss of fire across everything he could. His fellow dragon riders did the same. Soon, the entire rear of the enemy's line burned. The enemy infantry attack faltered.

Pater didn't care. His eyes stung from tears and smoke. He roared, "For Tamia and House Stygge!"

He settled Bromenen onto the ground. Once down, he let him have his will to thrash and bite and whip his tail. He didn't stay long; a dragon was a better warrior in the sky. Pater's heart a fractured vessel, he took wing again, the power of Bromenen's wingbeats throwing them from the ground into the sky.

Behind him, the other riders were screaming, one calling out, "Heave to, dragon rider. Let us coordinate." He ignored their wild calling. The earth-bound couldn't hurt him anymore.

His dragon's mind tore at Pater's own thoughts. Bromenen felt the loss of his mate acutely and couldn't keep the pain from washing through its link to Pater. Pater didn't understand it at all. All he knew was the loss of Tamia. He could see the fire in her eyes. He remembered the warmth of her embrace.

Pater pivoted for another round of burning. Bromenen shuddered, coughing up blood as a six-foot bolt of steel-capped wood burst through his breast and shattered his heart.

Pater fell again. This time Tamia wouldn't catch him.

Death did, the flash of his legs and arms and ribs all shattering on impact rifling through his consciousness before it mercifully closed its grip and tossed him into his next body.

💀 💀 💀

"General? General, are you alright, sir?"

Pater took a sip of whatever the goblet in his left hand held while he stared at the map on the table before him. Waking as someone else always required an adjustment. Sometimes, the bodies his soul joined were already in perilous positions. Pater grabbed the table suddenly as vertigo and the feeling of falling swarmed through him.

A cold wind whipped the cloak he wore. The cloak,

The Soldier

failing to escape, wrapped around his legs as damp air swirled through the tent flap. A page sealed the flap and then stood holding the tent closed. Pater no longer wore a dragon rider's garb but a general officer's rank. He now commanded an army. His old bones hurt, and gout twisted his right hand.

"Yes, yes. I'm okay."

He looked at the map. The world displayed before him lacked the clarity of familiarity, but something about it still fussed at the edges of Pater's memory. The names he recognized and the language he could read, but he didn't know why or how. He thought the map represented a battle line, hard-won and not entirely secure.

Slowly, Pater caught up with the mind planning the engagement. He learned a lot about war in these moments and recognized an enemy's line of advance. The whole of the invasion had stalled under Pater's counterattacks. Now, the enemy floundering, Pater had to find a way through the intruder's defenses, break his will, and push him out. It was King Stygge whom Pater had cornered, but not some teenage prodigy. This adversary was older, seasoned, and deadly dangerous.

Pater pointed to a series of bluffs on the left edge of the map. "What are these heights? Do we control them?"

"Yes, general, we do. King Mikel forbade us to move to the heights, though, for fear of starting a war with Berkan."

"They are our heights." He didn't know how he knew, but continued. "How am I to wage a war with every advantage removed from me?"

No one spoke. Silence coursed around the table in ungainly waves. Pater studied the contours of the map, noting the size and stature of a Stygian castle in the north. On the map, it held prominence, and the cartographer had surrounded it with a town.

"Stygian is enormous." He couldn't help decrying out loud.

"Pardon, general? Stygian?"

"Castle Stygian." He pointed. "There in the north."

"King Stygge changed its name last year. Sir, you worry me."

He waved off the concern, sighing at the slippage of time. "No matter. I thought I remembered it differently."

He knew the comment wouldn't help his officers with their worry over his state. He didn't care. He needed to continue.

Without the heights, he couldn't push the extreme left of his enemy's defenses. Without pressure on that flank, the enemy could pivot against the river to defend their siege equipment and subject his own line of advance to catapult fire. He remembered any number of times being in the line of Stygge's catapults. *What a cluster!*

But the river…A thought began to take root. "I want to damn the river, redirect it across their line."

"Sir, we discussed it yesterday. It is environmentally impractical and would change the value of this very fertile valley. We must attack the right, unhinge it, and then roll the enemy back to the river."

"We must?" Pater looked at the map. Reading maps hadn't changed despite his rebirth in another body. He pointed and spoke. "The right flank you speak of is a jumble of rocks, shrubs, gullies, and trees. No cavalry or infantry line is making it through that with enough punching power to dislodge an entrenched enemy."

Pater shook his head. The beginning was always like this. He had to sort out who he was and what he was supposed to do. Sometimes he did well enough to live for a couple of years. Sometimes not. He had only been a pikeman for a week or so. Long enough to survive two failed defenses and die in a third. He had been a dragon rider for less than a day!

He set the goblet of wine down. He didn't care for wine. Or, rather, his consciousness didn't. This body seemed fine with it. "So you're telling me we have to attack where they

The Soldier

want us to, fight a battle entirely on their terms, and try to do so without the aid of commanding height or overwhelming arms?"

"We are better than they are."

Pater drilled the man with an icy stare. "We better be."

"We are, general. Our battle mages are the best in the world. We will uproot them in the forest and toss them aside." The man who continued to speak, a colonel with an iron-gray mustache and matching beard, slammed his fist into his other hand with conviction. "You'll see."

Pater leaned forward and rested his hands on the table. The silence stretched in the chilly tent. He considered other options. "Are there any other surprises for me? Are there unicorns and pixies about as well? Dragons?"

The mood in the room shifted. He had crossed some taboo line. Pater glared at the colonel until the man relented and spoke. "General, it is because our enemy ruled unicorns closed to hunting that we are at war."

Pater fought the urge to throw his hands in the air. Inside, he raged that some of the lives he lived bordered on the surreal. Man never seemed to need a terribly severe reason for killing others. "Fine," he said demonstrably. He changed the subject. "Aside from our mages, what is our greatest asset?"

"Sir, are you sure you are okay? You slept a long time this afternoon, and perhaps you are with fever."

"I am fine," Pater insisted. "I am just reviewing the strength of our assets in how they relate to our present obstacles." For effect, he pounded the tabletop. "Tell me!"

They did. Pater listened carefully, categorizing every detail. Then he planned his assault. He had no illusion about its eventual outcome. Ignoring the heights was a monumental disaster, and it seemed everyone in the room knew it. They waited for the other shoe to drop. The following morning, with a reluctance well-hidden from his staff, he gave the order to attack.

His archers laid a brilliant covering fire through which

his troops advanced over the broken ground. His mages flung illusion and wove fear into the very air. They hurled boulders and trees and called lightning from the heavens. By midday, he had amassed enough infantry to form a solid wall of attack against the right flank.

The enemy had mages too, though, and they resisted. As the enemy mages revealed themselves, Pater had his own mages, archers, and siege weapons target and kill them. The work was sloppy and wasteful, but as the sun eked past midday and began to dive into the western sky, he had broken the line. His troops now reformed to shove the enemy into the river.

Then the dragons appeared. Six of them, with riders in colored armor matching the color of the dragons they rode. His mages killed two. The other four, led by a maniacal banshee of a man, burned his spell casters into ash and then commenced to blistering his mustered infantry and other reforming attack elements. He aimed ballista skyward, filling it with spear-length shafts of death. It served to kill two more dragons, including the banshee. The last two proved elusive and destructive. When night fell, he had retreated back through the rocks to where the day had begun.

Enemy soldiers charged after his retreating army. Pater tried to mount his horse for escape, but the advancing enemy shot it full of arrows. Its screams of pain chased Pater as he searched for another only to have it killed, too. Before he could find a third, Stygge's soldiers surrounded him and clubbed him senseless. When he came to, he was tied to a chair outside a camp commander's tent with strange faces eyeing him. They wore an unknown insignia, though it had the name Stygge in bold letters embroidered around it.

A troop of four stepped forward and hauled him before the king on the other side of the tent flap. The king, barely graying and supremely confident, wore the face of a man with a disquiet soul under brooding, blue eyes. As Pater watched, the king unclasped his cloak, his hand lingering on

The Soldier

the unicorn brooch holding it closed. He also stretched a parchment over his writing desk, securing it in the process before reaffixing the brooch to his chest.

"General." The king looked up from reading whatever tides the map told him and fixed Pater with an icy stare. "I am unhappy in your overly successful attack today. You killed a good many of my men." The disquiet returned in a rolling wave before the king continued. "I am not in the habit of congratulating fine officers for their fortitude against my army." A flash of unknown memory flittered across the king's face before he continued. "You would be the first."

Pater blinked. "Thank you, your majesty."

"But," the king bent over the document while his pause allowed the war on his face to finish. Pater saw his captor's heart set in the tightening of muscles around the other man's jaw. Pater knew what was coming now.

"You have killed our heir today, and that requires a more direct and personal response."

The king's anger shone through his tattered and broken countenance of calm. Pater bowed his head, understanding the role a ruler played over the ruled. More so for those captured in war. He stood unmoving, head bowed as his captor raged.

The king commenced pacing, absently flipping a knife and muttering to himself. On the third iteration of the king's march, he stopped in front of Pater as if seeing him for the first time. "Honor is its own reward."

With little additional fanfare, the king slammed the knife through the arm gap of Pater's armor. Pater gasped, too shocked to do more and certain the look of incredulity on his face would live with the king forever. It was a death blow, but not one that would kill Pater in the next few minutes. He would suffocate on his blood or bleed out internally over the next several hours.

The king withdrew the blade, having spent a moment holding Pater upright after the shock of being stabbed had threatened his balance. Pater blinked, marveling at how clear and blue the king's eyes were.

Astounding!

The king called his guards. "Take him to The Hollow and hang him."

Rough arms grabbed Pater and dragged him from the tent.

Strangely, the last thing he saw before darkness and chaos took over his mind were the shining cobalt eyes of the king's unicorn brooch.

How 'bout that. They match.

His mind held the two images in front of him as the rope chafed his skin and choked the remaining life from his shell.

💀 💀 💀

Pater leaned over the rail and offered the remnants of his lunch to the gods of the sea. All around him, other men made similar submissions. In the ropes above the heaving deck, deckhands scurried about their business, trimming sail and catching the wind. He'd been two weeks at sea, stopping in ports every third or fourth day to pick up oddities for their assault north. Every day on the water held these same deity-consorting moments. He leaned overboard again and prayed fervently, hoping to see his shoes pass out of his mouth in witness to how desperate his plight and how empty his stomach. His life had become hour after hour of rail-side retching.

"Mast, ho!"

The shout from high up in the rigging caught everyone by surprise. The languid grace of mariners about their job drew jealous stares from most of the land-walkers—those not sick, anyway. Fully half of the troop had no ill effects at all and took great pleasure in riding their brethren like rented mules. Pater heard men whispering about time, wind, and tide before he was leaning over the rail and puking again, the idea of mental arithmetic too much task for his addled brain's

The Soldier

single-mindedness of purpose.

Mid-morning was bad, afternoon worse, and gods help them all if there were a storm. The only mercy pinging in his mind centered on the singular absence of storms. It seems those in command had divined enough about the weather to send their fleet seaward without the threat of ship-rending gales.

A callous and ill-tempered voice tore the curtain back on his unit's pleasure cruise. "Listen up, you soft-sided mud-crawlers!"

The sergeant's voice rattled through him. Its enmity immediately calmed his belly. Pater turned to his taskmaster, certain the face he showed the sergeant looked as pallid as those around him.

The sergeant continued. "Seems that wee sail on the edge of the ocean is speeding happily toward us." He thumped his gauntleted fist against the banded armor covering his chest. "I've got it on good authority we are returning the gesture."

Half the troopers roared with like-minded enthusiasm, thumping their fists against breasts as well. The other half nodded morosely, offering what support their sea-weakened state could summon. Most didn't have armor on at the moment. The sergeant was peculiar in that aspect.

"I'm not interested in half-hearted fighting, you weak-kneed momma's-boys." He pointed over his shoulder to the other ship, now visible even from standing flat on the deck. A dozen men also saw the horizon and heaved back to the rail to renew their commitments and associations. The sergeant paid them no mind. "I assure you, dead is dead. No half-measures. If you don't fight with everything you have to survive, the other guy will kill you."

From somewhere along the rail, a sick trooper interrupted the sergeant. "I hear they use women in the ranks. Even sick, we should be fine."

The sergeant moved with such haste to the side of the

179

soldier questioning him, Pater swore magic played some role. Two men down from Pater's post on the rail, the sergeant grabbed the puke-stained tunic of the interrupter and jacked him clean off his feet.

"Maybe when you get lost in her pretty eyes, she runs her sword through your chest. Maybe, as she's stealing your life, she steals a goodbye kiss before dumping your lifeless carcass over the rail to follow your lunch." For effect, the sergeant shoved most of the man's body out over the beckoning sea. He pinned the man's legs on the deck-side of the rail to keep the guy from falling in, but the action had a sobering effect. For several tense seconds, all thoughts of seasickness seemed trivial. Their sergeant was good at getting his point across.

He settled the man back on the deck and stalked back to the wash pail he had been standing on. "It's true they use women in the ranks. They use dragons, too. Or used to, when there were still a few of them left. I don't care. We enter battle. We go as killers offering no quarter, taking no prisoners. If we can take the ship, fine. If not? Loot it, burn it, and let it sail to the bottom with its dead and those on the way. Don't bring anything back that needs to be fed."

Pater shifted. The task seemed easy enough—straight forward kill-or-be-killed kind of action. He'd get to use a pike again, probably just to push against the other ship or drag some unlucky soul over the rail and into the water between the two hulls. If the armor didn't drown the soldier outright, the crushing weight of the two ships smashing into each other at the mercy of the waves would. Of course, once soldiers started boarding, it would be swords and daggers. A few archers in the rigging could do a little distance work. So could the archers on the other ship.

A thundering crash from the rear quarterdeck meant the catapult now ranged the other ship. In front of Pater, the ballista operators in the bow cranked the winch back on the big crossbow and set a six-foot bolt in position. The bolt wore a thick sheen of oil.

For five minutes, the catapult and ballista rained their destruction on the other ship. Pater's ship took damage, too. Two different flaming bolts had torn through the sails, snapping lines and dripping fire on their way past. The man next to him disappeared as a third bolt sizzled through the space in which he stood, eviscerating him and carrying him over the rail on the other side of the ship.

The enemy's catapults were effective, too. Twice, huge casks of oil smashed down on the deck, saturating everything in foul-smelling combustibles. The fire of the ballista bolts ignited one of the kegs, and the sailors worked at fevered tempo to throw sodden sails on the fire and stamp it out. The burning men were shoved overboard. Pater used his pike to help with that as well. The screams of burning men ended in the bubbling sizzle of fire drowning in water.

When the ships hit, Pater hacked and swung at any movement he saw on the other boat. By locking his feet in a scupper and levering his toes up against the rail, he maintained his balance better than most. He hooked his pike on a man's shield and jerked hard enough to unbalance the fellow and drop him in the litter-strewn water between the two hulls. The man bobbed up only to be crushed by the boats as they slammed together, his scream joining the chaos of other wounded and dying men and women.

With the boats entangled, the sergeant took the initiative, bellowing. "Boarding party, away!"

Sailors dropped planks across the rails, bridging the gap. Men hustled up and over, the seaworthy and those less so. Pater's slot to storm as a boarder meant he'd be in the second wave. He continued to thrash with his pike, waiting while poking or pulling at enemies on the other boat. He had to beat back several attempts on him as well but fared better than the enemy with his defensive swatting. He'd become an adept pike-wielder during his sojourn.

"Boarding party two! Go! Go! Go!"

The swirling form of a woman blurred across the rail of the other ship as she raced to counter the boarding party. Pater couldn't quite reach her but hurled his pike with enough force to entangle her legs and spill her, screaming and surprised, from the rail. She stared at him, her youthful face passing from confused to terrified in the instant before she hit the water.

Pater leaped for the gangplank and scooted across, unsheathing his sword as he went. Once on the other ship, chaos made a formal introduction. Fire leaped from a hundred different places, many of them corpses. Men and women screamed in the throes of mortal wounds or adrenalin-fueled battle-lust. Blood and assorted pieces of flesh lay everywhere. Bodies blackened to char by the fire and too fearful of letting go of life screeched more hideously than the rest, but it was a near thing.

A knife-wielding hand stabbed out from behind a barrel. Pater hacked at it, severing the hand with enough force to drag the body attached to it from hiding. The kid tried to swing again, unaware the hand and knife were gone. When the youth saw the spray of blood, he stopped to stare. Pater didn't wait and flashed a backhand across the boy's neck before moving past the dead attacker.

Behind him, he heard the sergeant bellowing again as he led the third wave across the boarding plank.

Pater didn't have time to think, killing two more men in trade for a long cut on his left arm. A sword thrust swirled out of the smoke-consumed quarterdeck. He parried the blade quickly, hammering the thrust to the side before he turned his wrist and slashed. He recognized the satisfying draw of steel across flesh as skin parted under his blade. A snarl followed, surrounded by curses. The smoke cleared, and a blond-haired woman bleeding from a gash on her shoulder stabbed at his face.

She screamed, "Die, invader!" Her ferocious battle cry followed.

The Soldier

The move spoke of recklessness and lack of training. Fear, too, the whole of her attack hurried. Injuries often addled the mind and forced the body to do things it shouldn't. Her thrust at his face left her open to his counter.

Pater obliged, raising his sword in a clockwise circle and slamming her blade to the side. He didn't speak; words weren't necessary. The force of Pater's counter jarred the woman's body. She gasped as a new wave of pain from Pater's previous slash rippled across her face. He drove his blade down hers, pushing both further away. In an act of solid soldiering, he tore the sword across her midsection, parting boiled leather and flesh alike.

Entrails spilled onto the deck. The woman a moment ago awash with fury and anger slipped in her own blood and fell amid the gore. Her sword forgotten, she tried to stuff her spilling organs back inside. As a combatant, her fight was over. As a human, it would end soon as well. The sergeant flowed past Pater like a rising tide and killed her, saving time the job.

"Forward, men." The sergeant shouted, brandishing his sword in a terrifying flourish. "We have their number now. They'll be feeding the sharks soon."

Pater fell in behind the sergeant and continued their brief, brutal conquest, storming up the port stairs of the quarterdeck.

Ten minutes later, the sergeant stood astern, staring out at the beaten and burning ship. "I want fire set below decks. Find their stores and take everything edible off this scrap heap."

An enemy soldier crawled across the deck by the sergeant's feet. The sergeant was a brutal man of war, singular in focus and purpose. He leveled a kick at the crawling man's arms and spilled the hapless soldier face first into the deck. With an economy of motion, he then rammed his sword through the man, pinning him to the deck to die.

Straightening, sword quivering in the body at his feet, the

sergeant raised his eyes to stare down any moral objections before speaking. "No quarter to anyone on this boat. Kill them all!" He ripped his hand in a hard slashing motion Pater had come to recognize as an end to debate and discussion.

Pater helped strip the ship and aid the wounded into the afterlife. When finished, they sent the empty ship's burning husk into the sun. As she foundered in the waves, she sank. Pater joined his fellows in cheering. Nothing more invigorated the soul than a battle survived and won.

He'd won this one, true. He'd won many. But he always lost the last one in a given body. He enjoyed the adrenalin rush of survival and cheered with his shipmates throughout the day and into the night. The sergeant barked them into silence repeatedly with reminders of how far voices travel over water, but they still jested and recounted tails of the recent battle. Shouts of "Death to Stygge!" rang out every few minutes as well as a well-developed array of curses. King Stygge's grip on shipping had slipped mightily in the last two years.

Toward midnight, the moon disappeared behind a bank of clouds, and the temperature plummeted. A chill wind buffeted them, and calm seas became rough. A thunderous crack from the clouds pounded the ship. Bolts of lightning flashed across the night. The sea looked angry in those flashes with garish white foam glinting at the top of waves as high as a castle's walls. The seasick found their way to the rails and began their ordeal again.

The cheering of the rest turned to cries as even the most basic of human movement grew complicated in the heaving ship. Small lanterns about the hull tried and failed to illumine the dark. In the next flash of sky-borne light, Pater watched as his ship crashed down the back end of a wave and tunneled into the next, burying nearly a third of the ship into the briny ocean's grip.

Water piled on the old battle-barn and poured down unsecured hatches into the berths below. It proved too much.

The Soldier

In sound-shredding anger, her hull snapped. The violence of the break tossed men in a myriad of directions, all of them ending with a storm-swallowed splash. The fortunate few died instantly. Pater, still mostly clad in his armor, struggled to stay near the wreck and quickly tired, slipping under the waves.

A final blast of lightning illuminated the wreckage above as he sank. He fought for the surface, trying to shed his armor, but to no avail. His arms tangled in the rigging, and another rope around his waist tugged him down into the black. He spasmed for lack of air, his arms flailing and legs kicking of their own volition. With sudden desperation, Pater opened his mouth and breathed deeply.

Water rushed in and filled his lungs. His mind watched a little while longer.

💀 💀 💀

He lay on the soft and subtle furs of his bed and counted how many unicorns raced across the canopy above him. His daughter had spent months weaving the canopy. His youngest, she brought joy since her birth. She didn't have the clarity of purpose of her big sister, Tamia, but she could soothe a room with a smile. Truth be told, she reminded him more of her mother.

She had perished at the hands of his enemies a little more than a year ago, her caravan set upon and guards slaughtered. Slowly, Pater pieced together the king's memories of the manner of betrayal that had cost him his daughter. The pain in his chest dragged at him like a millstone. He had no recourse but war and had marshaled his army and ridden out immediately.

Now, lying in his broken and abused body, staring at the last remnants of his family and their history, he couldn't bring himself to face the reality of his failure. He would sue for peace today. He would give up the dream of avenging his wife, his daughters, and all the accumulated hurts of his reign as king. The pain of their loss burned him like a thousand knife wounds to the soul.

His body hurt, too. Wounds from decades of campaigning, half-healed from sleeping in the cold and damp, chafed at him. Shards of metal from a shattered crossbow bolt, decades-old, tore at his back with every breath. Knots in his muscles from overuse in the battle the day before screamed like a condemned man.

He stood, sinking his feet into the soft fur of his bearskin rug. Pater chuckled, remembering the many nights he slept on it instead of in the bed. He dressed carefully; he didn't want to call on anyone to help him today. Today was his cross to bear. Today was his failure. Pater sailed on a sea of memory in the old man's mind, waiting to piece together his next pilgrimage.

He threw a simple flame spell at a cast-iron pot loaded with wood. The pot was half-buried to help protect its form from the heat of the fire. He couldn't do much with magic anymore. Since the loss of Tamia, he hadn't the focus necessary to incant. His son, a stout and dependable leader keeping the wolves at bay on the other side of the kingdom lacked the culture of his sisters. The king fastened his breeches and turned his back to the fire, absorbing its warmth.

Pater's muscles came alive in the heat, offering more support for the rest of his morning routine. The name Tamia played around the edges of his memory, too, but the fog of jumping into a new life could leave him scrambling for days before he could sort out all his past lives. Pater checked himself in a mirror of high-polished steel. He looked respectable for a man about to surrender his hope, his throne, his people. The weight of history dragged at him from the rheumy eyes staring back.

Slowly, deliberately, Pater opened the small box on the edge of his trunk. His mind pirouetted at the site of the unicorn brooch, at the memories associated. The heritage

The Soldier

garnered in the precious pin carried a magic all its own. A lifetime of years tied together through filial love, uncompromising hard work, and the sharp edge of steel would collapse into history with the treaty today. In the final betrayal of his family and their sacrifice, he would walk away, alive, from their sacrifice.

Pater's hosts never knew he was present. Pater took over a man's conscious mind and did the dying for him. This time, he could feel the presence of the other mind. More than that, he shared the experience and the grief, getting the lesser half. He lacked control, too. Pater wondered if it had anything to do with the king's ability to use magic.

Pater held the unicorn and stroked its beautiful simplicity. Tamia, a great dragon-tamer, had made it at his kingdom's zenith. The design held simplistic brilliance. Its cobalt eyes even matched his. Tamia had imbued it with magic to help guide the empire. And then the image split, Pater watched Tamia fall from his dragon's back in one scene, and also as the king looking up pride turning to horror in an instant. That had never happened before either. He always lived alone in the death-bound. He could remember things, but never so vivid an image.

The king's tears of sorrow built, and Pater ground his will into them, driving them away. It took all of his effort; his control clearly diminished in this new life. Pater had given up on tears long ago. Now, his thoughts seemed more jumbled than usual. The lack of control stole from him the accouterments of a body's familiar behaviors.

He fastened the unicorn pin and called to his page, "Come in here, lad. I've a task for you."

A youth of a dozen winters opened the tent flap and hurried inside. "Sire?" The boy's blue eyes flashed as they took in all the king had done already.

"I am going to parlay today." The king tussled the boy's hair, his mind stirring at a flash of memory of his son at that age. With surrender, he wouldn't be leaving his son much.

187

"Ride forward with my generals and me."

"Sire, it isn't customary."

Smoothing a wrinkle, the king continued. "Indeed, it is. I will need a commoner witness. You are him."

Bowing, the boy excused himself.

The king smiled. Pater saw the smile from the other side of the king's mind, but the unicorn pin jarred something in him. It should mean something more substantial to Pater, but he couldn't sort it out.

With the boy gone, the king paced for several minutes. Every step caused pain, but less than the previous one as the king's body remembered its youth. With one last look in the mirror, the king squared his shoulders and set his jaw. Turning, Pater walked out into the glare of morning sun.

Several officers waited for him. He eyed each of them and nodded. They had served for years, fought many battles. They had come to this decision as a group of war-weary men. They couldn't win the fight. They could upend lives and drag the war out for several more years, but unless the enemy became magnificently incompetent, it wouldn't matter. Without the dragons and more men, they couldn't hold off the inevitable. Like death itself, the empire's collapse marched toward them.

The king and his council mounted their horses in silence. They rode to the tent midway between both armies in silence, too. His page had beaten him there and stood by the side of the table halfway across the shaded space under the tent.

Pater approached the table with his entourage, watching through the king's eyes. He took the offered chair but didn't sit. The stiffness in his legs had returned during the horse ride forward. While he had no control over the use of muscles, Pater felt everything acutely. The thought of standing again after sitting down engendered displeasure for the latter. The leader of the opposing army strode forward and took his position, too. Pater waited in stony silence, unable to direct

The Soldier

the flow of action or even force the king's body to obey the simplest of commands.

King Mikel obliged, breaking the silence. The man smiled ingratiatingly and spread his arms. "Your majesty, thank you for joining me. May I interest you in something to eat?"

He snapped his fingers and Pater watched as a boy the age of his own page strutted to the front. The boy's confident smile restrained Pater's host from saying anything until the lad had finished his preening walk.

"You are too kind, my lord. Alas, my age offers unusual challenges to diet. I must refrain. My compliments to your staff, it looks marvelous."

A flicker of anger danced across the younger ruler's face as he waived away his servant and continued. "Let us talk of peace, then."

Pater looked around at the assembled guards of King Mikel. They wore the weariness of battle on them as well. He saw pride and honor, too. In the middle of their ranks stood a dusty soldier, ordinary in every regard—the commoner. The man turned, letting the boy pass to the rear. As he did, the soldier casually grabbed the pommel of his sword and twisted it, unsticking the blade in its sheath.

Pater knew the man, motion, and moment. Intimately. The man had eyes holding no spark of the divine. They carried a cold and passionless glint, the eyes of a killer. Reaching up, Pater touched the brooch under his chin, never removing his eyes from the soldier's steely stare.

Pater knew where he was now. He knew the soldier. He had lived that life an eternity ago. From his perch in the king's mind, Pater could see himself before the curse, before the murder that drew it forth. Pater wanted to scream. He wanted to warn the king.

The moment flowed around memory. Pater recalled the anger boiling in the breast of his former self; he had lost many friends in the war. He remembered the orders his liege had given him if the king refused the food.

"So, Lord Mikel, how should we continue?" Pater heard himself say the words. He sat, regrettably. "I recall battles against your father, Lord Mikel."

Pater watched himself. The soldier facing him wouldn't recognize or even believe what had happened. Age and war-weariness bled into Pater from the king. He forgot the cue but saw resolution settle over the soldier in the whitened knuckles on the pommel-grasping hand.

King Stygge seemed amenable to the mild dictates of King Mikel. Who wouldn't be? The entire thing was a show. Trapped beside the mind of the king in whose body he rode, Pater could do nothing. His bones ached as he stood, a distraction laced with the wince of age and overused muscles. Pater sensed the start of an enchantment in the mind of the king as time came full circle. Pater's consciousness bobbed along the current of unfolding events. The king thought the enchantment a powerful omen of good fortune, something benign to bless the agreement. The king's spell tore his mind and Pater's away from crashing inevitability. When the sword struck home, Pater missed it.

His guards, or, rather, the king's, screamed and rushed forward. King Mikel's men met them. Men on both sides died.

Laying in a pool of expanding blood, head hard against the ground, Pater recognized the rumble of a mounted cavalry charge. Fear seeped into him. He grabbed for the power of the king's magic, wrestling with the king for control. The king fought back like a demon.

Pater failed.

The king, recognizing the internal threat, turned the magic on Pater as well as the man standing over them, unaware they were the same. In an instant, the taint of the curse rolled through him. His skin tingled. His mind raced. He had forgotten the effects and watched his former self shiver reflexively and then follow King Mikel as the cavalry charge thundered past and into the hastily retreating army of King Stygge.

His vision tunneled to the blur of rushing hooves and clouds of dust charging out of their way. Life dribbled out of his chest and seeped into the ground. He held the brooch closely and muttered, "I am sorry, Tamia."

Pater looked out over the battlements of the castle at the flaming ruin of Old Town. Beyond, the infernal army of the Royal Empire of King Mikel sat squatting like their fume-belching cannon. Next to him, on the right, rested a barrel overflowing with arrows and a second with pitch. On his left, a guttering wall sconce belched smoke and fire. High overhead, dragons screeched their return to the world. Normally, he restarted with a pike or a horse. Now he stood on a battlement. There'd been other battlements, for sure, but never cannon. His mind barely understood the idea. Perhaps there would be new ways to die as well.

Pater flexed his hand and knocked an arrow. All around him, others did the same. The dragons would ignite the arrows in flight. He remembered the instructions now. The methods of war had changed, cannon and arrows laden with dragonfire, but death still shepherded the results, and he and death shared an acquaintance.

~ *KT Morley* ~

KT Morley is a new author having spent twenty years conspiring to teach the youth of America about Algebra and the plight of a hopelessly lost X. He now manages his school's Humanities department, occasionally engaging his department's classes in poetry and prose. He has published in ezines, the Zimbell House anthology *Poseidon's Dream*, the recently released *Glass and Ashes* anthology by OWS Ink, and Rogue Blades Entertainment's *Crossbones and Crosses*. Writing has freed his consciousness to live in the interesting stories plaguing his mind. Perhaps his students were right and he has a screw loose. No matter! When not penning prose of some type, he enjoys a plethora of interests from weightlifting to fishing. A penchant for beer and food does seem to get the better of him most of the time.

Bhailgeth's Ransom
by Alfred D. Byrd

"Begone, monster, from Vlanseth's gate!"

Tlaquir peered up at the captain of the guard, barely visible in the long night, who had called down to him from the city's wall. *How many times has his counterpart given me the same order over my lifetimes? Do the Vlansethir recall nothing of their past?* In a calm tone, Tlaquir called back, "You know I must talk with your magistrate about the ransom my master, Bhailgeth, demands for—"

The captain sneered. "Bhailgeth's long dead. We've seen no sign of him in many lifetimes."

You've learned little of reasoning. Don't you know I'm a sign? "How can one who's given me life endlessly renewed have died himself?"

The question silenced the guard. After a moment, he answered it with bluster. "Leave now, Tlaquir of the Abominations, or the archers at my command will fill you so full of arrows there'll be no space between the arrow heads in your flesh."

A threat cleverer than most I've heard here. Tlaquir ran his gaze across the archers to the captain's left and right. Their bows seemed to Tlaquir shorter, thinner, and less recurved, and their arrows less well fletched, than he recalled. *The standard of weaponry's fallen in Vlanseth since my last visit.* Tlaquir doubted the arrows could penetrate his armor of boiled leather. Even if they pierced him through, they would do him no lasting harm. One who had endured Bhailgeth's rites of necromancy could not die—permanently.

Still, Tlaquir did not welcome even temporary death. He wished to avoid it for once. "Your men would just be delaying the inevitable. Why not let your magistrate do his job? If he rejects my petition, he can always order me killed."

For a while.

The captain made no reply, but turned and spoke to his archers. When he fell silent, one of them left the wall, Tlaquir guessed to take a message to Vlanseth's magistrate. After the archer had gone, the captain feigned to ignore Tlaquir.

Content to wait, Tlaquir took in his surroundings. Under a cloudless sky of months-long night in which the northern lights flared in ever-shifting sheets of green, Vlanseth's wall stretched away into darkness. What Tlaquir could see of the wall had fallen into disrepair since his last visit to the city unknown years before. Dilapidation did not astonish him; what did was that the city still stood. Although a warm ocean current and hot springs kept the city livable, the great ice was closing in from the north. If the ice ground the city under, the drama of Bhailgeth's demand for ransom would have ended, badly for the Vlansethir. *Why are they so stubborn about giving up what it does them no good to keep?*

Atop the wall there was a stir of motion. The captain called down, "The magistrate will see you now, Tlaquir of the Abominations."

Tlaquir held in a sigh as the gate groaned open. *I just hope that this magistrate is more reasonable than his predecessors were. If not*—Tlaquir loosened a double-handed broadsword swinging in its scabbard across his back—*I'll take him and as many of his guards as I can into the land only I will return from.*

When the gate stood fully open, the street leading inward from it was empty. Clearly none of the Vlansethir wanted to block Tlaquir's path. The street's emptiness complimented him, but also insulted. He called up to the captain, "Where's my guide?"

Harsh laughter greeted the question. "You need none. The magistrate's seat stands where it stood on all of your prior visits here. Surely, you haven't forgotten."

Tlaquir refused to dignify the captain's jibe with a response, but heading on, swept his gaze over buildings lining the street. Market stalls, workshops, dwellings—all had decayed since his last visit to Vlanseth had ended with his hacked, burned corpse being hurled through the gate he had just entered. He shook his head at Vlansethir's folly. *If they repaired the city with the wood they waste on funeral pyres, the city's splendor would last—*

—until the ice swallows it. As he went on, the city assumed a morbid familiarity. *Here's a place where I died—and there—and there—*

He caught sudden motion in a corner of his left eye. Startling him, a tall, burly man holding a massive ax stepped into his path. Not all of the Vlansethir, it turned out, feared to bother him. The man's flushed face coupled with an alcoholic reek told Tlaquir the fellow had been drinking recently enough to have bolstered his courage, but not long enough ago to have dulled his reflexes. He might have been the worst of foes for Tlaquir, had Tlaquir needed fear any single foe. Eyes wild, the man distorted his mouth into a rictus only passingly a smile. "I challenge you, Tlaquir of the Abominations, to fight me to the death. I seek vengeance for your killing my grandfather, Mrenselg, without mercy or justification."

Tlaquir guessed at his opponent's age. *It must've taken long for Bhailgeth to revive me this time.* "I don't recall killing anyone of that name."

"You wouldn't recall his name. He was just one of the guards you hacked apart when you slew the magistrate."

"I would've slain neither the magistrate nor his guards had they not first attacked me. May I know your name, Mrenselg's grandson?"

"Why? So you can forget it as you forgot my

grandfather's name?"

How can I forget what I never knew? "So I can use it to persuade you to give up your foolish quest for vengeance."

The word 'foolish' must have been ill chosen. The man, roaring with rage, swung the ax with speed and skill Tlaquir had not foreseen. Hurling himself back, Tlaquir could not wholly avoid the ax's head, which dug a searing path through his armor across the upper left of his chest. Still, the blow's strength dragged the man off balance long enough for Tlaquir to unsheathe his sword and swing it in a long-practiced motion. A neck parted, blood fountained, and a head and then a body struck pavement.

The wound on Tlaquir's chest was already closing when he swept his gaze over a once-again empty street. To unseen listeners, he called out, "Please, Vlansethir, don't die as namelessly as Mrenselg's grandson. I never attack. I fight only in self-defense. Yield to Bhailgeth's reasonable demands and Vlanseth will recover its ancient glory."

When no one replied to Tlaquir, he shrugged and headed for the magistrate's seat. *Sometime, somewhere in this city, I'll find someone who'll listen to reason.*

💀 💀 💀

Alone of Vlanseth's buildings, the magistrate's seat had kept its former splendor. *Rulers live well even while their subjects perish,* Tlaquir thought sourly. Still, the arched entrance at a colonnaded porch's rear lacked guards who should have been there.

Tlaquir wondered about the guards' absence. *Is the magistrate hiding from me in hope of my going away? If so, he'll be disappointed. Immortality teaches one patience, if nothing else. I can stay here till the ice covers me.*

Tlaquir climbed the steps to the porch and went through its entrance. Within, in a hall dimly lighted by oil lamps hanging from the ceiling, a table bore a single serving of food and drink. *For me?* Hospitality to him would be novel in Vlanseth, but the present magistrate might be more imaginative than his predecessors. *Maybe, he's even reasonable.*

Tlaquir was hungry. It did occur to him the magistrate might have poisoned the meal. Still, Tlaquir doubted any poison could touch him after his treatment by Bhailgeth. Even if the poison worked, it would just delay the inevitable.

Taking the seat in front of the setting, Tlaquir ate with good appetite fish, roast tubers, and bread, and drank beer, all of fine quality. *Am I eating a meal that'd been meant for the magistrate before I showed up at Vlanseth's gate? If so, I wish he'd share it with me. A man may be more reasonable at table than he is on his throne.*

Until then, the hall had been empty but for Tlaquir. Now he glimpsed furtive motion, a twitch of a hanging over a side entrance. Seizing his sword's hilt, he turned toward the motion, then his eyes widened and he froze at a sight he had never expected to see in doomed Vlanseth.

Unlike the land's short, stocky people, including Tlaquir, the woman who met his gaze was tall and slender, with moon-pale skin, silvery hair, and eyes of the blue of the ice that threatened to crush Vlanseth. A gown of shimmering white that fell from her shoulders to her ankles did not wholly hide charms that would have fired Tlaquir's lust had Bhailgeth left it to him. As things were, he admired the woman as a work of art even as he grasped that he had seen only one other like her—his master, Bhailgeth. *He told me he's an exile from his people, who live far off. What's another of them doing here?*

He could only hope she had brought reason to Vlanseth.

Taking a step toward Tlaquir, she gave him a smile that was winter and summer combined. "Hail, Tlaquir, Bhailgeth's servant. I hope you're enjoying your meal."

He was wary of any of his master's people. "May I have the honor of learning your name?"

She had taken another, almost imperceptible step toward

him. "Your master's taught you manners. You may call me Hallaquel."

Tlaquir noted the 'you may call me' instead of a 'my name is.' "My master didn't teach me to conjure. You're safe from spells with me. Are you Vlanseth's present magistrate?"

Hallaquel laughed in silvery tones. "Can you have forgotten that Vlanseth's magistrate must be a child of its nobility? Noble am I, but not of Vlanseth. No, I'm an advisor to the magistrate, who sent me to you to find, it may be, a solution to the present crisis that doesn't involve your hacking him and his guards apart until one of them returns the favor for you. The magistrate's brave, but no reasonable man seeks death."

Tlaquir made a smile rare for him. "I'm all in favor of reason, rare in these parts in my experience. As for my hacking the magistrate and his guards apart, I wouldn't do it if they didn't set on me. I'm never the one to start a fight, though I'm often the one to end it." Hallaquel winced, perhaps as what she took as a boast rather than mere fact, but Tlaquir went on. "Still, before you and I speak of the magistrate's business, may we speak first of you? You fascinate me, Hallaquel. Are you like my master?"

Somehow she had halved the distance between her and Tlaquir. "By that question, do you mean, 'Do I extend my life by Bhailgeth's abominable arts of necromancy and necrophagy?' No, I'll live a normal lifetime of my people and then go to whatever awaits me beyond it. I'm a traveler who's come from the south to learn whether rumors of a necromancer of my people were true. It saddens me they are."

Tlaquir sighed. "It seems to me you're no more prepared to be reasonable than a number of past magistrates were. You must know that Bhailgeth won't be diverted from his purpose."

"He won't, but maybe you will."

Bhailgeth's Ransom

'What do you mean, Hallaquel?"

"I mean you're brave, and the magistrate's brave, but Bhailgeth isn't. He's unwilling to endure the cycle of death and resurrection he's damned you to. Without you, he has no hope of getting his demands from this city—"

Tlaquir shook his head at Hallaquel's obtuseness. "His demands would benefit this city if those here had the wits to understand. He could drive back the ice and restore Vlanseth to its former glory if the city but yielded him its dead—those who are through with their bodies. What he'd do with them wouldn't bother their former tenants and shouldn't bother the living Vlansethir. Instead, they waste valuable wood, rarer each year in these parts, on burning bodies to keep them from him. Do you call what the Vlansethir do reason?"

Hallequel looked woebegone. "I'd hoped you'd served Bhailgeth out of compulsion rather than belief."

Again, Tlaquir shook his head at her obtuseness. *If you'd lived as I've lived, you'd know that what I believe and what Bhailgeth compels me to do have long since merged.* "Don't you understand that, unless Vlanseth lets my master drive the ice back, it'll cover this city within the lifetime of those just born?"

Again, she had halved the distance between her and Tlaquir. "The Vlansethir are willing to let the ice cover their city rather than save it through the abomination of necromancy. In the end, when the ice does breach Vlanseth's wall, they can sail into the south where there's still light and warmth. You could sail there with them. You could sail there now."

Sadly, Tlaquir recalled that the man he had once been would have taken Hallequel's offer. He sought a means to explain his fate to her. "Do you know what a geas is?"

She looked forlorn. "Are you saying Bhailgeth's laid one on you?" When he nodded, she said, "I'd hoped not to have to do what I now must, but—"

Mere steps from him, she moved with speed and skill he

199

had not foreseen from her. As she spun toward him, she drew from within a fold of her gown a silvery blade with an unearthly sheen that Tlaquir feared—or hoped?—could end his life for the last time. Still, as quick as she was, he was quicker. His broadsword sheared off her knife hand; then, as her beautiful features distorted in horror at her loss, his return stroke sheared through her neck. Head, hand, and sword struck the floor together, and the sword shattered into silver tears.

He looked down bleakly at beauty's ruin. *The captain of the guard was right. I am a monster.*

He had not long to mourn Hallequel or to curse himself for having slain her. Beyond the hangings across the room from him, a man's voice called out.

"I feared she would reach this end, but I promised her a chance to redeem the sorcerer's emissary. Both her death and his are on his hands. Guards, kill him!"

"Wait!" Tlaquir called out. "There's no need for blood—"

His plea failed to keep heavily armed and armored guards from surging through the hangings across the table from him. The men formed a wall armed with blades. He had never fought so many in a closed space; in his prior engagements with the city's guards, he had met them on the street or on the seat's steps, where there was room to maneuver. *Still, lack of room may hamper them more than me.*

It did not hamper the guards across from him. When they leapt onto the tabletop to get at him, he darted to his left. With a sweep of his broadsword, he cut the legs from under the guard at the end of the line. Even as the man toppled, a teammate of his rounded the table's left end and swung an ax at Tlaquir in a two-handed blow. As Tlaquir avoided this, he noted his foe was watching the tip of Tlaquir's sword.

Doesn't he know that a sword's hilt can be as deadly as its blade? With a two-handed blow of the hilt, Tlaquir taught the foe a lesson that his helmet's crumpling ensured he would not retain. Shoving the falling guard into a companion, Tlaquir called out, "We needn't fight. I'm here to help—"

Relentlessly, the remaining guards closed in on him. As he swung his blade with remorseless efficiency against them, emotions roiled within him. He mourned needless loss of life, and he seethed with frustration at his mission's repeated failure, yet he exulted in combat, at which he had been skilled even before Bhailgeth's sorcery had made him unparalleled.

Still, even he was but one man against a squad. As combat went on and a fey mood grew in him, he felt that even a squad might be too small to withstand him. He felt contempt of its commander, the magistrate, of whom he had seen no sign. "Where's your leader?" Tlaquir called out. "Hallequel told me he was brave—"

"I'm here, monster!" a high, but clear voice called out before him. A beardless youth in an elder's robes ran forward through a gap in the guards. It saddened Tlaquir that he must slay one who had barely begun to live, but the magistrate's face bore a purity of determination lacking to even the fiercest of his guards. "My life for my people's honor!"

To Tlaquir's astonishment, the youthful magistrate caught the broadsword's blade between his arms. He flung himself onto its point. For an instant, Tlaquir went numb with horror at the youth's act. *Why do he and his people hate me so much they throw their lives away?*

When Tlaquir's numbness cleared, he tried to pull his blade free of the youth, but the surviving guards, availing themselves of their leader's sacrifice, gave Tlaquir no chance. Blows from swords and axes dented and then breached Tlaquir's armor. The healing power Bhailgeth had given him fell behind the rain of blows. Blood fountained from Tlaquir as strength left his limbs. Combat in Vlanseth was again ending for him in his death—a death that would not be his last.

"Fools," he gasped out. "This victory of yours has gained you nothing. Hack or burn me as you will, I'll return to you. The ice will have closed in—"

A massive blow to the head sent him spinning down toward darkness. His last thought before it overwhelmed him was, *We'll do this again.*

His dying prophecy would, as always, come true. It led him on a journey oft repeated. As Tlaquir trudged, broadsword slung across his back, under a rippling aurora toward Vlanseth's gate, he swept his gaze over the city's wall. The ice, having encroached farther, almost overhung it in the north. The wall's dilapidation had but grown with however many years had passed since his last death. *Hallequel said the Vlansethir would sail off into the south at the last moment, but here they still are. Are they at last willing to listen to my master's demands? There's still time for him to drive the ice back.*

Pausing before the gate, he called up to sentinels on the wall, "I am Tlaquir. I bring you a message from my master, Bhailgeth—"

It disappointed, but did not astonish, the warrior, when a sentinel called down to him, "Begone, monster, from Vlanseth's gate!"

~ *Alfred D. Byrd* ~
Alfred D. Byrd has a bachelor's degree in

Medical Technology from Michigan State University and a master's degree in Microbiology from the University of Kentucky. He has worked for the past thirty-plus years as a research analyst in a plant genetics laboratory at the University of Kentucky. His short stories have appeared in *Quest for Atlantis* from Pill Hill Press, *Warrior Wisewoman 3* from Norilana Books, and *Past Future Presen*t from Copper Publishing. He has several works of fantasy, science fiction, theology, and Appalachian regional fiction available from Amazon.com and other on-line booksellers.

Sand-Devil

by Eadwine Brown

A CHANSON OF LEOFRIC DE BREDON

I

"Sweet Christ, did even you suffer this much?" Leofric de Bredon muttered, squinting against the hard light. Though it was far from noon, the sun already blazed down fiercely from a white sky. He pulled a skin from his saddlebag and drank sparingly, grimacing at the tepid water and the dust in his mouth. Leofric's companion frowned and adjusted the keffiyeh that he wore for shade over his Franciscan habit. Friar Leonard turned his blind gaze toward the knight.

"Peace, brother," he said lightly. "Another hour to Beit Ras." The eyeless priest smiled wryly and mopped sweat from his brow. "And then another two days to Damascus."

"That it is." Leofric grunted, his keen eyes drawn ever toward the distant Horns of Hattin, where the might of Outremer had been broken by Salah Al-din not ten years before. The road ahead of them shimmered in the heat, leading off to the east away from the ragged hills that hunkered around the barren plain. As the Frank watched, dust rose from some far-off hidden defile, and he caught the edge of a thin sound—a cry of pain, far off.

"I mislike that," he said, grimly. "Come, priest. Let's away."

He awoke with a cry. His mind was as blank as the pallid

sky above, but for the single thought that something of great worth had been taken. He stood, and saw that bodies lay around him—swarthy men in strange, dirty garb. Not one lived. Further down what he saw to be a ravine, dust rose and he heard shouting in a barbarous tongue. A broken sword lay nearby—the hilt and a curving length intact. He took it up, and strode down the ravine to find the thing that had been taken from him.

His long strides carried him swiftly, and before long he saw men ahead, mounted and riding hard. He cried out for them to halt. Pale faces turned to look, and the fleeing men cried despairingly. A horse stumbled and fell, screaming. The rider threw himself clear and tried to rise, but the man with the broken sword was upon him in moments.

The bandit stared up in terror, and the man saw himself reflected in wide eyes. Dark and gnarled, skin threaded with veins that gleamed red-gold; a shaven, tapering head; trophy bones piercing his ears and cheeks.

"Mercy! Please, lord!" The words came desperately from lips that trembled with fear. "I have a wife. Children! Show Christian mercy?"

"Christian?" the man asked, as though tasting the word. "What manner of thing is that?" He raised the broken blade in a dark, long-fingered hand, and spoke a word that made blood leak from the shrieking bandit's nose, that word in a tongue that had not been uttered for a thousand years.

"You have taken from me. Where is it?" the man demanded, although he was not truly a man. The broken scimitar fell upon flesh, and the bandit shrieked in pain and terror as his comrades fled.

💀 💀 💀

Hours later, when he had the answers he sought, and he'd extracted what was necessary from the hapless bandit, he stood on the broken ridgeline, golden eyes watching the

Damascus road. He had plundered the dead for garments and a poorly-balanced shamshir that was the best blade he could find amongst them. Much had returned to him in response to the rite, and the offered heart and eyes. He recalled his name, and the purpose that had sent him forth from the great gates of Erṣetu, but what had befallen him remained yet unclear.

"It is of no matter," Dahāka muttered, fists clenched. "Only the tablet matters." He set out down the ravine, in the wake of the fleeing bandits, the plundered blade gripped tight in his fist.

Dust swirled in the wake of the two pilgrims' horses as they followed the twisting path of the road. Leofric's keen gaze never settled, roving ceaselessly in search of the ambush he suspected. They paused at a spring amid the rocks for long enough to water their mounts before pressing on. The road painstakingly avoided even the lowest fringes of the rough hills to the west where thin groves of stubborn carob trees moved in the hot breeze. As the two crested a low rise, they caught sight of Beit Ras, its huddled buildings gleaming, seemingly only a stone's throw away over a spur of the ragged hills.

"What fool's path does this road follow?" Leofric growled. He twitched his reins, and his horse turned east again, away from glowering hills and far buildings alike.

"I have heard strange things said of the wild hill country between the Sea of Galilee and the new fortress of Qal'at 'Ajloun," Friar Leonard said. "The Bedouin here are Jabal 'Auf, traders and allies of Outremer for the most part, but their taboos are curious and their memories long. Perhaps the pagan Romans heeded such warnings."

Leofric did not reply immediately. His keen eyes had fixed upon a rising cloud of dust and a dark shape on the road below and ahead of them where the road curved back to the west and gently downhill.

"Pagan mutterings be damned, priest, there's something in the road ahead. Be cautious."

Leofric loosened his arming sword in its scabbard and touched dusty heels to his steed's flanks. The well-trained horse changed its pace, and Leofric spared a glance for the blind friar as he moved further ahead. In scant minutes, the shape had been revealed as that of a man sprawled in the dust. His clothing was ragged and dirty, and he smelled of smoke and stale sweat. Leofric dismounted, tucked the end of his reins into his belt, and nudged the prone figure with the toe of his boot. The man twitched and groaned, then came fully aware with a terrified shriek that made the horse snort and shy. Wide, staring eyes met Leofric's, and the knight held up his hands in a gesture of peace.

"I'll not harm you," he said in Arabic. The man blinked, cried out involuntarily, and rolled to his hands and knees with a cough. Leofric caught his arm, and helped him to his feet.

"What happened to you?" he asked. "Bandits?" He took a flask from his saddle and passed it over. The ragged man drank sparingly, and nodded his thanks.

"Not bandits, Frank," he rasped. "Something worse."

💀 💀 💀

Leofric bade the man wait until Friar Leonard caught up with them, then took food from his saddlebags and pitched an awning for shade in the nomad fashion.

"I am Sadiq Masoud al-Hamid," the ragged man began, "and I am, or I was, a bandit." He frowned. "I take no pride in it—Allah knows that I am sinful and greedy, but I was once a soldier and then, after Arsuf, robbing men became preferable to fighting them. When you came upon me in the road, I had been thrown from my horse. My fellows—whose names I spit upon!—left me in their flight, for we had discovered a terrible thing in the hills." He met Leofric's eyes, glanced briefly at Leonard's empty sockets and shuddered, then with an obvious effort, continued.

"It was...we thought it to be a careless traveler at first, a man who'd lain down amongst the rocks for shelter as he slept, but then Jalal saw that dust lay thick upon him, and the webs of spiders, too. He had purses at his belt, and there were a few coins lying about him. Someone muttered that it was a djinn, but that was foolishness. Shamsuddin used the butt of his spear to rouse him, while we all stood ready to rob him—but he didn't move. So we opened his purses and took his money—heavy gold, like dirham. Shamsuddin found a clay tablet, wrapped in cloth. When he took it, the man awoke. It was like lighting a lamp—one moment he might have been stone, and the next his eyes opened and he spoke. His eyes were gold and he...he..." Sadiq's voice shook with horror. He squeezed his eyes closed and muttered a prayer. Friar Leonard prayed with him and smiled kindly at the bandit.

"It was a devil of the sands, not a man at all." Sadiq muttered. "It slew five before we even knew what was happening, and then we ran for the horses. Jalal's fell. I think it broke a leg, and the creature...it must have tortured him, but it asked him questions, and then it cut out his eyes and his heart." His voice shook, but the words tumbled over themselves, so fast was he speaking. "It called fire from the air and burned them like pagan offerings, then Jalal withered to dust and it seemed to feed on the dust. Allah forgive me, do not punish my sins with this golden-eyed devil!" He fell silent, tears rolling down his cheeks.

"God does not punish with such terrible things," Friar Leonard said, softly. "He will forgive you, Sadiq Masoud al-Hamid, for you are repentant. This sand-devil is not God's work, but Leofric and I do as God wills."

II

The Franciscan and the bandit talked together for as long

as it took Leofric to clean and oil his war-gear. As the heat of the day began to give way to the lesser heat of the evening, Friar Leonard called the knight's name.

"Sadiq tells me that his band had a meeting place in Beit Ras. If any more of them survive, it will be there we'll find them," the priest said.

Leofric nodded. "And to what purpose?"

"There are more things in Heaven and Earth than are dreamt of by men, Leofric. Consider the sight that God has granted me in place of the eyes that Constantinople took from me, or the miracles of the saints. Some are blessings—others nightmares. I have heard whispered tales of a black-pillared city that once lay amongst these lonely hills in the time of the ancients when things were not as they are now, and of a pagan curse that damned all those who lived there."

Leofric touched his iron belt buckle in unconscious warding, but shook his head.

"Ignorance and superstition, priest. I'll wager that all this poor sinner's tales amount to is a sun-addled mind and ambushers themselves surprised, not some creature from a cursed city of the sands. Can such things be?"

Friar Leonard's face was grim.

"There is devilry here, Leofric de Bredon. In Damascus men whisper of lost Irem, the City of Pillars, in the same tones that the barbarous Welsh use for the Lost Land of Cantraef Gwaelod," the eyeless priest said. His blind gaze turned unerringly to Leofric. "I know a little of the horrors that lurk in forgotten places. I have read the terrible things the poet al-Hazred wrote of Irem, and of the fate he suffered by writing of it. Sometimes the old darkness of the world reaches out to reclaim a little of what we men have wrought."

"*Deus vult*," the knight replied.

The sun was all but set by the time the three travelers rode into the dusty streets of Beit Ras, and the call to prayer was ringing out. Sadiq, acting as their guide, had directed them to a small eating house in the Greek style, which doubled as a caravanserai, before hurrying off to the mosque. Their horses stabled, and lodgings for the night arranged, the two pilgrims now sat in the cool of early evening, talking quietly as they ate olives and bread.

"Whether al-Hazred's Irem and this city of black pillars are one and the same, I cannot say," Friar Leonard continued, wiping his hands on a cloth. "But that poor bandit spoke of strength many times that of a man, blades breaking against it, and veins that pulsed gold against dark skin."

"And golden eyes," Leofric said. "Hard to disguise something like that."

"Indeed," the priest replied. "Yet you saw no other tracks?"

Leofric had scouted wide as they'd set out toward the town, and found much evidence of Sadiq's fellows in panicked flight, but no sign of a pursuer. He nodded, and poured rich, dark wine for them both.

"If we are to believe what al-Hamid said, the thing spoke in Greek to demand that something be returned. If it hasn't found the thief already, I'll wager that it will come here and we'll see the truth of things."

"If it can speak and be understood, then it must be capable of reason, Leofric. It has slain men, aye, but so have you. I would offer it God's peace if we can."

"Aye, priest. As you say." The knight shrugged and drank.

As the evening prayer concluded, furtive, ragged men began to appear in the street around the small taverna, with Sadiq's return acting as a sign of sorts. They came together in a group, and he led the handful of men inside.

"This handful is all that remain, Father," Sadiq said, humbly. "This is Shamsuddin," he pointed to a rangy fellow with calculating eyes and a dark beard, "this Hadad, and this Nasir, Jalal's brother. Shamsuddin has everything that we took from the sand-devil."

A heavy pouch thumped onto the table, and the dirty men clustered around. Leofric undid its thong and thick gold coins chimed and rang as they poured out. A dark, curious tablet slid out alongside the dirhams, and this Leofric took up. It was thickly inscribed with rows of wedge-shaped symbols, separated by precise lines. It smelled of dust and the ages, for it was clearly not the product of any race of men that lived. He turned it over in his hands, skin prickling at the strange feel of the thing, then handed it to Friar Leonard, who ran his hands over its inset symbols.

"Fascinating," the priest said. "What hand carved this into clay? What meaning do these symbols hide?"

"It is the language of the old people, from long before the Greeks and the Romans came," Nasir said, hesitantly. "Wherever the ancient ruins are, we find things like this."

"Can anyone read it?" Leonard asked, and the former bandit shook his head.

"No," Nasir said, quickly, realizing his mistake, but the eyeless priest had noted the gesture in that oddly sighted way he sometimes did.

"No matter. You say that this was in the man's pouch, and it was removing it that awoke him?" The survivors nodded, and all became a babble of voices as they all sought to tell the tale. Presently, Leofric thumped the table with the handle of his eating knife, and they fell silent again.

"Enough! You'll take rooms here tonight—and bathe," he said. "Whatever you found in the desert is enough to turn you from your sins, or so the priest says, and I'll not condemn a man for repenting. Should this devil come looking for its tablet, it'll find us as well."

The call to evening prayer echoed from the sinister hills as dusk gave way to full night, and the bell of Beit Ras' small church summoned the faithful to Compline. Friar Leonard and Leofric attended mass, which was spoken in Greek, and passed a few words with an officer of what amounted to the town watch, a Copt, then the knight sat vigil with his longsword close at hand. Despite Leofric's admonishment, the bandit Hadad had refused to join his fellows at the little eating house. He'd spat at the idea of accepting the protection of Christians, and vanished into the gathering dark.

Deep into the night, long after Sadiq, Nasir and Shamsuddin had returned from Ṣalāh al-'Ishaa', a piteous shriek rang out over the sleeping town. Leofric sprang wolfishly to his feet, swept up his sword and plunged into the darkness. Within moments, a shouted challenge stopped him in his tracks, and even as he called his name in reply, a spear thrust from the night nearly impaled him.

"Damn you for fools, put those blades up!" he cried angrily. "You'd know me from the evening Mass, Hafik, if you but opened your eyes."

The guard he'd addressed, who he and Friar Leonard had spoken with on the steps of the church earlier that evening, muttered a shame-faced apology and called for torches. With Leofric aiding the search, they quickly came across a shabby dwelling at the edge of Beit Ras with a splintered door, cleaved asunder by heavy blows. Leofric pushed the timbers back and stepped inside, blade up and ready. A smear of blood marked one dirty wall, but the place was empty. The night breeze stirred its fingers through a thick layer of dust curiously mounded in the center of the small main room, and the Frank coughed as it caught his throat.

"Murder has been done here," he muttered. "But this dust hasn't been disturbed, for all that the blood there is fresh."

"God preserve us," Hafik said, his voice trembling.

"There is black horror afoot here, Leofric de Bredon—the dust is all that remains of the poor wretch whose blood marks that wall. The old people here whisper older tales of shadows in the form of men, the souls of those who've died without water on the burning sands. They cannot rest, instead trying to slake a thirst that cannot be satisfied with the blood and sweat of the living."

"Pagan nonsense," Leofric scoffed, but crossed himself and touched the iron pommel of the poniard at his belt. "Who dwelled here?"

Hafik scowled, his fear forgotten.

"A raider," he replied, spitting into the dust. "A man I would hang if I could—a bandit by the name of Hadad ibn Farouk." Leofric cursed, his eyes widening, and turned toward the broken door.

"Christ and all the saints! Thirsting shades be damned, Hafik, something else haunts the dark this night!"

💀 💀 💀

The tavern's door lay in flinders, strewn across the ground. A harsh voice called out in barbarously-accented Arabic as Leofric ran up the few steps and plunged inside.

A thing shaped like a man, clad in shadow and rags, whirled to face him. A battered blade was sheathed at his side, and he wore ragged garb not unlike that of the pitiful bandits. A gaze that shone molten gold fixed him—and Leofric found himself pinned in place, such was its burning intensity. As he shook off the nightmarish weight of the dark man's stare and stepped fully into the lit common room, Leofric saw that the fellow's skin was black and gnarled, yet wholly unlike that of the Moors, Numidians and Ethiopians he'd met in his travels. Sadiq cowered behind Friar Leonard, who stood tall and fearless before the shadow-thing, like a king pronouncing judgment. The eyeless Franciscan held the strange clay tablet in one heavy hand.

"Give unto me that which is mine," the man demanded again, still in Arabic. Friar Leonard smiled wryly.

"Gladly, but first I would know what you are," the friar replied in the same tongue. "I cannot behold you, but if I could, what manner of man would I see?"

The black one snarled something and sprang at the blind priest, his blade flowing into his hand. Leofric's grip was tight on his sword hilt, but even as he began to draw his own arming sword and move, a moment too late, to turn the deathblow, the priest's empty hand shot out.

"Stay thy anger, Dahāka of Erṣetu," the priest cried out. "Thou art seeking the thieves that waylaid you upon the road in ages long past, not this petty brigand." His voice had deepened into the mesmeric tone of prophecy that Leofric half-remembered from their first meeting, and it seemed that the light of the room's lamps flowed and roiled in response, wreathing the priest in a glowing halo. "In the name of the God I serve and his son Jesus Christ, by thy service to the Truth called Ahura Mahzda, in defiance of the Lie called Ahriman—Dahāka of Erṣetu, sit and speak with me."

Tension ebbed from the dark man, and the sense of threat left him. His blade-hand fell to hang at his side, and the fury in his golden gaze dimmed. Leofric's hand loosened on his half-drawn sword hilt, and the glowing light ebbed away from Friar Leonard.

"How is it that thou, Christ-priest, know the names Dahāka, or Erṣetu? I am a messenger, or perhaps that is what I once was, in a time that seems forgotten by all men but thee."

"I bid thee sit in peace and speak with us," Friar Leonard said, his voice returned to normal. "As thou hast said, I am a priest, and my fellow there a warrior of renown. We have recovered what was taken from thee, but pledge peace first."

"I swear it."

Sand-Devil

💀 💀 💀

"Know, oh priest, that I cannot utter a falsehood, for to do so would be to serve the Lie," Dahāka began. "My home is the golden city of Erṣetu, which lies in the barren hill country to the north. What unknown ages have passed since it was built, I cannot say, but my people have always held that we dwelled there at our god's direction, standing guard against old terrors and hidden evils in the boundless caverns beneath the earth. We had outposts and lesser cities, once, but whether they still live, hidden and shunned as it seems Erṣetu now is, I do not know. We were long-lived, blessed and transfigured by great Ahura Mazda. I recall that, in my youth, word came that other men had begun to build a city of temples, named Babylon, and I was a decade into manhood when Nebuchadnezzar, the son of Nabopolassar, led his army into Egypt."

Enraptured fascination lit the blind friar's face as he lifted his wine cup and drank. Leofric, still suspicious, sat between the dark man and the Franciscan, his sword hand resting near its hilt.

"Believe you this wild tale?" he muttered, but the priest did not reply.

"In any case, I was sent to one of our lesser cities—troubling omens had been seen by many in those days. The priests found nothing but misfortune in their offerings, and feared that the ancient evil was taking root there. The tablet I carried is a missive to the high priest, and a fell rite that would deny such things in the name of the Golden Truth. I failed in my task, or perhaps it was a tool of the Lie that laid me low—I remember a sudden attack and a heavy blow that laid me senseless in the dirt, then darkness, then awakening as the tablet was taken from me."

Friar Leonard frowned slightly, his blind eyes meeting Dahāka's golden gaze. "What manner of older evil did your priests fear?"

The dark man shrugged, and gulped wine. "I will not speak of it. Suffice to say that there are places of darkness and horror, ruins of black basalt where such things once ruled in eons past. It matters not—now that I have recovered the tablet, I must return to Erṣetu and discover what remains of my people." The golden eyes closed, and Dahāka muttered something with the cadence of a prayer in his own strange language. "You claim to serve a benevolent god, you men of Christ," he continued, "as do I. I know that I am an outsider, a stranger to this time and to you who are men, but will you aid me in this?"

Leofric's hard eyes shone as he glanced at Friar Leonard. The blind priest met his gaze and nodded in that strangely sighted way he had, and the Frank lifted his hand from where it had lain by his blade.

"By God and Saint Michael, you have our service, Dahāka of Erṣetu," he replied.

III

Three figures set out into the rising sun the following morning. Two rode—Friar Leonard and Leofric de Bredon—and the third loped easily alongside the horses. Every steed that Beit Ras had to offer had screamed and balked at Dahāka when he approached them, but the dark man, wrapped in a deep hood and long cloak, had only laughed, saying, "My legs are a match for your mounts."

Well into the morning, Leofric called a halt. He watered the horses, and passed a skin to the eyeless priest that he too might slake his thirst. Dahāka of Erṣetu's golden eyes watched them drink, but the dark man only shook his head when Leofric offered him water. They pressed on, making steady progress through the heat of midday, and eventually paused in the shade of a scrubby copse. The dark man seemed as immune to heat and dust as he was to thirst and hunger, but he showed no impatience at his companions.

"How far into the hills is this Erṣetu of yours?" Leofric

asked. Dahāka stood at the edge of the trees, staring out at the shimmering horizon.

"I cannot say. Since its earliest days, the city has been woven about with misdirection. One more line of defense against the Lie." His golden gaze turned to rest on Leofric. "Do not suspect duplicity, Leofric de Bredon. Erṣetu lies more distant than simple cubits."

The three pressed on as the sun passed its zenith and began, slowly, to sink into the west. After a time, Dahāka trotted ahead of the two riders, apparently following a trail. He returned just as quickly, his face troubled.

"I do not like the tale told by the signs before us," he said, bluntly. "They are old, but the spoor of a thing that should not be on Earth."

Leofric loosened his arming sword in its scabbard and the wicked axe that hung at his saddle. Friar Leonard prayed aloud, lifting his hands to the sky and calling upon the Lord of Hosts. Their dark companion flexed his gnarled hands and set his shoulders, then led them onward.

As they moved forward, the light changed—it seemed that the sun lifted back toward noon, and a strange haze fell about them so that the sun was always visible, no matter which way they looked.

"There is some devilry afoot here," growled Leofric, hand closed tight on his sword hilt. His cold gaze scanned the empty hills that surrounded them, and for a moment he thought he saw a dark flicker of movement off to what he thought was the east. Even as the thought came to him, the motion vanished, but Dahāka's golden gaze was fixed upon the same spot.

"That black shape was devilry, man of Christ. All else is the touch of Ahura Mazda." The battered sword sprang into his hand, and the Erṣetuan strode ahead faster. "Come—gird your hearts."

They crested a rise, and suddenly the descending slope before them was filled with stone. A city sprawled before them, pale stone gleaming in the strangely timeless light of the manifold suns, and Erşetu gasped and fell to his knees. The city was silent—no weeds grew in its streets and no ruin marked its buildings, but Leofric's skin prickled with a curious certainty that it was long dead.

"Something is wrong." The man of the desert rose to his feet. "At this hour there should be many of my people abroad, and sweet smoke rising from the great temples. What manner of homecoming is this to be? Be ready for anyth—"

Dahāka fell silent, and took a faltering step toward a tumbled heap of masonry nearby them. Ruddy-flecked gray, rather than the pale of the city below, it was the remains of a statue, toppled and broken. A stone face gazed up at them, high brows and wide cheeks above a firm mouth and a strangely-styled beard of long ringlets. Both eyes were gone—one seemed to have been gouged out, leaving a mournful cavity, while deliberate blows had smashed the other. The longer Leofric looked, the more he made out amongst the pile. Four—no, five—clawed but elegant limbs; long wings; a torso, curiously bull-like.

"This is the remains of a Guardian of the Truth," Dahāka said, hollowly. "Sacrilege and blasphemy! What madness has been wrought here?" He mastered himself, turning his strange golden eyes to meet Leofric's hard gaze. "Do you carry oil with you, Leofric de Bredon? For lamps, or sacred rites to your Christ?"

"Certes," the Frank nodded, and pulled a small flask from a saddlebag. "And a fire-making kit, for it's a poor knight that cannot make his own fire." He patted a leather pouch at his belt, and a rag of tow that he kept ready for such use.

"Keep both ready," Dahāka said, grimly. "And do not

question me if I call for its use."

They descended into the city, passing quickly amongst the outlying buildings. Leofric's cold eyes roamed everywhere, and he murmured a commentary to his eyeless companion, whose face was rapt with delight. The buildings were curiously proportioned, with tall doors of pale wood. Some had been smashed apart from without; others apparently broken from within. Everything was dry and barren, and charred burns marred the light stone here and there. Deliberate blows had smashed statuary and what Leofric took to be votive icons and symbols, and Dahāka turned his eyes from such marks with whispers in his own strange tongue.

"May you never live to see such hatefulness on the streets of your own home," the Erşetuan said, after a long time. They were deep in the city, on a wide street that lifted gradually toward what appeared to be a majestic temple. "The gifts of Ahura Mazda have kept me from suffering death's sting, but this day I feel all the venom of it." His dark skin was ashen, and his hands shook.

Leofric tensed as he heard movement behind them—a furtive sound as of something creeping along—and began to turn his head.

Friar Leonard's wide hand caught his shoulder. "Do not look back, Leofric de Bredon." The eyeless priest's words were sonorously prophetic. "Not yet. There are more ahead. Ready the oil, and flint to spark it."

Broken chains, their links tarnished and green with age, lay in heaps on the road before them, and Dahāka again whispered something with the rhythm of a curse. He led them onward, until the great pillars of the central fane towered above them. Its wide gates stood open, marked strangely with seemingly-burned patches. Ashes lay scattered across the paving stones, and more age-darkened bronze was strewn here and there. Tripods, and what looked like braziers to Leofric's eye.

Dahāka led them into the stygian heart of the temple, his cautious steps grinding and crushing the remnants of what Leofric presumed were once sacred fires. Darker shadows circled and rustled behind and around them, but their black companion stood tall and unafraid. A chant built on his lips, at once sibilant, guttural, and sharp. The words rose and fell like the waves of a great sea, until the vast chamber echoed with the brazen challenge of his voice. Dahāka fell silent, his gleaming eyes all that Leofric could see clearly.

"*Sub tuum praesidium,*" Friar Leonard began to pray, echoing the cadence of Dahāka's words. Something moved in the gloom—a dark shape, man-like, its eyes glowing red-gold. "*Confugimus, Sancta Dei Genetrix.*"

Leofric's senses swam in the gloom. The dark figure that emerged to confront Dahāka was a monstrous thing, stooped and malformed, only its golden eyes and gnarled skin betraying their kinship. Leofric felt the hairs rise on the back of his neck, and his hands trembled. Dahāka shouted something in his own language, rage shaking his words, and his adversary shook with a slow and terrible laughter. More figures, similarly marred, moved in the gloom behind their leader, who spoke a mocking reply to Dahāka.

"*Nostras deprecationes ne despicias in necessitatibus nostris.*"

The old shamshir Dahāka had taken from the fallen bandit shone as his black hand raised it high, and with another shout Dahāka sprang forward pantherishly, Leofric at his side. The knight's sword rang from the twisted figure as if from an anvil, but the shamshir cleaved deep into the thing's shoulder before Dahāka leaped back and away, crying, "Now, Leofric, give me fire!"

"*Sed a periculis cunctis, libera nos semper.*" Sparks flared as Leofric struck his flint. The rag of tow tucked into the flask of oil caught, and the flame was reflected all around them in dozens of pairs of red-gold eyes. "*Virgo gloriosa et benedicta, Amen.*"

Dahāka cried the name of his god, and thunder rolled above the temple. Leofric dashed forward, jabbed a hole in the hide flask with his blade, and squeezed the flask hard. A jet of oil spat at the wounded monstrosity, and Leofric hurled the flask and its makeshift fuse, burning merrily. The oil flared and caught with a *wumph* of heat, and a terrible shriek split the darkness. Flailing, tearing at itself, the twisted creature whirled and stumbled about, burning oil dripping from its body and catching in the dry wreckage of once-holy artifacts at its feet. It rebounded from another dark figure, caught desperately at it, and the two reeled away in a deathly embrace. Friar Leonard, the ragged sockets of his eyes shadowed by the dancing flame, called Leofric's name as he tossed a second flask of oil with curious surety. The crusader caught it and lit it, and hurled it into the mob of dark figures. Oil splashed and flared, and the heat was suddenly intense.

"Back! Back into the light!" Dahāka cried, and as he obeyed, Leofric saw that the black face was wet with tears. Dahāka carried the tablet he'd been charged with in place of the battered shamshir. Leofric caught the blind priest's arm and helped him back out into the bright light of noon. Dahāka followed, already reading from the clay tablet words that shook the ground beneath their feet. Thunder rolled again, and as he fell silent, arms upraised to the white, hazy sky, a resounding crack echoed from the barren hills around them. The earth shook, and the temple roof collapsed in with an awful shriek of tearing stone and panicked creatures that were, perhaps, once men.

💀 💀 💀

The city lay silent once more. Dahāka of Erṣetu was ashen-faced, his golden gaze dimmed with sorrow. Leofric laid a hand upon his rag-clad shoulder, and the dark head lifted.

"You will find the Damascus road an hour's ride north,

Leofric de Bredon," Dahāka said. "Serve the Truth of Ahura Mazda in all your dealings. I thank you for your aid, though my heart is broken for what I have wrought here."

"You did your god's work, brother," Friar Leonard said softly, his blind gaze tender, "and mayhap the work of mine, too. I bless you in the name of God the Father, His son Jesus Christ, and the Holy Spirit, that your grief be tempered."

"I am the last of my people alive in this city, priest," Dahāka replied. "Perhaps the last in all the world. I cannot follow those wretches into death, for I have not been corrupted by the Lie, nor can I walk the earth among your kind, as once I did. What is left to me now?"

"You said that your folk raised many settlements." Friar Leonard placed a hand upon Dahāka's other shoulder. "Tongues and nations may have changed, but your feet will know their old pathways, were you to seek them out. There are many secrets hidden upon the face of the world—might others of your kind not be among them, uncorrupted by the evil that took root here?"

"That tainted thing crowed that madness and horror had claimed all the cities of my people long ago."

"Will you believe that? Christ said that the devil has no truth in him, 'for he is a liar, and the father of lies.' Holiness—Truth—is in right action." Friar Leonard said, and the Erṣetuan nodded slowly. He raised his head, and drew in a long breath, his golden eyes bleak and distant.

"It could not have spoken the truth," Dahāka said, finally. "You are right, men of the cross. If there is any purpose left to me, let it be this."

"*Deus vult*," said Leofric de Bredon. "The good Friar has taught me that black deeds and black fates do not outweigh virtue. I pledge to aid you. Dahāka of Erṣetu, in the name of God and Saint John." The crusader took the dark man's gnarled hand in his own as he swore. The sound of thunder echoed again, faintly, as though far away, as if in reply to his oath.

~ Eadwine Brown ~

A native of Nottingham, Ead lives with his wife and two cats at the foot of the Malvern Hills, near the wild marches that separate England and Wales. His name is the Saxon spelling of Edwin, which is the answer to the question he is most often asked.

Shadow's Crossing

by Tony-Paul de Vissage

The boatman crouched closer to the little fire. It was a cold night, a raw night.

Aye, that it was.

Raw, like a bleeding wound, and the wind a knife slashing at its open edges.

Once again he cursed the fates causing him to be born into a family of ferrymen. *Why not a carpenter, a tailor, even a farmer?* Grubbing in the dirt would be more welcome than this eternal waiting by the river, with the water's ever-present cold creeping into his bones…

At present, however, his isolation was to be envied. In the village, a few miles away, great pestilence raged. Many had succumbed. It was said the contagion was spread to the Great House itself where even now the old lord lay waiting to die.

"I seek passage across the channel, boatman."

With a cry, the boatman scrambled to his feet, peering at the source of the voice.

Dark, to be sure. A figure dim in the mist rising from the river. The black horse was barely visible, its rider an even fainter shape, his face obscured by the shadows of a hood, body enfolded under a shapeless cloak. Both were like shades in the mist, appearing noiselessly from the fog.

"You can get it here, for a price," he told the figure, gruffly. He didn't relish having to leave the warmth of his fire so late at night, though it meant a fare.

"I have no coin." The traveler's reply was quiet.

The shadowed head turned, regarding the water somberly. The boatman had a glimpse of a pale oval under the hood before the mist surrounded him again.

"I must reach the other shore. It's most important." He shrugged. *Or the wind stirred the folds of the cape?* "But if you won't take me…Well, it isn't far. My horse and I will swim."

He turned the animal's head. It snorted, breath stirring mist into little uprising curls.

"Wait." The boatman held up a detaining hand, speaking into the gloom. "The channel's deep, bottomless in spots. Your horse will never make it. Besides, the water's too cold this time of year."

The other paused, looking back at him, eyes gleaming darkly under the shadow of the hood. *Is that a flicker of red under bloodless lids?*

"Be that as it may, there's no other way for me to get across…if you won't take me." The repeated words were a near-accusation.

The stranger didn't move. As the ferryman regarded the dark figure, he felt an unreasoning ripple of fear.

Why am I afraid?

His would-be passenger made no offer of violence. Nevertheless, there was menace, of a sort, and something else…in the set of those shoulders, a kind of *despair*. So real it seemed to reach out and pluck at the ferryman until he felt a whimper of terror wrapping itself around his heart.

He'd never been afraid, enjoying the solitude of the river, accepting its loneliness as part of his life. It never touched him before…

…until now…

The wind blew across the water again and the ferryman turned away hastily. If the breeze were to stir the cloak from the stranger's body, he feared he might not see a man of solid flesh but stark bones beneath the black wool.

"Who said I won't?" he demanded, voice harsh in the stillness.

The stranger didn't answer, merely waited while the ferryman untied the rope-gate, giving admittance to the deck of the barge, and gestured impatiently for him to enter.

"If you're so desperate to reach the island that you would swim…Get on, get on."

Obediently, the horseman dismounted, cape fanning like great ebony wings. When he led the black charger on board, it snorted and tossed its head as its iron-shod hooves touched the wooden planks, making the barge sway under its weight. Its master caught the bridle by the cheek piece, speaking soothingly to the animal. It quieted but rolled its brilliant, liquid-dark eyes in dislike at being on this strange, moving object.

The boatman cast off his lines. With a long pole he pushed the barge forward, guiding it to the opposite bank. The farther shore was barely to be seen in the mist, a few dark high shapes revealing themselves as trees, gathering around a lighter expanse of beach.

The rider stood by the black horse's head, staring silently at the approaching shore. The boatman, when he gave his attention from his task to look at his passenger, saw fair hair so pale as to appear colorless, and broad shoulders beneath the enveloping cape. The wind tugged at the cape's edge, lifting it slightly. There was the gleam of a metal-tipped scabbard at his left thigh. In it rested a broadsword, ancient and worn, but still deadly.

"There's sickness and death on the island." The boatman felt he should warn his passenger.

"I'll not be harmed," the stranger replied with certainty.

"It's the wrong time of year for travel," the ferryman continued. "Winter's wicked here. What's so important on the island you must go there *now*?"

His voice floated above the water, then was swallowed by the fog.

"I go to visit an old…friend. One by whose side I've often fought in days past. He's given me much, and now, I've come to repay my debt."

The traveler fell silent. Only the slapping of the waves

against the barge's sides broke the wordless quiet.

Presently, to the ferryman's intense relief, the distant bank was reached. The stranger swung onto the horse's back and only then did he speak again.

"My thanks to you, boatman."

The horse's hooves clattered on the boards as it leaped from boat to shore, splashing in the shallow water, urged on by spurred heels.

"Thanks won't put coins in my purse," the ferryman flung after him. "I'd be a fool if I did this often."

On the shore, the great horse whirled, hooves raking the air.

"My gratitude can be a valuable thing, boatman." The stranger's reply floated over the water. "When we meet again, you'll see."

Horse and rider disappeared through the shadowy trees, the curtains of fog closing about them, swallowing the sound of hoof beats.

It was as if they'd never existed.

Once more, the ferryman was alone in the river mist. Again, he shivered. Muttering, he tied the barge to the stake driven into the sand and set about making a fire, to await the stranger's return.

💀 💀 💀

It was colder now, the fog deeper. Huddled near the fire, the ferryman pulled his blanket tighter around his shoulders.

Since his passenger's departure, he tried to sleep but did so fitfully. Those last words continued to torment him and he couldn't understand why.

Of course, I'll see the stranger again. His ferryboat was the only way off the island unless one could sprout wings and fly like a bird.

Whom had the horseman gone to see? Who was the one waiting for the dark-cloaked traveler's appearance? Had given him so much? Was so important?

There was pestilence in the village. For a month it had raged. No one was untouched. Only the ferryman had no worry of sickness. His home was at the river's edge, located too far from the village for the winds to carry the fever.

Why had the stranger wanted to go where sickness reigned?

Sickness and death…

It struck as sudden as a blow to the belly. He knew the rider's identity. Had known it all along, if he dared admit, but refused to recognize it… and *he* would be returning to the ferry.

"'When we meet again,'" he had said.

The stranger would gather his harvest of souls, then return to the river.

"Me…He's coming back for me!" The words gagged in the ferryman's throat, blocking the scream rising within him. He had no care for the dying lord or his fellow villagers, only the ending of his own existence. *Will those pale, powerful hands reach for me, the deadly sword raised? Indeed, will I even know when it happens?* He wondered how much pain there would be…

The heavy thud of a horse's hooves pounding the earth broke through his doze. The boatman lurched to his feet, rubbing his eyes.

It was a dream. I merely dreamed.

All sleep vanished as the black horse burst through the fog, stopping before him, legs braced, heaving sides foam-slick with sweat-salt. Mist floated about the creature, blazing from its nostrils like silver flames.

Shadow and man stared at each other over the gleaming head.

Something is amiss.

The boatman could sense it. It was as though the dark horseman now carried a burden. The wings of the cloak drooped as with a great and heavy weight resting upon the rider's broad shoulders.

"Is your business now finished, sir? Did you find your friend?" the boatman dared ask.

"Aye, I found him…" The voice was reedy and hollow. "…and more…"

He sighed, a weary gusting of expelled breath forming a frosted cloud that dissolved like tears onto the sand.

"I didn't know there were so many needing me." He leaned toward the ferryman, holding out his hand. The gauntlet upon that hand was leather, fine-grained and old, stained and cracked from many years' wear. "I wish to dismount. Assist me."

The boatman hesitated.

"You also fear me?" His laugh was low, a mirthless sound, and sad. "Don't worry." The gloved hand beckoned impatiently. "It isn't your time."

"I'm not afraid." The boatman sprang forward, reaching out to catch the outstretched hand in his own, holding it tightly.

"No." There was surprise as well as satisfaction in the deep voice. "No, I vow you're not."

Leather fingers tightened around his.

How cold they are.

Even through the glove, the ferryman felt the chill. His fingers tingled as the blood within them slowed. He placed the other hand on the caped shoulder, grunting when he took the weight as the figure swung from the horse's back.

The hooded face peered into his.

All he could see in the glowing eyes was his own cowering reflection.

Why, oh why, can't I see his features? He didn't shrink away, forcing himself to stand firm.

In the distance, black smoke billowed. A red glow outlined the trees, their bare branches raised like arms beseeching the heavens, skeletal fingers grasping at the sky. Crimson shadows danced across the sand.

Within the hood, the stranger's gaze followed his own.

"They burn those I've claimed. When the last spark falls and the embers cease to glow, the living will thank God for their survival and once more go on with their lives." He released the boatman's hand and leaned against the horse, then dropped the reins and turned toward the fire.

The ferryman looked from the glow beyond the trees—*my village's pyre*—to his own pitiful flame. The stranger spread his arms, embracing its warmth.

The wind blew the ends of the cape across the fire. It swayed low over the flames, caressed the coals, resisted and escaped them unharmed.

"They feared me. Why?"

The question floated into the silence, borne by the wind through the last leaves remaining on the trees. It echoed across the water, as if it had been asked many times before and as yet remained unanswered.

"You're a stranger—"the ferryman began.

"A stranger?" His answer was dismissed impatiently. "I've been with each man since he drew *Firstbreath*, walked beside all until this moment. I'm as much a part of this world as Life itself, and yet…" The hooded head lifted, gazing at the starless sky. "Many call upon me, but when I appear, they struggle and are afraid."

The boatman didn't answer. He wasn't a man of much thought. Indeed, this night's happenings were beginning to befuddle his simple brain. It was a question men asked often, he reckoned, and one perhaps never resolved. He had no answer just as he could give no reason for the banishment of his own fear. He dared instead to ask another question.

"Your friend…did *he* fear you?"

There was a flicker within the hood. He thought the shadow smiled.

"Didn't I say we were *old* friends? He greeted me gladly. As a sword companion should. Clasped my hand with eagerness, knowing how long I've waited." The dark gaze turned toward the ferryman. "Your village has need of a new lord, boatman."

Marveling at the calmness he felt at this announcement of the old lord's passing, the ferryman asked, "And the others? My friends?"

"Ah…there were a few who bade me welcome. An old woman, weary of pain…a young girl…" The harsh voice softened. "She held my hand with the shyness of a maiden touching her lover for the first time…But joyfully. Oh yes…there was joy." Another sigh. "I took her quickly."

The hollow voice grew stronger, as if in telling of these few acts of acceptance, the shadow gained in strength and vigor. No longer was the sound filled with eternity's weight.

"There was an infant…I lifted him from his cradle…"

The gloved hands rose above the flames. The boatman could almost see the tiny form nestled within that leather grasp.

"He seized my finger, unafraid. I returned him to his place…his life is ahead." The hands fell away.

"I wonder…Could your barge hold all I've freed tonight?"

The boatman looked around uneasily. The boat was big enough for four people, no more than five. "Where…?"

"Don't worry," the shadow assured him, raising one hand in a calming gesture. "Their souls are released, and already gone to the *Otherwhere* to be judged, but as long as this fever enthralls the world, *I* alone am earthbound." Abruptly, he whirled, striding back to the black horse. It raised its head and neighed deep within its chest. "I must go. I've tarried here too long."

The weariness was gone now, the burden of souls disappeared.

The boatman hastened to open the gate and the horse obediently entered, no longer alarmed by the barge's movement. Once more, they crossed the water, this time in silence, the only sound the boatman's pole breaking the river's surface.

Again mounted, with the black charger churning the damp sand with impatient hooves, the darkling wayfarer looked down at the boatman.

"And now, your payment—"

"No," the man hastened to assure him. "I ask for nothing."

"*Nothing?*" That quiet voice at the same time mocked and challenged. Drawing off a gauntlet, the rider extended his hand, pallid and insubstantial as the mist, "My hand, boatman…"

…and waited.

Trembling, the ferryman reached out with his own. Strange joy stirred within him, coupled with a frantic eagerness. Aye, he would touch that frigid flesh, clasp the shadowy palm within his. Feel once more that coldness. This time, let it fill and consume him. And then…

"Nay." The hand jerked away, the gauntlet replaced, grasping leather reins instead of mortal fingers. The horse's head was turned toward the trees and the trail leading through them to the outside world. "We will meet again, boatman. A long time hence. Then, will I offer you my hand."

His own still outstretched, the boatman watched in silence as horse and rider glided into the fog. For a moment longer, he could see the charger's body outlined dimly, then the mist, like a soft white mouth, swallowed them.

His hand fell to his side. His own heartbeat became an echo of the horse's hooves, floating over the water to be lost on the farther shore.

Once again, he was alone. With the river and the mist and the wind…

… and his thoughts…

Another night.

Another winter.

The latest of interminable winters.

The latest of innumerable nights.

The wind blew strong and cold across the channel, making stiff, choppy waves splash against the sides of the barge, causing it to bounce and dip.

It had been a busy night, and the boatman welcomed the activity. More money for the family he now had, a wife and two little ones living in the village. The purse hanging at his waist was full and heavy. Even in the cold, people wished to cross the channel, many returning home, some merely traveling through.

There was a peddler, his horse laden with goods. It was a skittish, ill-tempered creature that resisted entering the barge, fighting with an iron mouth against the reins. The peddler finally forced it aboard by whipping it with a switch he broke from a nearby huckleberry bush, the tiny thorns down its length supplying a stinging incentive.

The creature fairly leaped aboard to escape the woody lash, dancing nervously in place while its owner held the bridle tightly and spoke soothingly to it.

At last they were ready to depart. The boatman turned to cast off…

"Do you have room for another passenger?"

He froze. Couldn't move.

It can't be.

Even after all these years, he recognized that voice, and the gentle, hollow sound of it sent a shiver into his very marrow. He didn't want to look, wanted to simply toss aside the ropes, and leave the tardy passenger on the riverbank.

"Aren't you going to answer him?" someone asked and looked back at the shore, calling, "There's room for one more."

Reluctantly, the boatman tried to reply but couldn't speak. He simply stood there, staring…remembering…

The rider looked as he had before, a tall figure swathed in black, not a bit of flesh showing, astride the great black horse with river mist swirling white around its fetlocks, making no move to approach the barge.

Not without invitation…

Without speaking, the boatman stepped aside, gesturing reluctantly.

The horseman dismounted, leading his horse aboard. It was calm this time, stepping daintily onto the rough-hewn planks, head down, eyes mild. The peddler's horse, that fitful creature, reacted to it with a violent neigh and a sudden shifting of its weight. The peddler attempted to quiet him as the barge bounced and splashed.

Silently, the boatman cast off. Silently, he pushed his pole into the water, guiding the barge across the swiftly moving water, the lantern hanging from one of the railings making oddly bright patterns on the waves.

They were halfway across when it happened.

Unnerved by the movement under its hooves, perhaps frightened by the water itself or the glittering lights reflected from it, the peddler's horse began to panic. Grunting deep in its chest, it reared.

The ferryboat dipped low, the passengers at the front staggering and clutching at each other for support. A woman gave a short squeal of fear as water sloshed over the side onto her feet.

The horse reared again, pulling its reins from the peddler's hands. It lunged forward, striking the railing with its chest. There were screams and cries as the wooden barrier splintered and people toppled into the water. The creature staggered backward. The opposite end of the barge tipped, tossing the boatman himself into icy darkness.

It was so cold he was stunned into immobility. Couldn't think, couldn't move. There was a heavy weight, something pulling him down. Briefly he fought against it, feeling himself weaken.

Abruptly, the weight was gone. Muffled through the water, he heard the sounds of the others' struggles. Above him, saw the light of the lantern hanging from the bow, its flame twisted by the moving water. Slowly, he floated toward it.

Sound was like a thunderclap against his ears as his head broke the water. Frantically, he tried to move, kicking, waving his arms.

He could see the dark traveler and his horse standing on the far shore.

How had he gotten there?

The horseman knelt, reaching out to pull the others, one by one, from the water.

Is that why he came back? To take all my passengers?

He tried to swim toward the shore, but he was so tired, and the water was so cold, the current too strong. He could feel himself getting weaker, moving slower and slower, face splashed by the waves, head sinking, cold water in his mouth…

"Here, take my hand."

He opened his eyes, saw the stranger. The dark figure had waded into the water, up to his waist, the cape floating around him like huge, wet wings.

How can he do that? The river was too deep at that point for a man to stand.

He extended that gauntleted hand. "Take my hand," he repeated.

The boatman hesitated. Another wave slapped him in the face. The current pulled at his tiring body. He grasped the offered hand, felt himself pulled up and out of the water and to shore. Toward where the others huddled together on the beach's soft, dry sand. Several of them hugged each other. Two of the women were sobbing softly.

The horse, the cause of it all, stood a few feet away with lowered head, nibbling at a shrub.

"You saved me," the ferryman said to the shadow.

"You're an old acquaintance." His reply was soft. "I wouldn't abandon an old friend."

The black charger snorted, flinging the air into little wreaths about its head. The shadow gathered its loose reins, swinging effortlessly into the saddle.

"But now, I've done what I came to do and it's time to leave."

"Wait." The boatman held up a hand. "Before you go, let me see your face." When the shadow hesitated, he went on, "After all, shouldn't old friends know each other's features?"

The figure seemed to consider. He gave a silent nod.

"Very well."

The worn gauntlets pushed back the hood so it fell against the broad shoulders. The ferryman gaped.

Truly, this wasn't what he expected at all.

"Why—y-you're beautiful!" *Did I think that or actually say the words?*

The face before him could have been an angel's, palest of hair like ashen floss lying against the pushed-back hood, skin the most pallid alabaster, and the eyes…so clear and brilliant they were like pieces of blue-tinted ice. He'd never thought Death might look so astonishing.

"Come." The figure spoke again. Once more, it extended its hand. "It's time to go."

The boatman understood that meant the shadow wasn't leaving alone.

"Why?" he protested. "I mean…You saved all of us. Why…"

"No," the quiet voice interrupted. "I didn't save *everyone*." He nodded to the little group crowding together.

Slowly, they parted. They hadn't been huddled in fear as the ferryman supposed but were gathered around a body, lying still and sodden, water still streaming from its hair and clothing, beach sand clinging to its arms and legs.

His body.

Someone pulled loose the money bag, holding it up,

testing its weight.

"It was too heavy. It pulled him down. If he hadn't made so much money tonight…" The fellow shook his head.

"I'll take it to his wife." Another took it from him. "She'll need it for the little ones."

They lifted the boatman's body in their arms.

He turned to look at the shadow.

"You *had* to pull me from the water," he said, wonderingly. "So the money could be recovered, so my body could be taken home."

There was a slight nod. "I've paid you now, boatman. Your family will be cared for. That's my gift." Again, he held out his hand. "Now, we must go."

Silently the ferryman regarded the outstretched hand. Once, so long ago, on another wintry night, he had frightened himself wondering how it would be when he grasped the stranger's hand. Now he didn't hesitate, just placed his own in it, feeling the fingers tighten around his.

Firm, gentle.

Friendly.

He was pulled onto the black charger's back. As the shadow released his hand to turn the horse's head, he clasped the dark figure about the waist, and his only thought was that it hadn't hurt.

It hadn't hurt at all.

~ *Tony-Paul de Vissage* ~

Toni V. Sweeney was born in Georgia after the War between the States but before the Gulf War (December 27, 1942, to be exact). She has lived 30 years in the South, a score in the Middle West, and a decade on the Pacific Coast and now she's trying for her second 30 on the Great Plains, specifically in Lincoln, Nebraska. Since the publication of her first novel in 1989, Toni divides her time between writing SF/Fantasy under her own name and romances under her pseudonym Icy Snow Blackstone. In March 2013, she became publicity manager for Class Act Books (US). She is also on the review staff of the *New York Journal of Books* online.

Rogue Blades Presents Titles

Rogue Blades Presents (RBP) Anthologies & Titles
Crazy Town: A Heroic Anthology of Fantastical Crime Noir
Crossbones & Crosses:
A Heroic Anthology of Swashbuckling Adventure
Death's Sting—Where Art Thou?
A Heroic Anthology of Immortal Protagonists
As You Wish! A Heroic Anthology of All the Good Parts
Reach for the Sky: A Heroic Anthology of the Wild & Weird West
SLaughter is the Best Medicine:
A Heroic Anthology of Mayhem & Mirth in Melee
Skovolis: City of Thrones (A Kaimer Collection)
We Who are About to Die: A Heroic Anthology of Sacrifice
No Ordinary Mortals: A Heroic Anthology of Supers

RBP Signature Series
#1 Return of the Sword:
A Heroic Anthology of Sword & Sorcery
#2 Rage of the Behemoth:
A Heroic Anthology of Colossal Adventure

Challenge! Anthologies
#1 Discovery
#2 Stealth

Clash of Steel Anthologies
#1 Demons
#2 Assassins

RBP Nonfiction
Writing Fantasy Heroes: Powerful Advice from the Pros

THANK YOU FOR READING A ROGUE BLADES PRESENTS TITLE

Copyright for individual works reverts to the individual authors.

"Sand-devil" by Eadwine Brown. © 2019 by Eadwine Brown.
"Bhailgeth's Ransom" by Alfred D. Byrd. © 2019 by Alfred D. Byrd.
"Immortality, a Poisoned Chalice?" by Adrian Cole. © 2019 by Adrian Cole.
"Shadow's Crossing" by Tony-Paul de Vissage. © 1990 by Toni V. Sweeney. First published in *Beyond: Science Fiction & Fantasy Magazine*, Issue 10, 1990. Reprinted by permission of the author.
"The Hungry Castle" by Liam Hogan. © 2019 by Liam Hogan.
"To Walk on Worlds" by Matthew John. © 2019 by Matthew John.
"The Death Of Sleeping Beauty" by Brandie June. © 2019 by Brandie June Chernow.
"Idol of the Valley" by Daniel Loring Keating. © 2019 by Daniel Loring Keating.
"The Immortal Contract" by D.K. Latta. © 2019 by Darren Latta.
"The Soldier" by KT Morley. © 2019 by KT Morley.
"A Thousand Deaths" by Kate Runnels. © 2019 by Kate Runnels.
"Red Horse, White Horse" by J.B. Toner. © 2019 by J.B. Toner.
"Just Add Holy Water" by Dawn Vogel. © 2019 by Dawn Vogel.
"Ghosts of the Staked Plains" by Keith West. © 2019 by Keith West.
"The Bull and the Djinn" by Logan Whitney. © 2019 by Logan Whitney.

Visit the RBE website to learn more about the authors and artists.

Rogue Blades Entertainment
~ We put the Hero back into Heroics! ~

Printed in Great Britain
by Amazon